Fran Annaford works in the entertainment industry. Enforced idleness during the corona pandemic led to increased activity on the laptop, and the eight volume 'Starnberg Set' series was conceived and written.

*If Time Were Not a Moving Thing* is the first part. It will be followed by *You Don't Own Me*.

Fran travels extensively in the course of her work. Home is wherever her partner and animals happen to be.

For L, my first reader

Fran Annaford

# IF TIME WERE NOT A MOVING THING

AUSTIN MACAULEY PUBLISHERS™

LONDON • CAMBRIDGE • NEW YORK • SHARJAH

Copyright © Fran Annaford 2023

The right of Fran Annaford to be identified as author of this work has been asserted by the author in accordance with sections 77 and 78 of the Copyright, Designs and Patents Act 1988.

All rights reserved. No part of this publication may be reproduced, stored in a retrieval system, or transmitted in any form or by any means, electronic, mechanical, photocopying, recording, or otherwise, without the prior permission of the publishers.

Any person who commits any unauthorised act in relation to this publication may be liable to criminal prosecution and civil claims for damages.

This is a work of fiction. Names, characters, businesses, places, events, locales, and incidents are either the products of the author's imagination or used in a fictitious manner. Any resemblance to actual persons, living or dead, or actual events is purely coincidental.

A CIP catalogue record for this title is available from the British Library.

ISBN 9781398480452 Paperback
ISBN 9781398480469 Hardback
ISBN 9781398480476 ePub e-book

www.austinmacauley.com

First Published 2023
Austin Macauley Publishers Ltd®
1 Canada Square
Canary Wharf
London
E14 5AA

My gratitude to my patient proof-reader is boundless.

*Hilfe…* She muttered the word inaudibly, slowly releasing a breath. It lessened the anxiety cramping her stomach muscles. *I will not be able to prepare Peter Clapton satisfactorily.* It was now nearly May, and the end of the season loomed. In the middle of July, the ornate red and gold curtain would fall for the last time. Until inevitably it rose again at the beginning of September after the summer break. And then it would be too late.

Arabella Cooper felt a pressure behind her eyes and across her forehead. If she was in Munich where she spent much of her childhood, instead of in London on a dismal dreary rainy afternoon, she would say it was a *Föhn* day. The *Föhn* is a curious weather condition, peculiar to the Alpine regions. A dry wind blows in from the mountains. The air is crystal clear; the peaks close enough to touch despite being sixty kilometres away, cars crash into each other on the autobahns because it is hard to concentrate, and the headache resembles a bad hangover. People suffer on *Föhn* days.

She was aware of silence in the room. Peter looked at her. She shook her head and felt a twinge of pain. "I'm sorry, just the start of a headache. Probably the weather. Could we open a window?"

It wasn't allowed during coaching sessions, because the noise disturbed the neighbouring studio rooms, and the tourists and shoppers on Floral Street were prone to whistle and join in. Add in the asphyxiating diesel stench drifting upwards from the constant stream of taxis and it was sensual overload.

Peter was not the brightest of men, but he was kind. "Nearly over," he said, opening the window. "Only another forty minutes." He was patently aware of his deficiencies.

Arabella's perfect German meant she was spared having to play endless Italian Rossini and Bellini works but trying to pound Wagner and Richard Strauss's difficult music into the hearts and minds of opera singers could be trying. And Peter was a character tenor, the sound they produced anathema to her. She preferred women's voices, apart from the very high sopranos. But she would rather work any day with the canaries as they were known, than with this sort of high tenor.

Peter sang mainly humorous roles. He had a piercing voice. Arabella joked it could cut through aluminium. The critics tended to agree with her. The role of Mime in *Das Rheingold,* which he was currently attempting to learn, was only borderline comical. *There are not a lot of laughs in the operas of Richard Wagner.* Arabella supressed a giggle. The realisation that the same role in *Siegfried,* the third opera in Wagner's Ring Cycle is twenty times longer and would be coming into rehearsal the season after next, now made Arabella's headache extend into the trigeminal nerve in her right cheek.

She knew it entailed working with him for at least four hours a week for the entire intervening two years.

There were two other pianists on the staff who specialised in German operas. It was so unfair that she was always scheduled with Peter. She cursed her best friend, Matilda, who ran the company office and allocated the coaching sessions. She did it deliberately, and lived for Arabella's complaints, never tiring of finding them funny.

"Let's go from Loge: *helfen will ich dir, Mime.*" She played the notes, and in addition sang in the Loge line to help him.

"*Wer hilfe mir? Gehorchen muss ich der lieblichen Bruder, das mich in Bande gelegt.*" They had worked on this section for several coaching sessions, but there were still three grammatical mistakes in the short sentence. *He doesn't speak the language, but why can't he just learn it parrot fashion?* Her cheek now throbbed.

Arabella faced the door of the room. A figure filling the glass panel distracted her. The panels had been installed to hinder #MeToo situations. There was some justification for this. She had on occasion been grateful the grand piano stood between herself and the wandering hands of a baritone or tenor. The glass reduced these incidences but had a negative effect on the soundproofing of the rooms.

Without knocking, the person entered. Arabella stopped playing.

"I have booked this room." The woman wore sunglasses and a full-length designer trench coat. The collar was fur lined, and it wasn't fake fur. It was a very expensive, but understated look. *Classy.* Her almost ash blonde hair was piled high in a chignon, increasing the impression of height.

Arabella estimated her to be about five foot seven, two inches shorter than her own five foot nine. She stood and took off her reading glasses at the same moment the woman lifted hers onto her head. Both took in a breath. Arabella looked into large steely grey eyes, as the women looked into her own dark blue ones.

Arabella was beautiful. From her Welsh father, she inherited the unusual combination of raven black hair and dark blue eyes. Her body was lean and athletic, but feminine. She was often blithely unaware of heads turning as she walked past.

As their eyes met, she heard a spark crackle in the room. They both flinched before a scowl settled on the woman's perfect face.

"I'm surprised. We have a coaching in here until five o'clock, and it's not even four thirty. I'll ring the company office."

Arabella reached behind her to the phone on the wall fixture and dialled 106. Matilda answered.

"Hi, there, enjoying your session?" She giggled.

"Hmmmm, enormously, but we've been interrupted. There's a woman here claiming she has booked the room."

From Peter came an embarrassed squeak. "Arabella, this is Marie Nyman."

*Oh shit*, she hadn't recognised her, and from experience she knew there is almost nothing worse than not recognising a diva. It was why the stage door keepers had regular coaching on knowing *who is who* in the international opera world. Four years ago, a star tenor left in a rage when he wasn't greeted by name, and Sir William, the Director General, had to pay a grovelling visit to the Savoy hotel to get him to return.

Arabella had never worked with, or even met, the Swedish star standing glowering in front of her, but she knew that was not an excuse. She felt herself blushing and turned slightly to the wall to avoid the soprano's hard gaze.

"Matilda, are you still there? Miss Nyman says she has booked this room." Arabella could hear Matilda tapping on her keyboard.

"Hold on." She hummed something which sounded vaguely like ballet music. "You are in number five, aren't you? Madame Nyman should be in number six." Lowering her voice, she said, "Come on over, when you finish. I have news."

"Yes, right, see you later." Arabella hung up and turned to Marie Nyman. She cleared her throat. "You are booked into the room next door. Number six."

Turning on her heel, Nyman shut the door hard, not quite slamming it. "Phew, charming."

"I worked with her last year," said Peter. "Actually she was quite nice."

"Well, she got out of the wrong side of her bed today, that's for sure."

"I doubt it," he sniggered. "She's married to Nicholas Miller. They are *the* golden couple at the moment. Don't you read the gossip pages?"

"Not very often, I admit." She looked straight at him. "I've been so busy lately, coaching *Das Rheingold*, and that means a lot of hours." He shifted his feet. "And James and I are renovating the house we bought last year, doing as much as possible ourselves. I don't even get to see the magazines at the hairdresser, because Barbara in the make-up department cuts my hair for me." She turned the pages of her music. "Anyway, Peter, after that breath of Scandinavian icy wind, we have thirty minutes left, so let's make the most of it, and try to get the next sixteen bars memorised, *correctly*, before the coaching ends."

Arabella brought down both hands heavily on the chord, using the sustaining pedal for good measure. Peter sang loudly to make himself heard, and they continued for another five minutes before the door opened again.

"How much longer is this going on?"

Arabella and Peter stopped and turned to Nyman, who suddenly recognised the tenor. "Oh hello, Peter, I didn't realise it was you." Her voice was much friendlier. Her English was perfect, almost too perfect, with just the slightest trace of an accent. "I have a rehearsal with Johannes Kirchner in an hour, and I really need to run through a few things in my role. *Porgi amor* for one."

Arabella felt guilty and reddened again. The Countess's aria at the beginning of the second act of the *Marriage of Figaro* was pianissimo. It must be quite impossible to concentrate on that sublime music with the unpleasant noises she and Peter were making next door.

Peter immediately closed his score and stuffed it into his briefcase. "Sorry, sorry, sorry. We are done anyway. Come on, Arabella. Let's go."

"Thank you, and I'm sorry."

*Well, things were looking up. An apology this time.* Marie Nyman hesitated at the door. Arabella didn't look at her, and with some force rammed her own music into her bag. When she did look up, the space was empty, and she heard the door to studio six close softly.

In a stage whisper, she said to Peter. "You go on down. I just need to check on something here."

Peter left. Arabella walked to the door and listened. The most wonderful voice began to sing the aria. Pure, but rich at the same time. The type of sound she adored. *Well, who didn't?*

Marie Nyman was at the very top of her profession. Arabella felt a little ashamed. Who was she to have been so rude to the owner of this glorious instrument? *And, she is hot too. And married to a hunk. Oh well, you can't win them all.*

Nicholas Miller was a relatively well-known English actor. Arabella had seen him onstage once, in a silly comedy-farce. She believed he did more TV and film work these days. She had to admit they made a golden couple, and would no doubt have beautiful babies.

*O mi rendi il mio Tesoro, O mi lascia almen morir!*—Either restore my dearest one's affection to me, or let me find peace in death!

"Whatever," Arabella closed the door, and tiptoed towards the stairs.

***

"Oh my god, that was so embarrassing. Do you think she will tell Sir William, or the music director? She has a call with him in," she glanced at her smart phone. "Thirty-five minutes. Shit."

Arabella threw herself down on the ancient sofa facing Matilda's desk. Sam, the leading baritone in the company's permanent ensemble was leaning on it, close to Matilda. Not for the first time, she wondered if something was going on between them.

Both were married, he in the process of a divorce, she not particularly happily. *I really must get Matilda to confess.*

Sam now sat on the desk. "I doubt it. I've worked with her four or five times. She's an Ice Queen, but totally professional, and a good and supportive colleague. And very desirable. But she didn't fall for my charms, though I tried." Matilda gave him a dirty look.

Arabella snorted. Sam had a reputation. He tried to corner her behind the piano on their first coaching session, but she had made very clear that it wasn't going to happen.

"Actually, I did wonder if she played on your team Arabella."

She expected the remark. If a woman didn't fall for him, she had to be gay. *Typical.*

"Really? But Peter told me she is married to Nicholas Miller, and that they are the flavour of the month. He was surprised I hadn't read it in the gossip magazines."

"I'm not sure they are actually married, but according to one I read they have bought a house together near Richmond Lock." Matilda did go regularly to a salon instead of using Barbara to style her hair. And Arabella had seen Gala on the table in her office.

"No house under three million in that area," said Sam. "If they are not married, I hope they sorted the finances." His tone was bitter. Everyone in the company knew he was having financial problems with the pending divorce.

His wife had been a promising singer, until she gave up her career to marry him and be the mother of their three kids. She was trying to get a settlement for twenty years of lost earnings. "On second thoughts, it's just as bad if they are married."

"Poor Sammy. Can I buy you a drink in the Nags?" Arabella got up from the sofa and stretched. The top she had tucked into her skirt rode up and showed a flat, tanned stomach. Sam almost licked his lips. Matilda looked daggers.

"Come on Matilda. The phone hasn't rung once since I've been here. There's no performance tonight. Sir William is in the States, and Johannes has musical calls, and anyway, his secretary can deal with his problems. Let's get out of here."

Matilda looked at the phone, sighed, and stood. "You are so right. And we are so dedicated. You buying me a drink as well?"

"No way. You owe me for four hours of Peter Clapton this week."

"Three and a half. The Swedish nightingale cut a half hour off your torture."

For a moment, she pictured incredible grey eyes staring at her. The perfect eyebrows. And those high Scandinavian cheekbones. And the soft skin on her long neck beneath the chignon. Had she imagined the spark?

She was being ridiculous. The woman was married and a superstar. Why would she even notice an opera pianist with conducting ambitions?

The three of them crossed the road to the pub.

\*\*\*

As usual it was crowded. Over in the far corner stood a group of singers, cast members of *Ariadne auf Naxos*, one of the productions playing in the repertory of the Royal Opera House. Arabella had played for some rehearsals, though it wasn't her allocated work. She was surprised to see the cast.

"What are you all doing here? The next performance is tomorrow." Arabella knew as she was on the schedule for orchestra pit duty.

"That's what I meant to tell you," said Matilda. "The old boy isn't feeling very well, so Timothy Wells will conduct tomorrow." Timothy was also a pianist colleague, but very senior to Arabella. "So, he wants to rehearse tonight, or at least the tricky bits, as none of them are enthusiastic about coming in tomorrow morning."

Arabella shrugged. There is almost no part of *Ariadne* which isn't tricky. She wouldn't like to be thrown into the deep end on the opera, although Timothy was the official assistant conductor and knew it well. Arabella was sometimes titled *assistant conductor*, but it didn't mean she would conduct a performance. In cases of illness, an experienced replacement was called in, usually from Europe

"That's absolutely fantastic for Timothy. But why aren't they flying someone over?"

Gemma O'Leary, the Irish soprano singing Zerbinetta, looked over to Arabella. It was dark in this corner of the pub, but there was no mistaking the desire in her green eyes. Arabella had noticed her interest several times during rehearsals but had chosen not to react.

After all, she had just married an American singer, some years her senior, but generally thought to be the love of her life. They had been waiting for nearly ten years for his divorce to be final. *I just do not want to know about that. Much too messy.*

Gemma's voice was husky, which was unexpected for a soprano regularly singing top F's. "Well, you know, Sir William is difficult to contact at the moment, and Johannes is not really interested. I think he is terrified of his upcoming prima donna production, and so we in the cast asked for Timothy. He conducted a lot of rehearsals before the old boy even turned up."

Arabella turned to Matilda. "Why aren't I playing the rehearsal tonight?"

"Because you have had too many sessions today. And anyway, Timothy said he would play the piano himself. He has better contact with the singers that way."

"There is something to be said for the argument. I wish other conductors thought the same."

Sam sniggered. "Some of them aren't musical enough."

"Bullshit," said Arabella, "I am forced to spring to the aid of my fellow conductors. Even the ones who can't play the piano."

Gemma sidled up to Arabella. She whispered softly, "Doing anything on Saturday night? We are having a small party, a sort of housewarming."

Arabella wanted to run screaming, but she had been working non-stop for weeks, and the alternative was tiling the kitchen. There was Sunday for that.

"OK, yes, thanks. That would be fun."

"I hope it will be. I'll text you the address. You don't have it, do you?"

"No, yes, great. Sevenish? Earlier? Later?"

"Sevenish is good."

Gemma touched her arm for rather too long, but Arabella felt nothing. In fact, quite the reverse. She wondered briefly about her reaction. She hadn't had sex for at least two months. Steely grey eyes came to mind and elicited a signal in her core. *Stop being ridiculous!*

The *Ariadne* cast gathered their things and left for the evening rehearsal. Other company members joined Sam, Matilda and Arabella. They took their time over two more drinks, Arabella changing to mineral water for the last one, before leaving the pub.

Parked outside the stage door was a top-of-the-range black sport Audi. The rear windows were tinted, but they could see the driver. It was Nicholas Miller. Matilda nudged Arabella as they approached the stage entrance. As they were about to push the stage door open, Marie Nyman came out.

She stepped around them, without really looking, then seemed to recognise Arabella. There was a hint of a smile, but it faded as she gazed expectantly into the driver's window. Nothing happened, so she went around to the passenger door and let herself in.

*Wow, so not a gentleman.* Arabella paused outside the stage door. Other singers were also leaving, and she stood aside while they passed her. *They are as bad as each other. Icy. Their central heating bill must be enormous. Nice and cool in the summer though.* She watched the car accelerate down Floral Street. The tinted windows obscured her view.

***

From the orchestra pit the following evening, she watched Timothy whenever she wasn't playing her piano part. Not every seat in the auditorium was taken. It was always the same with *Ariadne auf Naxos* performances. Box office poison they called it. So unfair. The music was glorious. Timothy was doing very well. Although he had his head down in the score rather too often, instead of being with the singers. *Oops, exactly, that was a moment when they weren't with him.* He could have avoided it. But they were back on course almost immediately.

Arabella swore to herself that if she ever got the chance to conduct an opera, she would be so secure she would not need to look at the score at all. She sighed. The chance would not likely come her way in the near future, if ever.

But she was wildly excited about her concert in two weeks' time. She was engaged to conduct a small chamber group. Rehearsals were to take place most evenings over the next fortnight. She had arranged it to fit into the gap where she was free, *The Marriage of Figaro* not being her allocated piece.

She allowed herself to drift away from the Strauss music for a moment. She turned her head and looked up at the staff box in the dress circle, wondering who was watching tonight, supporting Timothy. In the box next to it, sitting alone, was Marie Nyman. And she was gazing straight at Arabella. Their eyes locked. *We can't keep doing this.* The moment was over when Marie looked back onto the stage. She was following the singer singing the role of Ariadne. It would be a perfect role for her.

As far as Arabella knew, Marie was still singing primarily Mozart and Verdi roles, but surely she would be moving onto Strauss and even the lighter Wagner at some point in her career. How glorious that would sound. Arabella lost herself in an aural fantasy before she had to jerk herself back to the reality of having to play again. She was busy until the end of the performance, and when she turned to look up, the box was empty.

***

On Saturday evening, Arabella took the tube to Gemma and Pierre's new house. She could have ridden her bike as it was a lovely mild evening, but she knew she would be drinking, so decided not to. The house was an unremarkable narrow terrace house in the middle of a row which was obviously being renovated. It would soon increase in value. *A clever investment,* she took it in before ringing the doorbell. Since buying her own house she was interested and critical of renovations.

Pierre opened the door. She could hear voices. He gestured for her to follow the sounds, which she did.

She took in a breath. Attached to the rear of the house was a conservatory. It soared the entire two and a half stories up to the eaves. In the middle was a spiral staircase, at every level a small platform leading to a door, which in turn led into a room on each floor. It was a stunning idea, brilliantly executed.

There were a large number of fashionable plants filling the space, including a couple of orange and lemon trees. Gemma came over to stand very close and put her arm around Arabella's waist. She checked her out from top to bottom, rather too obviously liking what she saw.

"Hot," she breathed in Arabella's ear, who immediately regretted having dressed the way she had, in skinny black jeans, a black shirt and broad belt with silver trimmings.

"What would you like to drink?"

"White wine?"

"Coming up."

Pierre entered the room with two girls who sang small roles in the production. Gemma gracefully released her, letting her hand just brush against Arabella's butt. Luckily nobody could see it, unless they were looking into the glass of the conservatory wall. Nobody was.

"It's so lovely to see you. Thanks for coming," Pierre kissed her on both cheeks. They had worked on a production the year before last, and Arabella was very fond of this infinitely polite and generous gentleman. She began to feel awful about the situation with Gemma. He couldn't possibly know, could he? Or perhaps he did and was prepared to tolerate his much younger partner's tendencies.

Gemma came back with the wine, and Pierre looked at her so adoringly, it didn't seem likely. She handed Arabella her glass, and kissed Pierre bruisingly on the mouth. He almost melted. Arabella knew that the kiss was for her benefit. Gemma watched her the whole time. *Cheap.*

More guests arrived. They were about twenty in number, and she knew almost everyone.

She enjoyed the evening. She managed to keep her distance from Gemma. A few people left, and Arabella was about to thank her hosts and go too, when Gemma stopped her.

"I've noticed you looking up a lot. Would you like to see the rest of the house?"

Pierre smiled at her. "Oh yes, do, we are so proud of it." *No, he doesn't suspect anything.* Arabella was relieved and alarmed simultaneously.

"I don't want to take you away from your guests."

"We won't be long."

They walked up the staircase to the first floor. "Master bedroom, master bathroom. You see how the staircase from the conservatory leads into the bedroom." Gemma was speaking loudly, and they could most definitely be heard from downstairs.

"We have a guest apartment built under the eaves. I'll show you." They climbed the second staircase. Gemma closed the door, pulled Arabella towards her, and began kissing her wildly. At first, libido clicked in, and Arabella responded, moving her hips closer to Gemma's. Gemma moaned softly, and thrust her tongue into Arabella's mouth, chewing her lips. It was not erotic, and Arabella pulled away.

"No, Gemma. Really, not in your own house, with your husband a few metres away."

"Can we meet somewhere, soon. You turn me on so much" Gemma was breathless.

"Let's talk about it another time." *No way.* But she didn't want to prolong this conversation.

She opened the door, and said loudly, "What an incredible room," and hurried down the two flights as fast as she could. Pierre was at the bottom of the stairs. Arabella was so thankful her light lip-gloss had worn off during the evening. She had left no trace on Gemma's mouth.

She felt hot and uncomfortable, and wanted to get out of the house. Saying swift goodbyes to everyone, she walked out of the front door.

"Do you want a lift?" She was relieved to see two colleagues from the cast standing next to their car. Safety in numbers.

"We can drop you off at Covent Garden." It wasn't near where Arabella lived, but she could get a direct tube, instead of having to change lines from where they were now.

"Great, thanks."

They dropped her off. Instead of going straight to the tube, she wandered into the all-night warehouse store. It sold a lot of expensive rubbish for the tourists, but if you looked carefully, there were also little things, suitable for small gifts, and Arabella quite often browsed. The store wasn't busy. She noticed the cashier was reading a book.

*Gorgeous.* Not really her type, but at least on the soft spectrum of butch. They looked at each other. She had grey eyes. Arabella clenched her thighs as that most delicious of aches spread over her core. She walked over.

"What time do you get off?" A pause, and they both laughed at the innuendo.

"On the hour." It was ten minutes to.

"Shall I wait?"

"It would be my pleasure."

\*\*\*

Claudia lived in Holborn, quite near the store, and they walked to her apartment. It consisted of a small studio room and was clean and neat.

"A drink?"

"Water, please. I've had enough tonight."

"Are you drunk?"

Arabella laughed. "No, I know exactly what I'm doing."

They moved towards each other.

The sex was good, the first round hard and fast, after which they lay together on the bed until both were relaxed and their breathing steadied. Arabella stroked Claudia's stomach, which twitched. She rolled on top of Arabella, and her face came close. "Kiss?" They hadn't up until now.

Arabella caught Claudia's bottom lip and nibbled gently. The kiss was slow and deep, until it escalated, and Claudia slid down Arabella and kissed gently up her inner thigh. Arabella eased her legs open.

"May I?"

"Yes please."

Her climax was deep and satisfying, and she reached for Claudia, who shook her head. "No need, I took care of myself."

They lay sated next to each other, until Arabella slid her legs over the edge of the bed, to get to her clothes.

"You won't stay?"

"I don't think so."

"OK. I'm going back to Australia next week anyway."

Arabella was relieved and sorry in equal measure.

"Don't get up."

"Thank you for tonight."

It was heartfelt. Arabella looked once more into the grey eyes, seeing another face in her mind, but she refused to let that thought go any further. She brushed her lips against Claudia's, walked to the door and let herself out. She felt good.

\*\*\*

The next morning, Sunday, Arabella woke and stretched languidly. She felt muscles which she hadn't exercised for a while. She would like to stay in bed longer but heard James and Ian downstairs banging about and cursing, so with a groan she made for the shower, dressed in overalls and went to join them.

Tiling was her speciality. The kitchen was half finished and looked awful. She prepared the cutting tool and got to work. They stopped for coffee and toast at three o'clock, and by eight, she had finished the job. The men applauded. Now she felt other muscles aching, and they were not nearly as pleasurable.

"Indian take-away?" Ian asked.

She made a face. "It's too late. I won't sleep. Too heavy. Can I make us a quick spaghetti?"

They agreed and drank a bottle of wine together with the meal, all three frequently smothering yawns. Arabella was exhausted. Saying goodnight to the men who were clearing the table and loading the dishwasher, she dragged herself up to her room. As she lay in bed slowly letting her muscles relax, she turned on the radio.

A gorgeous voice was singing Agathe's aria from *Der Freischütz*. She waited for the announcement. It was Marie Nyman. She fell asleep, leaving the radio on. At five o'clock, she was wakened by white noise. And remembered what she had been listening to. She turned the radio off and drifted back to sleep.

\*\*\*

Arabella woke at seven forty-five, and as she gained consciousness, her stomach flipped in nervous anticipation. She would begin rehearsing for her concert this evening. First though, she had two hour long coaching sessions at the opera house, after which she planned to return home to study, eat a snack, and prepare herself unhurriedly for the rehearsal at six o'clock in Golders Green.

She had been learning the two orchestral works for months and knew them so well she could conduct without the score. But she felt too inexperienced to do that.

She was far too nervous to eat more than a slice of toast and a banana. She chose tea instead of coffee, much as she loved her morning latte. But tea was easier on her slightly nauseous stomach. She had a brisk twenty-minute walk to the tube station. The sick feeling receded.

At ten minutes to ten, she was in studio room number three, waiting for her coaching session. Penelope knocked shyly on the door. She was one of Arabella's ensemble favourites, a tall south African contralto, who seemed never to quite believe she deserved to be where she was.

Born in Soweto and given the chance to study after her voice was heard in a church, she won a scholarship to the Royal Academy in London and was engaged by the head of casting at the opera house in her final year. She had difficulties with languages, but Arabella did not mind at all helping her to get her tongue around German. They worked on Erda's monologue for the hour. It was a delight to listen to the rich organ like tones Penelope produced.

Her next session was with Fabien, the youngest fixed contract singer. He sang only tiny roles but studied larger ones for the future. He brought the Tamino aria from *The Magic Flute*. Arabella had played a hundred auditions in her four years at the opera house. This aria came up at practically every tenor audition, and she could play it in her sleep. She found Fabien arrogant and bumptious, and the hour seemed very long. Five minutes before the end, Arabella was itching to pack her music and to be on her way home.

The phone on the wall rang, surprising them both. She reached for it.

"Good you're still there." It was Matilda. "Hmmm, sorry, I've got some news, and I don't think you are going to like it."

"What's the problem?"

"Andrew just sneezed, three times."

"And?"

"He's playing for *Figaro* rehearsals."

Arabella groaned. For someone not involved in the opera business, the news of Andrew's sniffles would have meant nothing at all. But singers are hysterical about catching colds or flu. Most guest artists didn't get paid for rehearsals at Covent Garden, which meant living at their own expense for between three and six weeks in one of the most expensive cities in the world.

The fees they earned were paid per performance. If they didn't sing, they didn't get paid. A cold or even worse, laryngitis, could affect a singer's voice for weeks. It was possible to miss an entire run of performances and be woefully out of pocket.

"He's been sent home. The divas are jumping up and down. The staff producer has sent them away, but he must rehearse again this afternoon, or they won't get through the opera. They are on a tight schedule. So…"

"But I can't! You know I have my first rehearsal tonight. At six o'clock. If I have to work until five here, I can barely get to Golders Green in time, let alone have time to prepare."

Arabella felt her voice getting louder. Fabien shrugged and left.

Matilda sounded rattled. "Oh come on, I know how well prepared you are."

"But I've never even played *Figaro*."

"You are a great sight reader. It's not Bartok for god's sake."

"Where the hell is Timothy? He's supposed to be working on it."

"He must conduct the rehearsals. Johannes has a concert in Hamburg this week and is missing."

"Fuck!" Arabella checked to see no one was outside and could hear her. "What a great time to be AWOL."

Matilda chuckled. "Well, he couldn't have planned it better. It's the second act for the next three days. Who wants to be in a room with the three divas? I mean, well you are going to have to be. Sorry. The rehearsal starts at two o'clock on rehearsal stage one."

Arabella looked at her watch. It was just past midday. She would have to dash home to collect her scores. There would be no time at all even to eat, let alone to prepare herself for tonight.

"Buy me a sodding sandwich, can you please? Bacon." She slammed the phone back onto its fixture and ran down the stairs.

\*\*\*

Somehow, she was back in Matilda's office at ten to two. Having run whenever she wasn't in the tube she was frazzled and out of breath. Matilda looked apologetic and handed her the sandwich. She ate half and folded the rest into the paper bag, stuffing it into her heavy case.

She didn't bother to wait for the lift but ran up the three flights of stairs to the largest rehearsal stage. She was conscious of two women talking quietly in the far corner. Richard, the staff director was sitting at his table with Janet the stage manager. Her deputy was writing in his interleaved score. Timothy sat on his tall stool behind the conductor's stand, silently conducting a passage he was studying.

Arabella edged onto the piano stool and opened the lid of the Steinway. "*Nein, das gibt es nicht!*" Occasionally under extreme stress, she slipped into her mother tongue. She had forgotten to bring her *Figaro* piano score with her.

The two women looked up surprised by the outburst. One was Marie Nyman, the other Katharina van Mechelin. Marie's eyes opened wider. Katharina seemed amused. Janet hurried over to Arabella.

"I forgot my piano score." For a second, Janet, the ultimate professional, pursed her lips, but she was kindness herself when she saw Arabella's anguish.

"Where is it?"

"In my locker."

"I'll fetch it for you. Use mine for now." Janet walked fast to her table and brought Arabella her score. It was also interleaved, and thus heavy and cumbersome. Arabella gave Janet her locker key and she hurried away. The lockers were across the road in the administrative block. It would take her ages to get there and back.

It was now after two, and Richard looked at his watch. "We seem to be waiting for Madame Cortez."

"What's new," muttered Katharina, and Marie laughed.

The door burst open, and Ivelisse Cortez made her entrance. She was petite and pretty, with an angelic bell like voice, but looks deceived. She was considered not quite sane by almost everyone in the music business. Arabella saw Katharina and Marie simultaneously take a deep breath through their noses, and she would have laughed if she wasn't wound up like a top.

"Has the room been fumigated?"

It was Janet's responsibility to answer and to calm the woman, but thanks to Arabella, she wasn't there to do her job. Arabella felt a wave of guilt, and looked over to Paul, Janet's deputy. He swallowed hard.

"We aired the room for two hours and washed all the surfaces with disinfectant."

Arabella wrinkled her nose. That explained the unpleasant smell coming off the keys.

"It's not good enough."

Marie intervened. "Come on, Ivee, I'm sure they did their best, and we don't even know if Andrew really has a cold. Maybe it's just hay fever."

"Are you healthy?" Cortez looked at Arabella.

"Of course she is." Marie said soothingly. Arabella threw her a grateful look. Marie very slightly rolled her eyes in the soubrette's direction. Arabella looked down at her music, feeling her cheeks redden.

"Number twelve please," said Richard.

Arabella let out a relieved breath. The Cherubino aria. She had played *Voi che sapete* at auditions even more often than she had Tamino's aria. Thankfully the awkward score wouldn't hinder her as she turned the pages.

The three singers took up their positions. Richard explained what he wanted them to do, and Arabella began to play.

At over forty, Katharina was old for the role. But her figure was lithe and flexible, and she had played Cherubino in every major house worldwide. She brought enormous experience to the part, and Richard needed to say very little.

He concentrated on directing Marie and Ivelisse Cortez, especially the latter. It was a joy to watch Katharina's nuanced performance, as she convincingly played the pubescent teenager. The other singers were able to react naturally, and the scene was over in a flash. Everyone applauded. Katharina laughed off the applause but was pleased none the less.

"This will be my last Cherubino. I'm hanging up his breeches after this run." Arabella thought the gay community would go into mourning when the news broke. The lesbian fans loved the character, and they loved Katharina in the role.

Janet returned with Arabella's piano score just in time as they moved onto the next scene. Now she had to sight read. It wasn't difficult to play, but during blocking rehearsals, sections were staged, then repeated, and a pianist had to be on his or her toes to know exactly from where they were picking up. Arabella always learnt the operas she was scheduled to play inside out, but now she was winging it.

She had several times to search for the cue, flicking the pages back and forth. It didn't help that she was only half-proficient in the Italian language. Cortez sighed impatiently every time. Marie looked puzzled. Arabella began to feel annoyed that nobody on the staff defended her and told the singers that it was not her piece, and that she was only helping out in an emergency. But she was damned if she was going to say anything herself.

She was glad when the break came. She would have loved a coffee but had no energy to go all the way to the canteen. Janet looked at her and asked if she wanted anything. It was not for the senior stage manager to bring a pianist coffee, but Arabella nodded gratefully.

She was left on her own, remembered her half sandwich, ate it quickly, and turned the pages to see what was coming. She hoped they wouldn't reach number fifteen, which was a notoriously difficult and very fast little duet between Cherubino and Susanna. She started practising just in case.

Ten minutes later, the door opened, and Marie Nyman came in carrying two coffee cups. She brought one over to Arabella, who looked at her confused.

"I...I...for me? But Janet is bringing me one."

"It is from Janet, but she was called to the company office, so I volunteered. Apparently, it's the way you like it. Latte, no sugar?"

"How did you know?"

"The canteen lady knew immediately. She seems to be a fan of yours."

"Thank you so much." Arabella blushed, which was intensely irritating. It seemed to be her go-to mode whenever Marie spoke or looked at her.

"You haven't played *Figaro* before, have you?"

"No, oh god, is it that obvious? How embarrassing. I had to jump in and had no time to prepare. And I had to rush home to get my scores for a concert rehearsal this evening. So I couldn't practise and…"

Arabella stopped. *Idiot!* As if Marie Nyman would be interested in her excuses.

"Really. Are you playing? In the concert I mean?"

"No, conducting. It's a great chance for me."

"Well, this rehearsal couldn't have come at a worse time, could it? Poor you."

They were interrupted by the rest of the team and cast coming back from the break. Arabella was touched by the sincerity in her voice. She wasn't only an Ice Queen it seemed.

"The recitative after Susanna's aria please." Richard started the rehearsal again. "Please run it to the Count's entrance, then we'll stage it."

In the previous aria, Susanna and the Countess have dressed Cherubino as a girl. This was lesbian fan heaven. A woman in breeches, playing a boy, being dressed as a girl. Marie and Katharina played up the looks between them and the brief touches and caresses. The Countess sent Susanna out of the room to be alone with Cherubino for a moment.

"Take advantage of this situation please," Richard instructed Marie. "You are alone with the boy." Instinctively, Arabella slowed the recitative. Marie looked at Katharina and ran her tongue slowly over her top lip. The atmosphere in the room thickened.

Arabella stopped breathing. It was just about the sexiest thing she had ever seen. Katharina stumbled over her recitative, then laughed and pushed Marie away.

"Want to come home with me tonight?" She asked her suggestively.

"Maybe." Marie laughed. As did the team in the room. Arabella squeezed her thighs together and hoped she wasn't looking as flushed as she felt.

Richard spoke to Marie. "Only the front stalls would actually see it, but it would be fantastic if you could create that atmosphere every time."

She drawled, "I'll do my very best." Laughter broke the tension.

"Fine, we won't repeat it for now. We don't have Sam this rehearsal so let's skip to number fifteen." Arabella's shoulders sank.

"We have twenty minutes left. That should be enough. Miss Nyman, you are finished for the day. Feel free to leave."

Marie waved her hand in acknowledgement and moved to the row of tables to the right of the Steinway. She undid her rehearsal skirt and stepped out of it, leaving her in her designer polo shirt and comfortable but slim jeans. She took off the character shoes she was wearing and slipped into her own stilettos.

*Hot!* Arabella would like to have savoured the perfectly innocent striptease, but Timothy wanted to run the duet musically before the staging. Ivelisse did not look happy about the attention Marie had enjoyed in the previous scene and stomped over to the conductor. Arabella played the introductory bars after the

Count's exit and Ivelisse jumped in a bar too early with *Aprite, presto, aprite.* Timothy held his hand up to stop.

"How can anyone work with this pianist? I can't."

Arabella fumed but said nothing. Timothy was also too cowardly to say anything other than 'I'll cue you in.'

Which he did, and this time it was correct. But two bars later, Ivelisse made another error, and then another. The atmosphere was fraught. Arabella had not made a mistake but was struggling with the fast music and page turning. Then she was aware of a musky, lemony scent behind her, and a hand placed lightly on her shoulder.

Long fingers reached down and turned the page, making her life much easier. They got through the duet, and Arabella let out the breath she had been holding. The hand on her shoulder lingered a moment longer. She turned and looked into the grey eyes, which seemed a little darker than usual.

"Thanks," she breathed.

"It's nearly five o'clock, let's leave it there and pick up tomorrow, together with Sam. Have a good evening, everyone." Richard packed his things together.

"Go, run, and good luck." Marie touched Arabella's cheek briefly and turned to collect her rehearsal skirt.

Arabella bolted for the door, took the stairs three at a time, and flew out of the stage door. She could feel her cheek burning. Marie Nyman was just being kind. It meant nothing. Artists often touched each other.

The black Audi was parked directly in front of the stage entrance. Arabella caught a glimpse of Nicholas Miller fingering his smart phone. Her gut twisted uncomfortably with a pang of jealousy. She didn't have time to pursue those thoughts. She pushed her way through the crowds and ran down Floral Street, cutting through onto Long Acre and into Leicester Square Tube Station.

*\*\*\**

*Please, please let there be a Northern Line soon.* She arrived on the platform. It was the middle of the rush hour and very crowded. This is so not how she intended to get to her first rehearsal. She squeezed onto the train and tried to wriggle herself to a corner next to the door, where at least bodies pressed against her on only two sides.

She used her heavy case to make a shield. She wasn't in the mood for some man pressing his dick against her. It happened all too often on crowded trains. Half an hour later at Golders Green, she hurled herself up the station stairs, and ran to her destination, slowing only for the last five minutes to catch her breath.

She arrived at exactly six o'clock, which was highly unprofessional in her book. An orchestra could never be kept waiting. She should give the downbeat on the dot of the hour.

The orchestra were tuned and ready. She slid to the desk and unpacked her score and baton.

"Ladies and gentlemen, I am very sorry. There was an emergency at the opera house, and I had to come here directly after a rehearsal. Let's start with Michael Nyman."

She almost laughed. The identical surnames. What an idiot she was, not having noticed until now. She walked around the harpsichord to shake hands with the talented young soloist from the Guildhall School of Music, and introduced her to the orchestra, who knocked gently with their bows against their stands.

"OK. Here we go with Michael Nyman's concerto for harpsichord and strings."

They began the first reading.

At the end of the three-hour rehearsal, she was exhilarated. It was a difficult work, and the young members of the Chamber Orchestra struggled, but they were enthusiastic, and she knew they would go home and practise.

"See you all on Wednesday. Goodnight, and thank you."

Arabella was overcome with exhaustion. She waved at a cab. It would be expensive, but she couldn't stand the thought of the tube. She remembered to pull up the call sheet for tomorrow. Matilda had taken pity on her and put a reserve pianist onto the morning rehearsal. She had only to play the afternoon session. She could practise the second act finale in the morning. She texted Matilda: * 'Thank you darling. Can I please do Wednesday morning, not the afternoon. Tonight was hell.'

\*\*\*

Arabella arrived on the rehearsal stage a good ten minutes early. Janet was already there. The stage management usually needed half an hour to prepare the set and check the props.

"Act three already? I thought they would still be labouring through that duet and the second act finale."

"Miss Cooper, you were well out of it this morning. Miss Cortez continued to struggle with the duet. Richard had called the rest of the singers for the finale, so they were sitting around. The atmosphere was so unpleasant, Richard sent them away, apart from Sam. We worked on the scene we skipped yesterday, and then the duet. Until it was secure. Miss van Mechelin was patience itself, although it wasn't her fault. Richard decided to dial down a notch or two and leave the finale for tomorrow. This afternoon we are doing just the beginning of the third act with Sam, Miss Cortez and Mr Winter."

Patrick Winter was singing the role of Figaro in this revival.

"Then continuing with the other singers for the Sextet."

"The Countess?" Arabella blurted out, rather too quickly. Janet's left eyebrow lifted a millimetre.

"Richard gave Miss Nyman the afternoon off." Arabella fought not to show her disappointment. Janet was sharp.

"Damn it. I practised the second act all morning."

"Language, Miss Cooper. I'm sure you will do perfectly well. Yesterday was the baptism of fire. And your practise won't be wasted. The finale is scheduled for tomorrow morning and afternoon."

The sight-reading kept Arabella on her toes all afternoon. There were no tantrums, and they got to the end of what Richard had planned.

***

The Wednesday morning rehearsal also went smoothly. Arabella had time to practise and was relaxed enough to watch the singers as well as playing. She wasn't glued to her score as she had been the first afternoon.

Marie Nyman wore a full skirt falling to just under her knees and a long loose pullover. Arabella could admire her legs for the first time. Long and perfect. The singer leant down to take off her heels and put on her flat rehearsal character shoes. Arabella's breath hitched. The pullover hid the lines of her full breasts, which Arabella had enjoyed so much under the much tighter polo shirt on Monday.

There was no contact between them until the break, although Marie seemed to relax when she realised Arabella was on top of the music. She smiled.

She decided to continue practising during her break and didn't move off the piano seat. The others started for the door.

Marie hesitated and turned towards the piano. Walking over she asked, "Want a coffee?" Arabella felt herself blushing yet again. It was bad enough when Janet had asked her, and there was no way she could accept a star singer bringing her a coffee.

"No, no thanks, but thank you. I just need to practise a bit more."

Marie nodded and left the room. *That sounded really ungrateful.* But it would not have been ethical to accept. She feared Janet's disapproval, and no one could afford to get on the wrong side of the powerful stage manager.

Ten minutes later, Marie came back in, again bearing two cups.

"I didn't believe you. Here. And how was the rehearsal yesterday?"

"I…I…thank you so much." In her confusion, Arabella took a sip, and just avoided choking on it. "The rehearsal went well, for a first reading. It's a difficult work."

"What is it?"

"We do Richard Strauss' *Metamorphosen,* and in the first half Michael Nyman's *Concerto for Strings and Harpsichord.* The Nyman was on yesterday."

Marie looked amused. "No relation." She was quicker to see the connection than Arabella was. Both laughed, as other people began to come back. Luckily, Janet was a little late, and Marie moved onto the stage floor before she returned. Arabella was grateful.

\*\*\*

For her second rehearsal in Golders Green, Arabella arrived half an hour early and could relax and take in the atmosphere of the room before the others materialized. She wanted to check on a few sections, but the harpsichord was being tuned, which made concentration next to impossible. She moved back to the foyer of the rehearsal hall.

A pretty cellist was taking her instrument out of its case, half turned away from Arabella; who was checking her out when the woman looked up quickly.

It was too late for Arabella to turn away. The woman's eyes opened wide, and a grin spread across her face. Arabella decided there was no way to pretend she hadn't ogled her, and walked over, hand outstretched.

"Hi, I'm Arabella."

"Well, I do know that. Chloe…Spencer." They shook hands and Arabella looked down into pretty brown eyes, green flecks giving them extra sparkle. Chloe's hair was short, but stylishly cut, brown with a hint of copper. She held on just a bit longer than a normal first handshake. Arabella smiled. *Oh my, this is nice.* Although she felt a little awkward. She had no problems picking up girls from clubs and bars, but she was cautious now. Chloe played in an orchestra she was conducting. She dared not abuse her position. Nervously, she put her hand up to her own thick black hair, layer cut to her shoulders. She combed it out of her face, so that her forehead was clear. Chloe followed the gesture with her eyes, and it was obvious she liked what she saw. They looked at each other, but before either of them could speak, a group of the orchestra came in from outside.

The rehearsal went well. It was evident the musicians had practised. Arabella told them they would split Friday's rehearsal. A first half run-through of Nyman, before moving onto the Strauss work.

Everyone packed up their instruments. Arabella was aware Chloe was taking her time, but the orchestra manager came over and offered her a lift before they could speak to each other.

They lived in the same area. After meeting at a couple of neighbourhood concerts she told him about her conducting ambitions, and he gave her this chance. She thanked him now and was grateful. Glad even. She wasn't sure it was a great idea to get involved with Chloe.

\*\*\*

The next day Arabella was scheduled to play for both morning and afternoon *Figaro* rehearsals. Normally, she would have kicked up a fuss with Matilda, but she was looking forward to being in the same room with Marie Nyman for six hours. She was now feeling confident playing the score, so she knew she could watch the singers more. Especially a beautiful Swedish soprano.

The third act was scheduled, and she presumed they would pick up from where they left off on Tuesday. After the sextet. That was the plan on the call sheet. When she arrived, the room was empty. For a moment, she felt disorientated. A rehearsal room was never empty fifteen minutes before a rehearsal was due to begin. She considered calling Matilda. Then the door opened, and Marie walked in.

"Where is everyone?"

Marie laughed. "My fault. I wanted to stage my aria *Dove Sono* without hordes of people watching and waiting, so I asked Richard last night if we could do it with just him and the pianist in the room. The others will be here in thirty minutes."

Arabella blinked. This was close to heaven. Peace and quiet, and the glorious music to revel in. She had played the aria several times at auditions, always hearing mixed results. It was notoriously difficult.

"You want to sing it at ten o'clock in the morning?"

"I might mark a bit." Marie meant the technique by which singers sang softly down an octave from the original key. It was customary rehearsal room practice.

Marie moved over to the rack of rehearsal costumes and took her rehearsal skirt off its hanger. Arabella felt her mouth go dry as she watched Marie pull it over her slim hips. She was wearing tailored dove grey slacks and a matching pullover.

"Can you do me up?"

Arabella stood shakily and moved over to Marie, who turned, holding the skirt up at her waist. Arabella tried not to fumble as she closed the button and pulled up the zip. Marie's lemony musk perfume smelt wonderful. She wished she knew what it was. She tried to breathe in deeply, but silently, through her nose. Marie turned. They were so close. Marie looked at Arabella's lips. The door opened and she stepped away. Arabella walked back to the piano on wobbly legs.

"Do you want to run through the recitative musically," Richard asked, unpacking his director's score. "Before I stage it."

"No, let's just do it."

Richard explained what he wanted from the scene. Marie started to sing. She seemed agitated during the recitative, but Arabella presumed that was how she felt the Countess would react. Arabella read the English translation of the text. *...my husband is so impulsive and jealous. He's behaved with an irrational mixture of infidelity, jealousy and scorn; he loved me at first, then he offended me, and finally betrayed me...*

Marie was a consummate actress. Arabella wondered from where she was drawing such emotion. At the end of the recitative, she sat on the chaise longue centre stage for several seconds. Arabella's hands hovered over the keyboard. She held her breath.

Out of nowhere, Marie sang the first phrase, barely opening her mouth. Arabella played the accompaniment as softly as she could.

*Where have they vanished, those tender moments of sweet pleasure? What has become of the promises sworn by those unfaithful lips? Everything has changed to grief and pain. But why does that past sweetness still possess my memory? Ah, my constant heart, whose love survives my suffering, gives me some hope of regaining my husband's affection!*

Marie did sing with full voice, but pianissimo, as softly as was possible in order to maintain the pitch of the notes. It was the most beautiful sound Arabella had ever heard. The notes swam in front of her eyes. Richard was openly weeping.

"Was that OK for you, Richard?"

He gulped and nodded. Arabella knew she had to blow her nose and reached in her pocket for a tissue. *Damn*, there wasn't one. She moved to Janet's table and pulled two from the ever-present box on the table. She handed one to Richard.

Marie watched them, her expression inscrutable. Then she jumped up.

"What's wrong with you two? Unhappy love lives?" That broke the tension and they all laughed.

"We have ten minutes before the others arrive."

"Who wants coffee?" Arabella seized the opportunity.

"Oh well, if you are going to the canteen, a cappuccino please."

Richard shook his head. "I have my thermos with me."

Arabella ran. Ten minutes wasn't long to get to the canteen and back. Luckily, it was too early for an orchestra or chorus break, so she was served immediately. She ran back and handed Marie her cappuccino. She reached towards her purse.

"Please, no," Arabella was horrified.

"Then it's my turn next." The thought of a next time gave Arabella a warm feeling.

The rest of the cast came in, and they continued the rehearsal. They blocked through to the end of the act, Arabella singing in the chorus part. This was standard practice for a rehearsal pianist. Some were awful, but Arabella possessed a warm alto. Untrained, she could never sing on a stage, but in a rehearsal room it was pleasant enough. Marie looked at her surprised and nodded slightly.

Richard announced he wanted to run the whole act during the afternoon rehearsal, so they all went to the canteen for lunch. Arabella was wondering how she could manoeuvre to sit near Marie, when Matilda grabbed her and took her off into a corner, from where she didn't even have a view of the long cast table. Disappointed but resigned, she gossiped with her best friend until the hour break was over, before running over to the pianist's room to freshen up. She used a little lip-gloss and renewed her eye shadow. She looked in the mirror. *Not bad.*

Marie certainly looked her over when she took her seat on the piano stool. Then they were off. Richard let it run without stopping, so she had to concentrate hard. When they got to the aria, Marie marked her way through it almost inaudibly. Nor did she play out. Arabella was glad. She didn't want to share the morning magic with anyone else.

Richard was happy. "That was a good rehearsal. Thank you everyone. We'll go back to the second act tomorrow morning, and act one in the afternoon." Most of the cast groaned. Arabella was so happy she wasn't playing the afternoon rehearsal, firstly because she hadn't practised it at all, and secondly because the Countess wasn't in it.

She was also grateful to Richard for going back. The thought of having to sight-read act four was not a good one.

She pulled up the call sheet to check the rehearsal plan but smelt Marie's perfume before she could read it.

"Undo me?" *Oh yes, you do.* From her sitting position, it was easy to open the button and the zipper. Marie let the skirt slip down and stepped out of it.

"You haven't answered my question."

Arabella was confused.

"Do you have an unhappy love life?"

Arabella's blood pounded in her ears. "I...I..."

Marie laughed. "I presume not, by that reaction. See you tomorrow." She ruffled Arabella's hair and, looking a little disappointed, joined Katharina. They left together.

Arabella looked down at her smartphone and checked the morning call. She wasn't down for the rehearsal. Andrew was. Obviously, he had recovered. Her usual reaction would have been a whoop of joy, but instead she hurried over to the wall phone, and dialled 106.

"I'm not down for *Figaro* tomorrow morning." Her tone was accusing.

"Yeah, sorry, forgot to tell you at lunchtime. Andrew is better, and we really must give you the time off you were promised. Enjoy it, sweetie."

Arabella could only think of the 'see you tomorrow' Marie said as she left. She grabbed her things and hurled herself down the stairs to the stage door. Marie was talking to Nicholas Miller. They both seemed tense. They were about to go out of the door as she rushed up to Marie and blurted out.

"I'm not playing tomorrow. Andrew is better."

Marie turned. Her eyes were as cold as they had been the week before in the studio.

"That's a shame. Never mind. It won't be such a struggle for you." Arabella flinched from the blow.

Nick looked at her curiously and took Marie by the arm. "Come on, we'll be late."

They left and climbed into the Audi. Marie looked straight ahead.

\*\*\*

Arabella couldn't get out of bed the next morning. She was too mortified. Every time she replayed the scene at the stage door, her skin crawled. The Ice Queen nomenclature was apposite after all.

She was again early in Golders Green. Chloe was already there, but so were several other orchestra members, including the first violinist, and Arabella needed to talk to him about a number of things in the Strauss piece. The Nyman went even better than on Wednesday. She was happy with this orchestra. They were hard workers.

Chloe joined her during the break, but there was no opportunity to talk privately. Arabella still felt raw, and she was very nervous about the Strauss. Her instinct proved to be correct. As she feared, it needed a lot of work, and she hoped that the three rehearsals the following week would be enough to achieve the sounds she heard in her head.

The orchestra manager again offered her a lift. She had a moment of regret as she looked at a disappointed Chloe and determined to at least go out for a drink the following week. After all, she was free as a bird. Entirely uncommitted. Any fantasy she might have about Marie Nyman had been blown out of the water. Had she been so cold because she thought Arabella was in a relationship? She chastised herself for clutching at straws. The woman was a straight super star, married to a handsome husband. They were both A-liners. Way out of her league.

Together with James and Ian she worked on the house on Saturday and Sunday. They were happy she did her share on both days, and she felt guilty for leaving them to do the brunt of the work most weekends. They went grocery shopping on Saturday morning, and Arabella bought the ingredients for one of their favourites, shepherd's pie.

She also bought things for a suet pudding. On Saturday, they ate the pie, and on Sunday a salad followed by the fattening pudding. Arabella looked down at her stomach. She really must be careful. Luckily, the work on the house combined with her hectic week meant she was fine, but she resolved to do some serious cycling the following week.

Which she did. She cycled to the opera house on Monday morning. She held her breath going in but saw nobody as she went up to the wardrobe department. One of the seamstresses had made her a new outfit for the concert and she had the final fitting. They designed it together.

The optic was important for a conductor during the performance. The hard work was done during the rehearsals. At the concert, they had to exude charisma and mesmerise both orchestra and public. If the rehearsals were successful, the job at the concert was more or less directing traffic.

An audience spent almost the whole evening looking at the conductor's back. Most of them were used to watching a man, and a man's back was broad, tapering to the waist. Unless of course they were fat. Many star conductors were attractive men. Sex appeal and power were important ingredients in whatever it was that constituted a successful conductor.

Arabella was lucky to have broad shoulders and she designed a jacket to emphasise this, with visible darts tapering to her waist. Under it, she would wear a black waistcoat shot through with silver thread, and a slim wrap around ankle-length skirt in the same material as the jacket. It was very important that the jacket didn't move up with every arm movement, so the setting of the sleeves was crucial.

The suit fitted perfectly, and she was over the moon.

"You can pick it up on Thursday," the seamstress told her.

Arabella left, again encountering no one. She sighed with relief.

***

Her Monday and Wednesday rehearsals went as well as could be expected. There was still something missing, probably due to over cautious playing. The orchestra were not free enough to let go and just make music. She hoped for a miracle.

"See you all for the final rehearsal in St. Johns, Smith Square," she said at the end, her stomach plummeting with nerves at the thought. Chloe looked questioning, but she shook her head. For now, she couldn't think of flirting, let alone kissing someone. She was sure her nervous stomach gave her penetrating halitosis.

On Thursday, she went back to the wardrobe to collect the suit. She knew the *Figaro* rehearsals had moved on the main stage, so she wasn't worried about bumping into anybody.

"Have you heard the latest?" Betty, one of the dressers asked, "It was amazing. Cortez could be heard shouting right down the corridor."

"What happened?" Arabella's thoughts were instantly with Marie, hoping nothing had happened to her. *How stupid. She couldn't give a damn about me.*

"How would you allocate the dressing rooms?"

Arabella had no idea about the etiquette, but frequently delivering the conductor's musical notes, she visited enough artists in their rooms to have a feeling about it.

"Countess in one, Susanna in two, and Cherubino in three, or maybe in this case, Cherubino in two as Katharina is so famous in the role." The dressing rooms were identical, but it was a matter of status.

"Exactly. But Madame Cortez insisted on number one."

"You have to be kidding," Arabella stared at Betty. "And…did the others agree?"

"Katharina just laughed, Marie Nyman was very gracious, and Madame pranced into number one and started unpacking her stuff."

"They let her get away with it?"

"No way. Janet marched across to Sir William, who came over and went into number one. He left ten minutes later, and Cortez emerged with her stuff soon afterwards, screaming her head off in Spanish, and flounced into number three, slamming the door. Everyone thought she would leave in a huff, but I guess she can't really afford to do that to Covent Garden. She has a terrible reputation in lots of houses. She is sulking of course."

"And who is in number one?"

"Nyman of course. She is so lovely to dress. Am I glad Cortez didn't get her way. My hair would have been grey by the end of the run."

*She's lovely, is she? Well, not always.* But then, she thought back to the coffees, and the hands on her back and ruffling her hair, and she could smell her scent. She sighed and threw the dress bag over her arm.

\*\*\*

It was Friday. Arabella packed her scores and left for the concert hall. At least half of the orchestra was already there tuning and practising. Arabella sat on her tall stool behind the desk and zoned out, narrowing her concentration onto the music in front of her.

The Nyman piece went well. Arabella gave some notes. The harpsichordist asked to repeat a few passages where she felt not quite together with the orchestra. Arabella changed the balance between band and instrument a few times. In the break, the harpsichord was wheeled off.

The orchestra manager asked to say a few words. He had arranged for a photographer to be present before the concert the next evening. The orchestra needed new photos and they would be dressed in their concert outfits. It was a good opportunity. He asked Arabella if she could pose with them.

It meant being earlier than usual as they had to be finished before 'the half', when the public would be allowed into the auditorium. Arabella wasn't thrilled. It meant hanging around in her dressing room for that half hour, and her nerves would escalate, she knew it. But she couldn't refuse, and the advantage was she might have some good photos of herself in her new outfit. She knew the time had come to make a website, so she agreed.

The rehearsal resumed. The Strauss piece was fine, but again, a lack of inspiration worried Arabella. Was it her fault? Was she just not good enough?

Chloe kept her distance, realising that Arabella was not in a receptive mood. She appreciated that. Chloe was good news.

***

Arabella managed toast for breakfast, but nothing else. She rested as much as she could, packed her scores and a banana and set off for the concert hall. In her dressing room, she changed into her suit, and began her make-up. She had decided to go for just a hint of gothic.

Image was everything in the conducting business. Talent was in abundance. It needed something else to tip you over into the sought-after, and onto the first rung of the career ladder. She used a dark eye shadow and lightly rimmed her eyes with kohl.

She decided against black lipstick. That would be going too far, so she applied an almost colourless gloss, which made her lips sparkle. There was a knock on the door, and the manager collected her for the photo call. His appreciative look made her feel good.

The orchestra stopped talking and tuning when she mounted the rostrum. There were a few whistles and claps from the boys. She saw Chloe sitting holding her cello with her mouth wide open.

The orchestra members were not dressed in white tie and tails, but as befitted a young chamber group, they wore unisex black shirts and jeans and a thin grey leather tie. It was a good look, and complemented Arabella's outfit perfectly. The photographer snapped pictures of the whole group, from a variety of positions.

Then he asked Arabella for a few action shots. He was done in twenty minutes. Arabella asked him if he would photograph her in her dressing room, to which he agreed. Luckily, the light was good, and he said he had some good shots. She would pay privately for anything she accepted.

Over the loudspeaker in the room, she could hear the audience coming into the hall. *At least there were more than a dozen there.* It was every artist's fear to play to an empty auditorium. Then she remembered the manager said they were almost full and expected to sell out.

The players were applauded as they took their seats. The first violin took his place, they tuned, and Arabella narrowed her concentration. She let the harpsichordist walk ahead of her, then stepped onto the rostrum, raised her baton, and they were off.

The applause for the soloist was gratifying, and she played two short encores. The orchestra listened appreciatively and joined in the applause by tapping their bows against their stands. Arabella did the same with her baton.

Then it was time for Strauss, and Arabella came out alone, after the orchestra were seated and had tuned their instruments. The applause greeting her was much louder than was usual at this midway point in a concert. She was surprised, and it made her more nervous. *Oh god, please let it be better than yesterday.*

And it was. It was sublime. There was complete silence as she lowered her baton. It seemed endless, then came a loud 'bravo' from the back of the hall. Followed by a storm of applause, which went on for several minutes.

She lost count of how many times she went off into the wings, and came back on, each time gesturing for the orchestra to rise and take the applause. On her last entrance, they refused to obey her command, and remained seated. She turned to the audience and took a solo bow. The applause level rose again.

She got back to her dressing room and sank onto a chair. There was loud knocking. Matilda headed a group of pianist colleagues, and some of the younger members of the singing ensemble. She hadn't known they would be there, and she felt tears pricking behind her eyes, but managed to control them when Gemma and Pierre came in.

Gemma pulled her into a hug and kissed her, letting her lips linger for as long as possible. Luckily, Pierre interrupted with a 'My turn,' which was much more welcome.

Everyone left except Matilda. "Are you going somewhere with the orchestra, or shall we go and eat?"

"I think they are going to the pub next door. Can we go too for a bit, then we can eat something later."

"Sure. Get changed. Or are you going in that outfit. You look like a pop star."

Arabella laughed, closed the door and changed into grey skinny jeans, a top and a light anthracite coloured linen jacket. She was about to remove her makeup, but Matilda stopped her.

Arabella put her arm around Matilda's waist, and they left the dressing room laughing. Chloe stood outside and her face fell when she saw Matilda. Matilda looked at her for a long moment. "It's not what you think," she said, poking Arabella unsubtly in the ribs.

"Chloe plays cello. Chloe, this is my colleague from the opera house, Matilda." Chloe looked relieved, but still uncertain.

"Come on, we are all going to the pub." They left as a threesome. James and Ian were waiting in the street, too shy to have come into the backstage area. She hadn't known they would be there and was deeply touched. So, they came to the pub too.

Chloe looked wistful as the group said goodbye, and Arabella whispered, "I'll be in touch," before realising she didn't know how to. She could get the number from the orchestra manager. They hugged, and Arabella kissed her cheek, which was deliciously soft. She felt a slight flutter in her core. *Another time.*

***

Arabella had coaching again on Monday. Her mini holiday was over. There were two sessions in the morning, followed by two in the afternoon, so she went over to the canteen for lunch. It was crowded, and she sat down at a table with some chorus members and young soloists before she noticed Marie at another table, reading the *Times*. Arabella took in a breath. Marie had not seen her.

"Hallo there, superstar," Andrew said loudly, rubbing her back as she tried to bite into her sandwich.

"Have you seen the *Times* critic, with photo. Wow. You look great, and the review actually says, '*a star is born*'. Sorry I couldn't be there." Arabella blushed and mumbled, as more people congratulated her.

She was aware of Marie looking up. Her expression gave nothing away, but her eyes were not the steely grey from last week. She looked back to her paper and turned pages. Arabella got a glimpse of her own photo. Marie was reading the review. The conversation at the table moved on, and some chorus ladies were giggling about the Cortez dressing room scandal, which had become even more dramatic as the story did the rounds.

Arabella was aware of Marie standing and reaching for her bag. With a swift, elegant movement, she put the newspaper into it, and moved towards the door. Was it her own copy? Or had she stolen it from the canteen supply.

***

Arabella read on the call sheet that the dress rehearsal of *Figaro* was scheduled to begin at ten thirty on Thursday morning. She wanted to watch it, but Matilda gave her coaching at ten and twelve o'clock. At the end of her first session, she hurried down to the stage, entering on the side away from the stage manager's desk.

Paul was running the cues, and Janet was sure to be wandering around, but Arabella hoped she would be near Paul and not on the side where she stood. The scene change to the second act was due to take place in a few minutes. Figaro's military aria was coming to an end. It wasn't allowed for staff to get in the way of scene changes, so she squeezed into the gap next to the duty fireman and hoped she was invisible.

She saw Marie coming from the dressing room. Of course, she would go on stage from this side. Arabella hadn't thought of that. She wanted to stay unseen, but at the same time she didn't.

Marie looked unbelievably beautiful in her chiffon nightgown. It shimmered around her curves as she walked. Instead of a wig, her own hair was sculpted on top of her head, revealing her long neck. Arabella eyes drifted to her exposed collarbone, and she had to stifle a groan.

"Excuse me, ma'am," said a stagehand to Marie and gestured to where Arabella was hiding. She also had to be out of the way for the change. It could be dangerous. As she neared Arabella, she stumbled slightly over the hem of her gown, and Arabella's arm shot out instinctively to steady her. Marie whirled round and her mouth opened slightly in surprise.

"It's you," she breathed. "Thank you."

At that moment, the curtain came down, the blue scene change light came on, and twenty stagehands and electricians went into action. The fireman moved onto the stage to make sure things were safe, and Marie and Arabella were alone together in the dark corner.

"How did the concert go?"

"Well. Thank you. I think it was a success. The orchestra have invited me back in the autumn for another programme."

"That suit you wore is really something," Marie whispered in her ear.

Before she could reply, the lights went back on, and they moved subtly back from each other. Janet appeared.

"Miss Nyman, let me take you to your position."

"Wish me luck."

"Toi-toi-toi," mumbled Arabella, feeling suddenly cold as Marie's warmth and heavenly smell moved away from her.

Janet came back. "Now, Miss Cooper, you know I don't approve."

Arabella hoped she meant the rule about being backstage during performances. She chose to react to that.

"Please, Janet. I'm coaching again in ten minutes, which means I can't go into the house. I did play rehearsals after all."

"This is an exception. Please no more than ten minutes and stay in this corner." She moved away to go back to the other side of the stage. The curtain went up and Arabella marvelled at Marie's glorious singing. And at her beauty.

The chiffon negligée left nothing to the imagination, and Arabella felt that most pleasurable of aches in her core. *Why was she so friendly again? What had been wrong last week?* There was a smattering of applause from the few people in the auditorium, and Ivelisse Cortez entered the scene from the other side. Arabella hurried back to her coaching, her crotch damp against her jeans.

\*\*\*

Arabella wanted to go to the premiere, but of course it was completely sold out. She was annoyed with Matilda who didn't think to give her a ticket for the staff box, which was also full.

"Come on, I thought after your moaning about having to play for *Figaro* rehearsals, the last thing you would want is to watch the first night. Andrew and Tim are in there, and the Italian coach. As well as the Barbarina understudy. It's packed."

Arabella was not going to reveal her, what she now acknowledged to herself, major crush on Marie Nyman, to Matilda who would not keep the information to herself. Sam would be the first to know, and he was playing Marie's errant husband in the opera. It was bound to get back to her. The thought made her blood run cold.

"You should get some rest this weekend. You are playing the short rehearsal week for the second run of *La Boheme*, and you know Laura Kandinsky is singing Musetta. It could be a heavy week for you." Matilda winked and giggled. Arabella hadn't forgotten, but she had been so busy she had pushed the thought to the back of her mind. She groaned.

"Don't remind me." Laura was a brassy Texan soprano, who liked both men and girls in her bed. She also liked to party and drank too much. Last season, they had somehow fallen into bed together. Several times in fact, until Laura changed tack and moved on to her tenor partner.

That hurt a little, but she had to admit she was relieved. The hard drinking hadn't suited her at all. And now they would be in the same rehearsal room for a week. She hoped Laura had forgotten or best of all, that she had some new plaything with her.

In the meantime, she had a free weekend and a serious date at home with Ian.

Arabella was not a social media fan. She found Facebook crass, hating the stupid, banal postings, and the even sillier videos. She couldn't believe anybody would have the remotest interest in an Instagram page about Arabella Cooper, she felt too old for TikTok and Snapchat, and knew that parts of her concert were already uploaded onto YouTube from a wobbly smart phone.

But Ian, who worked in IT, had convinced her that an informative homepage was essential for an up-and-coming conductor, and after all, she now had some great photos, which, he assured her, should be in the public domain.

It took them most of Saturday to finish the page, and Arabella was technically challenged, but happy with the result. The start side was simple, with a stunning photo of her in conducting modus. Her biography was in English and German. She would ask the language coaches to translate them into Italian and French, but there was no hurry. Perhaps she should have Spanish, Russian and Japanese as well, but that seemed rather pretentious. Her career certainly did not yet merit it.

She also put up more photos from the St. Johns session, and a normal head and shoulders, which looked very tame up against the conducting ones. She had a button for her Calendar of engagements, but that was not yet activated, and she decided against a press section. Just about everybody put their best reviews onto their homepages, but who really cared, let alone believed they were true.

She settled for a banner with one line from the *Times* review on the start side: *A conducting star is born.* What hubris. She shuddered a little, but Ian was insistent.

The Contacts link was important. Fortunately, she was on the books of a boutique agency in St. Martins Lane. They had yet to get her any work and hadn't come to her concert but had called her enthusiastically after the *Times* review. At least she didn't have to use her own contact details.

Ian activated the page. She sent a link to Matilda, who could be relied upon to spread the word. As she was browsing, and on a whim, she internet searched Marie Nyman wondering why she hadn't done so before. No homepage. She was as reclusive as Arabella. No Facebook or Instagram either. They obviously had that in common.

Her Wiki side was not overlong considering her status. Daughter of two teachers, born in Stockholm, Bachelor in biology, of all unlikely subjects, then musical studies in Stockholm and a Master's degree in Hamburg. After winning the Lieder Prize at the Cardiff Singer of the World competition, she was taken up by one of the largest agencies in the music world, and there was no looking back.

She had sung at the Metropolitan in New York, Chicago, San Francisco, Paris, Madrid, Hamburg, Munich, and the Vienna State Opera. She was thirty-five years old. Her birthday was on February the fourth, which made her a Pisces. She was six years older than Arabella, who was a Cancer. *Complimentary zodiac signs if nothing else.*

She searched Nicholas Miller. Naturally he had Instagram. There were pictures of them together, even one of them kissing. Arabella scrolled down. There were hundreds of pictures of celebrity actors and directors with Nicholas. *Yeah, actors needed to self-promote.*

In one photo, he and Marie were sitting in a beautiful garden with a honey-coloured house wall behind them. There were others around the table, and all held full wine glasses up to the photographer. Marie's sunglasses sat on her head. She smiled but it didn't reach her eyes. She looked a little sad.

***

Feeling nervous, Arabella walked to the piano in the rehearsal room. The morning session had been a *La Boheme* first act rehearsal. Everyone in the cast had done the production before and it was fun. There were five men on the stage. Arabella and the pretty Italian singer Giulia Romano were the only women present.

There was a lot of testosterone in the room, and the boys came on to both of them whenever there was a break in the rehearsal. Both just rolled their eyes and let them get on with it. It wasn't seriously *#MeToo*. Giulia said they would run a mile if either of them responded.

Things would be different this afternoon. And they were. Laura Kandinsky had a way of creating chaos.

She came in with Sam, who was singing the role of Marcello, laughing loudly. Arabella kept her head down behind the Steinway. Laura seemed to be sober. The afternoon rehearsal was advantageous for her as she suffered badly from jetlag. She couldn't be relied upon to be punctual for morning rehearsals for at least ten days after arriving from Houston.

Andy the staff director introduced everyone, but they all knew Laura, and vice versa.

"And our rehearsal pianist, Arabella." Laura looked over and crooked her finger. Arabella got up reluctantly from the piano stool and walked over.

"Hello, gorgeous," she said huskily, and kissed Arabella on the mouth. Whistles and catcalls echoed around the room. She whispered in Arabella's ear, "My husband is here this week, but after that…"

A weight fell from Arabella's shoulders. If she could get through this week, she thought she could avoid Laura once the performances started.

At the end of the rehearsal, she held back, talking to Andy. Laura looked over to her, shrugged, and left the room. Arabella dawdled for a further ten minutes to give Laura time to leave the theatre.

She sauntered down the stairs, intending to drop in and visit Matilda, who would want a blow-by-blow account of the rehearsal, but stopped when she saw Gemma was in the room. She most definitely didn't need that. Although, a minute later she wished she had gone into the company office where she would at least have had Matilda's protection.

Standing together at the stage door, blocking the exit, were Laura and Marie in conversation. Marie saw Arabella and rolled her eyes just a fraction. Arabella could not go back. There were other people behind her. The only way was forward. She hoped Laura wouldn't see her, as she muttered, "Excuse me," and tried to sidle out of the door. Laura caught hold of her hand and pulled her back.

"This is the sexiest pianist on the planet, aren't you, gorgeous. Marie, do you know Arabella? I know you don't play on her team, but would you in all honesty kick her out of bed to get to Brad Pitt? Well, if the bed was big enough, I think I would just invite him in too. Heaven. Does anyone have a number for Brad?"

She laughed loudly and leaned over to kiss Arabella. "Sweetheart, I can't wait for my husband to leave so we can resume where we left off."

Marie's face froze. The steel returned to her eyes. Her mouth turned up in disgust. Arabella wanted to die. No moment in her life had prepared her for this sense of horror, despair and embarrassment. Gently, she released Laura's grip on her hand, and pushed open the door.

"Gotta run. Bye."

She fled to the car park in a daze, unlocked her bike and cycled, her long legs pumping the pedals, away from the theatre, and home.

\*\*\*

Somehow, she got through the next two days. Laura flirted with her outrageously, much to the amusement of the rest of the cast. She managed to avoid being alone with her, rushing away at the end of every rehearsal.

She knew there was a *Figaro* performance on the Wednesday evening and prayed that she wouldn't bump into Marie. Ivelisse Cortez came in just as she was leaving the theatre, but she was spared barely a glance, let alone a greeting.

On Thursday morning, there was a dress rehearsal of *Boheme*. Arabella sat in the front row of the stalls, directly behind the conductor who gave her notes to jot down on things he wanted to say to the singers. She was busy with that during the interval, doing a round of the dressing rooms with him.

She entered the stalls before the beginning of the third act and was sliding between the seats and the orchestra pit, when she looked to her right and froze. Marie was sitting with Katharina van Mechelin in the seventh row. Katharina waved at her. Marie lifted one eyebrow, but her face was otherwise impassive.

They turned to talk to each other. For the rest of the act, Arabella felt her back was burning. Her face certainly was, and she was thankful for the darkness. When she turned slightly during the scene change to the fourth act, she saw out of the corner of her eye, that the seventh row was empty.

\*\*\*

Matilda offered Arabella a seat in the staff box for the *Boheme* revival on Saturday. She wanted to refuse, but Matilda would have found it beyond odd, especially after the dust she kicked up about *Figaro*.

She sat back and enjoyed the performance. What wasn't to love about this most perfect of Puccini operas. It was well sung. Laura was on form. Giulia

Romano was gorgeous in the role of Mimi, and the men sang and acted up a storm.

Arabella was dressed up for the first night in her black cocktail dress, so she wandered into the bar in the interval. As usual she turned heads. The General Director, Sir William, noticed her, and beckoned her over to where he stood at his usual place, the far corner of the bar. Here he entertained sponsors and visiting managers, and the occasional celebrity. She was immediately nervous, but he smiled warmly and set her mind at rest.

"Arabella, I wanted to see you in my office next week, but as you are here, and this revival isn't interesting to sponsors or theatre directors, let's have our chat now."

She waited, not really thinking it was up to her to start a conversation, whatever he meant by the word *chat*. He offered her a drink and she accepted a glass of sparkling water.

"At least three people have told me about your concert, and my assistant pushed the *Times* review under my nose. But not just because of that. I have been hearing good things about you for a while. I know you want to conduct. You are a woman," Arabella suppressed a desire to giggle, "and although times are changing fast, it still isn't easy. To give you some help, I would like you to start working with James Staples."

She drew in a breath. Sir James Staples was Covent Garden's conductor laureate. He was in his mid-seventies, which was no age for a conductor, but had for years been crippled with arthritis. He rarely stood in front of an orchestra, but he was a legend, and had taught many of the younger generation of star conductors.

"That would be such an honour, Sir William." She was lost for words. The chat was rather one-sided.

"Good. I've already spoken to James, and you should call his assistant next week to fix a first meeting."

When Sir James was in London, he lived and worked in a small apartment in the opera house. It was the only one and was curiously located high up at the top level, where only the electricians ventured into the auditorium dome to adjust the lighting equipment. Not surprisingly a session with Sir James was known as *visiting heaven*.

Arabella was barely aware of the second half. She watched and listened mechanically as she tried to digest the news. The opportunity it gave her to improve her conducting technique was unique. She went through the pass door and congratulated the cast backstage after the curtain calls. Laura was on her best behaviour in front of Sir William, and Arabella escaped unmolested.

***

It was a relief to work with James and Ian on the house all day Sunday. Before they moved in, the small rear garden was used as a tip. Rubbish was still piled high. The best of it was dusty building debris, the worst was unidentifiable and disgusting.

James ordered a skip, which was positioned outside their front door. They had to carry everything through what was going to be the library/dining room, which had French doors onto the garden. For Arabella, there was nothing better than to eat in a room lined with bookcases. She knew it was eccentric, but it had been the plan for her own house ever since she could remember.

They spread plastic sheets along the whole route and started the laborious job. They dragged and carried everything down the corridor, past the room she would share with the men as office and music room, and up the half flight of stairs to street level. It was physically exhausting. Arabella found it at first exhilarating, then numbing.

She wore thick gloves to protect her pianist hands, and a hazard suit against the dirt, which was probably in some part poisonous. After five hours, her hands felt sore, and her throat ached from the noxious fumes, but they were just about done. The skip was full, and the garden was a patch of dirty earth, cleared of the debris. James and Ian pulled up the plastic sheets and dumped them in the skip. They were too ripped to think about keeping.

Arabella called a delivery service for three large pizzas, and they moved upstairs to the living room, each with a beer. Arabella's back hurt so much; she lay on the floor to stretch it.

As the beer relaxed her and gave her a slight buzz Marie Nyman's beautiful face flooded her thoughts, and for a moment she fantasised about kissing her neck and nibbling down to that delicate collarbone. She felt herself getting wet, and crossed her legs, swallowing a moan. There would never be a chance of realising that dream.

Laura said Marie didn't play on the team. And Arabella would never forget the look of disgust on Marie's face as she realised that there was something going on between them. Or was it jealousy? She knew it was wishful thinking but couldn't quite discount the mixed messages she had received before the stage door debacle.

After devouring the pizza, Arabella couldn't keep her eyes open. In bed, she could feel how wet she was and knew action was needed if she wanted to sleep. She slipped her hand down, closed her eyes and imagined those long fingers stroking her, and the grey eyes staring into hers. She put a pillow over her face to suppress her moans and came as hard as she had ever done.

***

There were no rehearsals the following week, and all the pianists were assigned to coach. Tuesday morning had been kept clear for the annual music staff meeting where plans for the following season were thrashed out. Johannes, the music director, was in the chair.

They were given full cast lists, and went through each new production and revival, discussing who would need coaching on each role. Most of the older members of the fixed ensemble had sung their roles before, but the younger ones needed to be taught almost everything. The international guest artists came to rehearsals fully prepared and were not the responsibility of the music staff. On rare occasions, they too had to be helped.

Johannes allocated each pianist the operas they would play and coach. Everyone had preferences and hoped they would get put onto pieces they loved.

Arabella knew she was on the opening production, which was *Das Rheingold*. Her language ability was an asset, especially as in this case the director was German and had a habit of returning to his mother tongue whenever he got excited, which was often.

She crossed her fingers. She knew the production beginning in November was Richard Strauss' *Der Rosenkavalier*, but she didn't have much hope of being on it. It was the plum of the season and her much more experienced colleagues would surely take priority. She was completely flummoxed when Johannes said, "Andrew, Paul and Arabella, with Arabella as assistant conductor."

There was a stirring in the group and Timothy Wells did not look too pleased, but he managed to congratulate her.

Johannes looked at her. "This is Sir William's idea. I admit I think it's a bit soon, especially as I will be guest conducting elsewhere and not present at all rehearsals, so you will be thrown in at the deep end. I can only advise you to learn every word, and every note."

They all looked at the cast list. Arabella couldn't contain her groan. The good news was that two legendary German singers were coming to sing Oktavian and Baron Ochs. Suzanne Weigl and Gunter Schmidt. But Gemma was cast as Sophie and Laura as the Marschallin. Arabella didn't need to voice it. Andrew said it for her.

"Why Laura? She is so unsuited for the part, and it beggars' belief to think she is a good enough actress to pull off the subtlety required for the Marschallin."

Johannes shrugged impatiently. "I agree, but there was some sort of agent skulduggery and Sir William was pressured into the decision. And I believe an important sponsor has the hots for her, so he was left with no choice."

Andrew sighed. "Nyman would be my ideal Marschallin." This time there were murmurs of agreement.

"Yes, but she is due to sing it for the first time the year after next and wouldn't anyway be prepared for the role next season. It is as it is. Maybe Laura can surprise us all. Next."

*No way.* Arabella was sure every pianist in the room agreed with her.

They moved on through the season. Arabella had revivals of *Don Pasquale, The Magic Flute, Fidelio* and the inevitable *Boheme*, and she would be preparing *Die Walküre* for the opening of the following season.

She had a fantastic set, and to cap it all, tomorrow she would have her first session with Sir James Staples. Now she hurried to the library to collect a full score of *Der Rosenkavalier*. She owned an ancient piano score, but she needed the orchestration. She was going to learn every crochet and quaver of that huge work before rehearsals began in November.

***

The first week of June came and went. A second series of *La Traviata* was in rehearsal, which would complete the repertory for the present season. During the summer months the Royal Ballet tended to have more performances. *Ariadne auf Naxos, La Boheme, Marriage of Figaro* and *Traviata* filled the opera slots. The final performance of *Figaro* was scheduled for the end of the following week leaving the other four operas to play until the end of the season.

Arabella had only coaching duties until the beginning of July when she would stop in order to play for two weeks of *Rheingold* on the rehearsal stage. The music staff began to feel in a holiday mood, and the weather was glorious, so they cajoled Matilda into scheduling as few coaching sessions as possible. Arabella used her free time to memorise *Rosenkavalier*.

She had had three sessions with Sir James Staples. He was tough with her, but she appreciated that. At the last session, she asked him if they could begin work on *Rosenkavalier,* but he shook his head. "Let's walk before we can run, shall we." They continued working on *The Magic Flute*, practising cueing in the orchestra at the end of the recitatives which, Arabella had to acknowledge, was hard enough.

She more or less scuttled in and out of the theatre, keeping a low profile. She avoided the canteen, but needed, and indeed wanted, to see Matilda, and perhaps go to the pub and catch up on some gossip, so at the end of her Sir James session, she gingerly made her way to the company office. Thankfully it was empty of singers.

"Oh hi, I just gave Marie Nyman your mobile number. Hope that was OK."

"You what! Why…how…what did she want?"

"Something about needing a pianist to play for her for a TV thing. I don't know. She was a bit vague. I know I should have asked you first, but you were up in heaven all afternoon, and I didn't think you would mind being called by a superstar. A straight one, anyway. Believe me, I wouldn't have given your number to Laura or Suzanne Weigl."

"Suzanne Weigl is happily married to her manager and has been for at least ten years. And Laura already has mine…unfortunately." Thankfully, she had heard nothing from Laura. Either her husband was still in London, or she had picked up somebody new, the latter being the most likely.

"Anyway, I told Miss Nyman that you were busy conducting all afternoon and unreachable, and that she should call you this evening. Want to go for a drink in the Nags?"

"A quick one. I promised Ian I would take him out as a thank you for creating my homepage." The lie slipped easily off her tongue. She had honoured her promise the week before, but Matilda didn't know that. All she could think about was getting to a place where she could wait for her phone to ring, but she certainly didn't want Matilda to know. She was as sharp as Janet. They had their drink. Matilda's gossip was in short supply. Arabella made her escape as soon as she could. Luckily Sam came into the pub, and Matilda didn't fight her on it.

She had ridden in on her bike today. It was faster than taking the tube. Whenever the weather was good enough, she cycled to and from work. It kept her fit. She had also started using the simple rowing machine she and James installed in their communal office.

Conductors needed a lot of strength in their arms and shoulders. Her arm and leg biceps were both harder and more pronounced than they had been in the winter months. Not that she wanted to look like a butch, but no, she was far away from that. Just fit.

\*\*\*

She had never ridden so fast, and she had to admit, so dangerously. She practically jumped lights and overtook cars, garnering a few dirty looks from drivers along the route. In just over twenty minutes, she heaved her bike down the stairs into the basement area and locked it to the old coalhole door. It was hidden from the street and had been safe up until now.

Then she ran back up the stairs to the front door and let herself in. She was alone in the house, for which she was grateful. She threw herself down the stairs to the kitchen and yanked a bottle of mineral water out of the fridge. She was so thirsty, her tongue stuck to the roof of her mouth, and she couldn't have said a word. Taking her water into the library, she extracted her smartphone from her bag, turning it on. It had been on silent during her Sir James session. Too late, there was a message from an unknown number. With trembling fingers, she pushed to hear the voice mail.

"Arabella, I hope this is your number." Of course, it wasn't obvious. Arabella had never got as far as recording a personal message. "I...could you call me back on this number. It's urgent I'm afraid."

*Oh god, no, is something wrong with her? How stupid, she wouldn't be calling me if there was.* Matilda had said something about her needing a pianist... and TV. She steadied her breathing, and pressed recall.

Marie answered on the second ring. "Arabella? Thanks so much for calling back. I want to ask you a favour." There was a slight pause. "Are you busy on Friday morning, or could you make yourself free?" Arabella heard her take in a breath. "A Swedish TV production company have been following me around for a few months. They are filming an hour-long film portrait and will be taking scenes from the last *Figaro* performance on Saturday. But they also want to film me working on some songs. I'm sorry about the short notice, but I would be very grateful if you would play for me. I have reserved a rehearsal studio for ten o'clock. They need time to set up their cameras. Would eleven be alright?"

"Of course. I can do it." Arabella paused, and before she could think what she was saying, blurted out, "I thought you were mad at me." There was a long pause.

"I'm not mad at you. What would give me the right? We just don't share the same tastes."

That was a low blow, and Arabella cringed. "Oh really. I happen to like my pizza with tuna and onions. How about you?" It was cheeky, but she didn't think Marie had the right to criticise her tastes in anything, though she did have to agree about Laura. There was a pause, then a chuckle.

"If you add some black olives and extra mozzarella, I'm with you all the way."

"Still, I'm sure Andrew or Timothy would be over the moon to play for you." She felt like making Marie beg.

"Yes, but they aren't as pretty as you are," came a low purr over the line.

*Where am I with this woman? Now she's flirting with me.* "Um… what do you want to work on?"

"Do you know the Grieg Heine songs? I thought I would keep it Scandinavian."

"Yes, I do, but I don't think I have the music."

"I'll bring it with me."

"What should I wear?"

"One of your normal coaching outfits. We should look natural."

"OK, I'll be there before eleven."

"Thank you so much. Goodbye until then. Oh, and Arabella, just a touch of kohl round your eyes would be lovely." The line went dead. Arabella typed in *Marie Nyman* and saved the number in her contacts.

\*\*\*

Friday morning was warm. Arabella had no intention of arriving hot and sweaty, so she took an early tube to get her to the opera house in plenty of time.

She went first to an empty studio and warmed up her fingers. She wanted to play at her best on Swedish TV.

She followed up with a visit to a staff cloakroom where she carefully refreshed her make-up, adding just a little more kohl. She knew that TV cameras put on ten pounds in weight and made a person look washed out. She used foundation, as she didn't want to run the risk of pink cheeks.

She had on fairly tight black jeans, a black sleeveless t-shirt, and her anthracite linen jacket, freshly ironed. Low heels completed the outfit. Her stilettos would have been much more elegant, but she remembered Marie had said to be natural, and who wore three-inch heels to coach a Grieg song?

She opened the door to the rehearsal studio. Lights and two cameras were being set up around the Steinway. She did not see Marie, so decided not to walk over to the piano, but stayed just inside the room, leaning against a table near the door, until Marie came in, deep in conversation with a good-looking man in his thirties. They were speaking Swedish.

Marie wore elegant grey trousers, and a button down fitted silk shirt in a slightly darker colour. The top buttons were undone, revealing a hint of her generous cleavage. Her hair was up in a chignon. Arabella felt a flutter move southward. She moved slightly to attract attention, and the Swedish couple turned. Marie's eyes darkened and she coughed.

"Sven, this Arabella… my pianist. Arabella, Sven, our director." Sven's eyes moved up her body onto her face.

"Are your eyes really that blue, or are you wearing contacts?"

"Yes, I am. I thought my reading glasses would reflect the lights. Or so I was told once when I did a TV interview."

Marie cut in. "But I can assure you her eyes really are this colour." Arabella was glad she had used foundation. She felt her cheeks flare.

"You are a beautiful woman. I'm happy we can work together."

"Sven…down boy." Marie made light of the situation, but Arabella could see she was far from pleased. *How interesting.*

"Ladies, take up you positions please. Let's film a complete version of the first song, then you can pretend to work on it, or even better, genuinely work on it."

Marie handed Arabella the music for two of the songs Grieg wrote in German to texts by Heinrich Heine. She turned to Sven.

"I don't hold out much hope for a good first take. We haven't ever worked on them together. But we can try."

Arabella opened the photocopies out wide on the piano. Luckily, she wouldn't need to turn the page.

"Tempo?"

Marie indicated with her hand what she wanted, and Arabella began playing *Zur Rosenzeit.* They were filming with two cameras. One of them was trained on her, and the other on Marie who stood in front of the piano behind a music stand on which she placed a second copy of the songs.

Arabella had played the songs some years previously for a graduate student in college, and she found she remembered them almost perfectly. It meant that she could look at Marie most of the time, only glancing occasionally at the music. Marie looked back at her, as she knew the texts by heart. They were immediately on the same wavelength.

Arabella could follow exactly when Marie wanted to breathe or to hold a note a little longer. It was an almost perfect rendition of the song and would normally have been achieved only after many hours of practise together.

"That seemed pretty good to me," said Sven.

The spell broke and Marie said drily, "Try to top that...anybody."

They began a filmed working session, in which Marie asked for a slightly different tempo in a phrase, or Arabella corrected a note or a pronunciation. It was totally unnecessary, and only for the cameras, but they did it. Then they sang and played a full take of the second song, *Ein Traum,* and the same thing happened. They simply gazed into each other's eyes and made perfect music together.

"This time, I would like a different camera angle. Marie, could you go around and stand behind Arabella. Look over her shoulder."

Marie did and they began working. Arabella was now tense. She could feel Marie's warmth behind her back and smell her scent.

"That's good. Now, Marie, can you please lean over Arabella's shoulder. I want a shot of your heads together. The black and blonde hair contrast is rather wild." Arabella felt a line of sweat trickling between her breasts.

"Phew, it's so hot in here. It's the lights. I'm afraid my hands will slip on the keys."

"You can take your jacket off, if you are decent underneath." There was no mistaking the slight leer. "We'll film you taking it off, otherwise there is a continuity problem. Ready?"

Arabella slipped out of her jacket and threw it on to a chair next to the piano stool. Marie leaned over her shoulder and pointed to a phrase in the music. She put her other arm around Arabella's back and her hand skimmed softly and slowly down Arabella's left arm, until it rested on her bicep.

She coughed slightly as if she had choked on her own saliva. Arabella clamped her thighs together. She was so turned on she thought there would be a puddle where she sat. But Marie was the consummate professional, and they played the scene; Arabella even noting things in pencil on the page, which she thought was a brainwave, and would make the take look more convincing.

"I think we have everything we need. We can wrap it there. Marie, please come with us. We need some shots of you at the front of the opera house and walking around to the stage door. And another one in the corridor, arriving at your dressing room. You have brought the outfit you want to wear tomorrow, haven't you? It will have to match with giving autographs after the performance. Arabella, thanks a million."

She felt dismissed and picked up her jacket. She handed the music back to Marie and turned to go. Marie hurried after her. "Wait," she took hold of Arabella's arms and turned her, looking into her eyes. "Thank you so much," she said softly and kissed her lightly on both cheeks.

Her hands lingered on Arabella's biceps, and she took in a breath. Arabella was sure she heard an appreciative hum, before she was released.

"Are you coming to the performance tomorrow?"

"I'm sorry I can't. I have a dinner date." She was meeting her cousin, a journalist who edited a small magazine. Marie's face closed down and her expression was inscrutable. The cameras and crew made for the door, and Arabella hurried away, slipping her jacket back on. She had goose bumps all over her arms, but they burned where Marie had held her.

*\*\*\**

She had a full afternoon session with Sir James, and was terrified she wouldn't be able to concentrate, but the work with him was always intense, as well as being fascinating, and she pushed all memories of the morning to the back of her mind.

When she turned on her phone at home that evening, there was a text from Marie: * 'I really am so grateful. Sven is bowled over by you and says if you ever want to get into films…I am leaving for Paris early on Sunday, so we won't see each other again. I haven't said goodbye to Laura, so please give her my best.'

Arabella's first thought was to text back, or even call her, but she wouldn't really know what to say. It was obvious Marie had jumped to the wrong conclusion about her dinner date. Why hadn't she explained in the rehearsal studio? She couldn't really answer that, but suspected it was an instinctive reaction. Marie's private life was a closed book. Why should she open her own to Marie? Anyway, to deny her relationship with Laura would sound pathetic. She decided dignified silence was the best reaction. She tossed and turned half the night.

\*\*\*

She led a routine existence for the next three weeks. Coaching, working with Sir James and studying her music for the following season, especially *Rosenkavalier*. One evening, as she shopped on her way home, a long queue at the supermarket cashier was backed up to a magazine rack. She did a double take when she saw a picture of Marie and Nicholas on the front cover of a magazine. She put a copy in her basket.

In the middle was a four-page spread about the *super couple*. She now knew what Marie was doing in Paris. She had a concert to sing, but principally she was being the supporting wife. Nicholas had a role in a mini-series being filmed there.

There were several loving, smiling photos, one of them both in swimwear. Marie's figure was perfect. She could so easily have been a model, although she was a little too full breasted. Arabella salivated over the long neck, flat stomach, and elegant legs. A grinning Nicholas Miller beside her was just too irritating. Arabella tore the article out and cut Nicholas out of all the pictures. She put them into the bottom drawer of her night table, apart from the bikini photo, which she slid carefully into a side pocket of her wallet. *Like a spotty teenage fan.* She shuddered but left it there.

*Rheingold* rehearsals began at the beginning of July. They would only manage to work on the first two scenes, so Peter Clapton had a stay of execution until August. Arabella felt ripe for her holiday and let even the hysterical outbursts from Helmut Kirsch the director, wash over her.

The last two performances were ballet, which meant the opera ensemble could all leave on Thursday afternoon. A large group of them occupied the Nags Head public bar until they were thrown out at closing time.

***

Arabella took a plane to Munich the next morning. For the last five years, she had spent two weeks there with her grandmother, followed by a week in Wales with her parents, and a week doing whatever she pleased. Her relationship with her *Oma* was her most important.

She got on fine with her parents, but they didn't really understand her chosen career or her lifestyle. It was to her grandmother, Clara, that she first came out as gay, during her time studying at the Hochschule in Munich. Clara hadn't been at all surprised.

It crossed Arabella's mind more than once that her grandmother's relationship with her closest friend Mia might hold secrets. They had studied together and shared an apartment. Six months after Mia married, Clara married a second cousin. It was a marriage that was neither happy nor unhappy. The couple seemed indifferent to one another. There was only one child, Arabella's mother. They provided her with a stable and loving home life, until she met her husband, Arabella's father, on an exchange trip to Cardiff. They married and moved away from Munich.

He worked for an NGO and was sent all over Africa. As a baby she travelled with them. When Arabella reached school age, Clara intervened, and Arabella lived with her and her husband Wolfram for significant parts of her childhood and adolescence, going to school both in Cardiff and to the international school in Munich which had the same syllabus as the school in Wales. Wolfram died when she was a young teen, and Mia's husband two years later.

Since then, there was never a day when Clara and Mia didn't see, or at least speak to one another. Arabella once asked why they didn't just live together, but she got no answer.

Clara lived in a spacious apartment in Schwabing, a lively area of Munich, full of ethnic shops and cafes. Often artists, students and wealthy business executives lived on the same street. It had been very convenient when Arabella studied at the Hochschule. It was a ten-minute fast walk away, or three minutes by bike. And when it was raining, there was the tram, which also stopped at the main station, and followed by a short walk, she reached the Bavarian State Opera, where she sometimes worked as an usher on duty in the top tiers. They were four to a tier, which meant they took turns watching the evening performance. It was bliss, and it was where Arabella met her first love.

She dated boys from the age of sixteen. Her classmates were pairing up from thirteen onwards, but she resisted until it was no longer credible. The remarks from classmates became unbearable and cruel. As often as possible she used piano practise as an excuse. Eventually she started going out too, with an admittedly great looking boy a class ahead.

They made out, and Arabella could get turned on by their kissing, but she could not understand the way her friends described their relationships. She didn't feel like that. Until she met Eva, a Czech mezzo-soprano, also studying at the Hochschule. For a while they were on the same roster in the State Opera. Eva took her breath away, and it was mutual.

Eva lived alone in a tiny studio apartment in a grungy district of Munich, but it didn't matter as they rarely left the bed. She was experienced, and Arabella was a fast learner.

After six months, she felt Eva becoming distant, and she decided to jump before being pushed. She confronted Eva who admitted she had begun a relationship with a singing professor, a man thirty years her senior. Arabella was heartbroken but resilient and discovered the rich world of gay bars in the city of Munich.

She became a player. Never more than one night, and never waking up with a partner. She became a heartbreaker herself.

In London, she mellowed, but remained happier sticking to her rules, although she had affairs which lasted for as long as a month, and on occasion did stay the night.

Her relationship and house purchase with James and Ian suited her perfectly. She settled down with them. They were close friends with no messy emotional attachment. She was happy.

***

Arabella spent a week almost exclusively in the company of her grandmother and loved it. They gossiped, went shopping, took Clara's car down to Garmisch and walked in the Alps, and on her birthday, the nineteenth of July, to Lake Starnberg, where they took a round trip on a ship. The lakes outside Munich were where celebrities or the fabulously wealthy lived, with huge houses and gardens accessing directly onto the water.

Some were smaller of course, but all were gorgeous. On a windless sunny day, the Alps were reflected in the water of the lake. "I could live here."

"That would be nice, you could visit me more often." Both sniggered. It was a ridiculous idea.

At breakfast the next morning, Clara looked at her granddaughter. "You should go and have fun, that was no way to celebrate your thirtieth birthday."

"But I love being with you Omi, and we did have fun yesterday."

"At least tonight, go to one of your clubs or bars, for a different kind of fun." She winked. Arabella acknowledged she did have an itch. She felt the familiar slight throbbing in her core.

"I'll see how I feel later." It was a hot day. They went for a walk and ate a light salad in an outdoor café on Leopoldstrasse. Clara yawned.

"The heat is tiresome at my age." At home, they both lay down in their rooms for an afternoon snooze. Arabella grilled a steak for dinner.

"I'm going to watch TV. Mia is coming over. Please go out, Arabella, and enjoy yourself." She realised Clara and Mia wanted some time alone.

There was no point getting to a bar until eleven at the earliest, so Arabella took her time showering and grooming herself. She dressed in her cruising gear, skinny black jeans, tight black sleeveless t-shirt, wide black leather belt, and armfuls of thin silver bracelets. She also put on silver earrings. She was not butch, or even soft butch, but she did favour a slightly androgynous look when she went to a bar.

As she applied kohl to her eyes, she thought of Marie. She had thought of her thousands of times of course, keeping it to herself. She decided not to tell Clara, as there was nothing to tell. Where was Marie, tonight? Wrapped in Nicholas's arms somewhere. No, she wasn't going there.

She chose a bar in Tal, near the Isator, and as she was early, and Mia had already arrived, decided to walk. It was still hot, but now pleasant for strolling.

She cut down onto Leopoldstrasse, and walked its length, passing the university buildings, and on up to the Odeonsplatz. There she turned left, past the Residenz and reached Max Josef Platz.

The State Opera was directly ahead. People were streaming out. The performance must have ended. She wondered what it was. The month-long festival at the end of each season featured the crème de la crème of great singers. It included a new production, concerts and recitals, as well as the standard repertoire performances, which were packed with illustrious star names.

The seat prices mirrored what was on offer. Arabella would have to take a mortgage on her house to buy two stalls' seats. But Munich was a wealthy city, and the performances were always packed.

She watched people for a while, either walking to eat at a fancy restaurant, or fighting to get out of the underground garage before the fumes became life threatening or being driven away in the chauffeur driven cars lining up outside the entrance. When it was quiet, she crossed over into Maximillianstrasse, which would take her past the stage entrance.

As she turned the corner, she saw crowds of people on the pavement, spilling out into the road. *Shit, autographs*. She was about to cross over the wide street, when she saw the black Audi. Nicholas Miller, looking bored, leant against the driver's door. *Marie must be here.* Arabella had only Paris on her radar, and never thought to look at the performance schedule in Munich.

She walked a little closer to the group, and then she saw her. Wearing a wrinkled black linen button down dress with sneakers, and a scarf wound into a turban, to hide what the wig had done to her hair on a hot July night. But she was still ravishingly beautiful.

She was being gracious as ever, signing photos and programmes and even some CD covers, talking to each person, smiling, posing for selfies, although she probably couldn't wait to get away and under a cool shower. Arabella shivered at that image. Something made Marie look up quickly and then they were staring at each other.

"Bella, what are you doing here?" *Bella*…nobody called her that, apart from her mother. She saw Marie looking her over and saw her gulp as she looked first at Arabella's bangle encased biceps, before coming to rest on her kohl-rimmed eyes.

"I'm here visiting my Oma, sorry, Grandmother. I didn't know you were here. I wanted a rest from opera, so I never looked at the performance schedule. Anyway, I could never afford a seat." She was babbling and stopped.

The fans were moving away. She saw Nicholas open the car door.

"If I'd known you were here, we could have had coffee…or something. But we drive out first thing tomorrow morning."

"Marie, are you done?" Arabella did not like his tone.

"Coming." *I wish.*

"Well… goodbye… have good holidays, and maybe we can meet in the autumn." *She said can.*

Marie climbed into the car. This time Nicholas held the door open for her, and then shut it with more force than was necessary for a car in that price range. Arabella quickly crossed the road and started walking down Maximillianstrasse. The Audi did a U-turn but had to wait behind a tram taking on passengers.

Arabella knew Marie was watching her. The tram moved off, the Audi followed, and passed her just as she turned to her right down Falckenbergstrasse. Then it was gone.

*\*\*\**

When she arrived at the bar, Arabella turned heads. She always did. She ordered a beer and leaned against the railing to check the room. She was still shaken by the unexpected encounter. And she was very turned on.

She visualised Marie standing in front of her, and then calling her *Bella*, and was torn between banishing the image with a pickup and wanting to go home to relive the meeting and revel in fantasy thoughts. Then she thought of Clara and Mia and didn't want to burst in on them.

There were a lot of baby dykes in the room. That was not her scene, although several of them looked longingly at Arabella. Then she saw her. Tall, blonde hair piled on her head. Around forty at a guess. Jeans and a black button-down shirt, the sleeves rolled to the elbow, a hint of cleavage.

Arabella's gut lurched. The face was much broader than Marie's. She had a strong jaw, with an almost clenched chin. *Marie as a dyke.* Their eyes met. The woman walked over. "You buying, or am I?" *So near and yet so far.* Her voice rasped. Arabella guessed she smoked.

"On me." She lifted an eyebrow inquiringly.

"Hi, Hefe Weisse please… Mareike."

"Annike." Arabella had no idea why she gave Mareike the wrong name. She had never done it before. She ordered the Bavarian speciality beer, sometimes known as champagne beer because it was very much fizzier than lager.

"You speak perfect German, but I hear something else."

"Yes, I'm Swedish." It slipped out before she stopped to consider that Mareike might speak the language. She was lucky. There was no sudden torrent of a language she spoke not one word of.

"Over here on holiday?"

"Yes, I go back tomorrow."

"Are you in a hotel?"

"No, I'm staying with friends in an apartment."

"Pity."

What was she doing! Sabotaging the evening before it began. Although, she couldn't take Mareike back to Clara's, and there was obviously a reason why Mareike couldn't take her to her own home. She glanced down at Mareike's right hand and saw a ring.

Germans wore their wedding rings on their right hand, as opposed to the British way. She realised she had never noticed a ring on Marie's finger. *How odd.* Mareike saw her looking.

"Husband." OK, well it was better than wife. "I would take it off, but it's too tight. Shall we dance?"

Arabella was glad, and they danced wildly, at first keeping a distance between them. She felt exhilarated and tension left her body. Then they danced closer. She grabbed Mareike's hips and ground them against her own. It felt good. She was getting very wet.

"Bathroom," whispered Mareike in her ear. Hand in hand, they wove their way through the now very full room. Luckily, the bathroom was relatively empty, and it had a row of quite spacious stalls. Arabella pulled Mareike roughly into the one furthest from the door.

She undid two buttons on her shirt and pushed Mareike's bra cups down. She grasped her right breast and put her mouth to it, sucking hard on the nipple, which hardened immediately. Mareike yelped with pleasure. As she moved to the left breast, Mareike tried to force Arabella's head up to kiss her, but Arabella was stronger, and bit down on her nipple.

Her right hand moved down to Mareike's jeans, and she popped the button, and tore down the zip. A musky, not unpleasant smell tickled her nose, and for an instant she thought she would like to go down on the writhing woman she held, but it would be impractical in the stall. She pushed her hand down Mareike's boxer shorts and rubbed the slick folds.

Mareike's head fell back, and she gripped Arabella's back. Her nails were rather painful through the thin t-shirt. She entered Mareike with two fingers and started thrusting.

"Oh god, yes, yes, please, harder." Arabella turned her and pushed her against the door. She increased the speed, curling her fingers between thrusts. With a low growl, Mareike climaxed, her walls pulsating against Arabella's fingers.

She sagged against her, and again tried to kiss her, but Arabella moved her face away, and Mareike's head fell against her shoulder. They stayed like that for a minute, until Arabella pulled her fingers away, and gently eased up the zipper.

"Your turn."

"No, I'm good. I…I must go." She unlocked the door, trying to ignore the painful pulsing in her clit, and walked quickly out of the bar… and home. She was still wet and turned on when she reached the flat. Clara was in bed, but she had left a light in the living room.

Arabella didn't bother to shower, though she wanted to. She lay on her bed and pulled the sheet over herself. It was too hot for any other covering. Her hand stroked her folds. This wouldn't take long. Her clit was swollen and hard. She closed her eyes and played back her meeting with Marie. She heard her say 'Bella' and came hard, whimpering softly.

*\*\*\**

She had given herself a holiday from music in Munich, but after flying home to London, she packed her *Rosenkavalier* score, and her music for the October chamber orchestra concert, which had now been decided. Benjamin Britten's *Simple Symphony*, Samuel Barber's *Adagio for Strings*, and Brahms *Variations on a theme by Haydn* in the second half. The latter work was not much longer than twenty minutes, but they would play his *Hungarian Dance* number five as an encore. It was a rousing piece, calculated to get an audience cheering.

Her suitcase weighed a ton, and she needed all her strength to heave it on to the train taking her to Cardiff. Her mother met her at the station. Arabella was amused that she now spoke German with a faint Welsh accent. Her father was at home. He was also on holiday.

They always had plenty to talk about but avoided the subject of her sexuality. They didn't disapprove, though Arabella always felt they were disappointed. They wished for a husband and children for their only child.

Her father had stopped much of his travelling to Africa, and acted as a consultant, so they decided to buy a house outside the city of his birth. He worked from home a great deal. Both her parents enjoyed gardening, and had created a gorgeous back yard, with a terrace leading to a small pool. This was extremely optimistic considering the Welsh weather, but it could be covered with a glass construction, and heated during the winter.

This year the weather gods were on Arabella's side, and she spent most of the day swimming and studying her music by the pool. She stayed for ten days, and when she left Cardiff, she was at peace with her parents and sported a flattering golden tan. She deliberated going somewhere for the last six days of her holiday, but the weather kept fine, and she could spend her days in the little back courtyard of her house, where a gardener had put up the planned high fence and laid out a good half metre of fresh earth underneath it.

Arabella and James went garden centre shopping as soon as she got back, and she spent the money she would have invested in a trip buying large numbers of creeping plants which she then planted and cared for every day that week. It was a much more satisfactory use of her money. She sighed with pleasure as she planted the last jasmine. The blossom was already giving off its heady scent. The middle of the plot had not been paved as they couldn't afford it yet, but the weeks of good weather had hardened the earth, and it was no problem to lie there on an inflatable bed.

She not only maintained her tan, she deepened it, and Arabella was aware as she dressed for the first day of the season in a knee length skirt, sandals and a short sleeved blouse how good she looked.

Peter Clapton voiced what the other male members of the cast were thinking with a 'Wow, good to *see* you Arabella,' and even the director, Helmut, looked her up and down and smiled his greeting. She went to the company office in the break, where Matilda and Sam were deep in conversation.

"Arabella, I have to say, if I ever turn to women, you are at the top of my list." They hugged, and Sam pretended to pant.

"My turn."

Matilda looked daggers, but his hug was no more than brotherly. She really liked Sam.

"Any gossip?" They looked at each other. "Oh, I see."

"No, you don't," Matilda was flustered.

"Your secret is safe with me. Pub later?"

"Definitely."

The holiday had been fine, but it was great to be back at work.

\*\*\*

*Rheingold* remained on the rehearsal stage for a further two weeks, before it moved over to the main stage. The pianists and conductor were now in the pit, and Arabella could no longer see what was happening above her head. It was the part of the rehearsal procedure she liked the least.

And there were a lot of technical problems with the complicated stage design, so she sat for long periods of time not playing, and able to see nothing. She could not leave the pit in case they wanted to resume. She downloaded the music for her concert programme onto her iPad and surreptitiously worked on it. A lot of musicians now had all their music digitally downloaded and some pianists and even string quartets played performances from their screens. Arabella shuddered. She wouldn't dare, terrified of what would happen if the screen went black. For learning purposes, it was fine.

The piano dress rehearsal was gruelling. It almost always was. Theoretically, all aspects of the production, except for the orchestra, came together for the first time. That meant the completed set, the singers in costume and make up, and the lighting plot, with its dozens if not hundreds of cues making magic on the stage. There was a wide margin for error, and this time it seemed magnified out of all proportion.

If this was the way it was going to be for *Rheingold*, which had a running time of two and a half hours, what was *Walküre* going to be like next season at double the length? Instead of playing the opera through which was strenuous, she and Andrew agreed to split the rehearsal between them, but as everything ground to a halt every few minutes, it was still exhausting. The atmosphere was tense and there were often raised voices on stage and in the auditorium.

She heard Sir William intervene, which improved things, and after a long six hours, the run-through finished. There were piano dresses after which the cast, team and director went to the pub to wind down, but this time everyone crawled out of the theatre, barely exchanging looks, and went home.

The orchestra took over. The conductor now had precedence over the director. The singers rehearsed onstage in the set, but without costume and make up. They concentrated on musical matters. Arabella was called to attend the rehearsals but had little to do. Timothy took the conductor's notes.

Sometimes she was asked to move around the auditorium to check the balance between orchestra and singers, but mostly she sat in the stalls, watching and listening, and concentrating on how Johannes conducted. Occasionally her mind wandered. Often she thought of Marie and wondered what she was doing.

She tried to search where she might be performing, but came up with very little, other than that she had a series of performances in Hamburg in October, and Vienna in November. But on September she drew a blank. *On holiday probably, with her husband.*

The premiere of *Rheingold* was also the grand season opening, and the last rehearsal week was filled with the final two dress rehearsals, one on Tuesday, and one on Thursday. Everything had come together, as it usually did in the theatre world, and apart from a few barely noticeable technical hitches, which were greeted by the old hands positively, *bad dress rehearsal, good premiere* was the old adage, the buzz was good after the rehearsals. Friday was given as a free day before the first night on Saturday.

Arabella was lazing in bed when her phone rang. It was Matilda. "Johannes, Andrew, Paul, and your sweet self, have a meeting with Sir William at two o'clock sharp. In his office."

"What the…"

"Yeah. Must be something big. Can you be there? Well, that is not a serious question, sweetie. You will be there, won't you?"

"Of course."

"Bye. Pop in afterwards. I'm dying to know what's up."

Arabella moved fast out of bed. She had time, but she dared not be late for this appointment. She showered and made sure her hair sat perfectly. She dressed in slacks, a top and a light jacket with mandarin collar.

She took no chances with the tube and arrived half an hour early. She went to the pianist's room. Paul was already there.

"Any idea what this is about?" He was nervous.

"Nope. I was thinking. The only thing we all have in common this season is *Rosenkavalier*. Please god, it won't be cancelled."

"I doubt it." Andrew came into the room. "We would not be summoned to be told that. We would read it along with everyone else on the blog." That was true. The music blog in question was filled with the latest gossip.

Heavily tilted towards the USA, it still came up with worldwide news about the music business before anyone else. The forum was the worst. Deeply insulting things were written about artists and arts organisations. Arabella had given up reading the comments years ago.

"Let's go."

They took the lift to Sir William's office and waited for a few minutes in the outer office. Johannes was already in with the general manager. They were asked to enter, and Sir William stood up from his desk in greeting, gesturing to them to sit at the big conference table in the corner. Johannes joined the group.

"Thank you all for coming at such short notice." He was old school, with impeccable manners. "You might have guessed this is about *Rosenkavalier*." Arabella's heart rate picked up alarmingly.

"We have a major cast change." Nobody said anything. "Yes, I know you are wondering why that would entail you all sitting in my office on a Friday afternoon. You could have read that on the blog," he said drily. They laughed politely.

"The thing is, Miss Kandinsky has asked to be released from her contract, claiming she has decided to stop singing the role of the Marschallin." Arabella drew in a breath and prayed nobody would look at her.

Sir William went on quickly. "I don't believe a word of it, and my sources tell me there is some sort of Hollywood film being made, in which she has been offered a role playing more or less herself. I could sue her of course, but quite frankly, I think we are all relieved. She was never right for the role."

He said this as though he had no responsibility for her casting in the first place. Johannes raised an eyebrow but said nothing.

"We have checked the availability of all the best singers who have sung the role, but at this late date, of course nobody is free. Our production is so important, I don't want to start going down the list to the second tier and making compromises. This morning I phoned Marie Nyman. She is scheduled to sing the role for the first time the year after next, in our production. We all know that it takes months to learn a difficult part like this, and we have just six weeks before we begin rehearsals." He paused for dramatic effect. "I am thrilled to say that Miss Nyman has agreed to sing the new production."

The pianists were too stunned to speak. The music director looked at them.

"I am too, and this is where you three come into the picture. Marie has relatively few engagements this autumn. We are incredibly fortunate. She had blocked off the time in her calendar to study new roles, among others the Marschallin. That is so lucky for us. Now, starting immediately, whenever she is in London, she requires daily coaching. Matilda will need to make sure one of you is always available."

Sir William took over again. "She will generally come into the opera house for coaching, but I have agreed, as a special favour, that if it suits her better, one of you will go down to her house in Richmond to work with her there. Are there any questions?"

The pianists looked at each other and shook their heads.

"I hope you are all musically prepared so you can give her the help she needs." They all nodded.

"Would you please go over to the company office. Matilda will coordinate everything. I trust you to be as helpful and supportive as possible. We simply must make this work."

They left the office and trooped over to Matilda.

"Spill the beans. I'm dying here."

Andrew spoke. "We must teach Marie Nyman the Marschallin in six weeks flat. No, probably less, as she has some performances and concerts in Europe during the period. It will probably mean in less than a month. Sir William says you must schedule us, so that one of us is always available whenever she crooks her little finger. Oh, and some of the sessions will take place in her house."

"Wow. OK. That will take some organisation, but we'll cope. It will be most difficult for Paul who is playing *Norma* starting on Monday. Andrew, you are only coaching until the first week of October, then you go onto *Falstaff*. Arabella, you are not playing rehearsals until *Rosenkavalier* begins, but you have your concert in October, and a great deal of coaching other members of the cast."

"Luckily, my concert is over by the time Andrew starts on *Falstaff*. I would be mega grateful if you could do the afternoon sessions on my rehearsal days, otherwise I'm sure we can make everything work." She looked at him. He nodded.

"Well, I guess I should ring the lovely lady and find out when she wants to start." She punched in a number. "Miss Nyman... Company Office, Covent Garden here, Matilda speaking. We are so thrilled about the news. When do you want to start working?"

Marie spoke, but Arabella couldn't hear what she said.

"Arabella, Paul and Andrew are going to be working with you. I think you know them all... Tomorrow. Fine. Paul can be available from eleven to two."

Arabella wanted to speak. Matilda held out her hand to stop her, while Marie continued.

"Arabella and Andrew have performance duty tomorrow. It's the premiere of *Rheingold*, but from Monday they are both available. Perhaps you could mail me details of when you are not free, so that I can coordinate everyone's schedule. They are all really looking forward to working with you. Bye for now."

Arabella wanted to protest. She could easily have worked tomorrow morning, but she didn't want to seem overly eager and wake Matilda's suspicions.

"Andrew, I will schedule you for Monday and Tuesday, Arabella for the rest of the week."

She would have to wait.

*\*\*\**

The first night of the season was a black-tie event. Both Arabella and Andrew had seats in the informal staff box, but they still had to dress appropriately. *It's so easy for the men*, Arabella grumbled to herself, as she pulled her black sheathe calf length dress from the cupboard.

She took time getting ready, and as the dress was not suitable London underground apparel, Ian offered to drive her to the performance. *I love my men. Who needs other relationships?* He dropped her off in Floral Street, and Arabella went to the pianists' room to leave her coat and bag.

She needed to take nothing with her as there is no interval in *Rheingold*, and a sponsor provided drinks and food at the party afterwards in the neighbouring Floral Hall.

She did a quick round of the dressing rooms, wishing everyone good luck. If she was a singer, she would barricade the door. People popping in every minute was a distraction. In fact, some singers did lock themselves in, but the others expected to see the team before the performance and were insulted if the pianists didn't turn up.

Arabella found every premiere she worked on nerve wracking, but she knew that she could be proud of her contribution. The singers she coached were perfectly prepared. Even Peter Clapton was rock solid.

The applause was frenetic. After congratulating everyone behind the curtain, this being allowed by Janet, Arabella went back to her room with Andrew and they gossiped about the cast performances for a while, leaving time for the singers to get out of costume and dressed in their party finery. Then they went back to the dressing room area, joining a group to walk through to the Floral Hall party.

The sponsors and their guests had made sterling inroads into the buffet. It looked as though a herd of locusts had been through, and as if these wealthy people had not eaten for a week. It was the same at every similar function. Sir William instructed catering to keep back food for the artists, and as they appeared, the buffet was restocked.

Cameras flashed from multiple directions. Arabella was photographed several times in conversation with various people. The two basses, singing the giants, put their arms around her shoulders. They were both well over six feet tall and made even Arabella look short. Peter Clapton who was a typically vertically challenged tenor, sat at her feet. There were several flashes as they grinned at the cameras.

It was a late night and it cost her a taxi home. Arabella lay in bed with feet sore after spending six hours on medium high stilettos and thought of Marie. Three days and she would see her again. Every part of her body buzzed in anticipation.

***

Matilda scheduled a three-hour coaching session for Wednesday afternoon. Andrew reported very positively. Marie was a fast learner. But masses of work remained to be done, and the memorising of the reams of text could only be done by the soprano herself.

Arabella dressed comfortably in jeans and a light V-necked pullover. She was just a little embarrassed Marie had seen her in her cruising outfit. But maybe she hadn't really taken it in. She hoped. The encounter in Munich was so brief.

She was practising in studio six when Marie came in. Arabella had a nervous lump in her throat, and her first sight of the beautiful woman wearing a grey pencil skirt, white shirt and heels, threatened to close off her airway altogether.

"Hullo," she said softly, "so we do meet again, and much sooner than I expected."

*Dared to hope.* Arabella stood.

"Don't get up. Let's get down to it. I must be mad to have taken this on." They worked hard for nearly two hours. "I need a few minutes."

"This time I am getting you a coffee. No arguments. How do you take it?" Arabella had noticed black coffee on the two previous occasions, but she wanted to be sure.

"I think I need a cappuccino right now. I usually take it black, but I'm going to splash out this afternoon."

"Sugar…sweetener?"

"Two sweeteners in black, nothing in cappuccino."

Arabella hurried to the canteen. When she got back, the room was empty. Marie returned five minutes later. She had probably been to the cloakroom.

"How was your holiday? You look very brown. Were you on a beach somewhere, or maybe in Texas?" Her tone was teasing, but her eyes were flinty.

Arabella took a deep breath. She had to stop this. "Look, it was two years ago. I'm not at all proud of myself, but it happened. OK? And Laura threw me over after a week to make out with the tenor. That hurt my pride, but I was actually relieved. She made me feel like…a whore."

"And last May?"

"Nothing… of course not. Please, Marie, believe me. That meeting at the stage door was one of the worst moments of my life."

"Are you upset she is not going to sing the Marschallin?"

Arabella looked at her in amazement. There was a hint of vulnerability in the question. Did Marie Nyman really believe that Arabella would be missing Laura? She didn't know what to say and shook her head. After a brief silence, she said softly, but firmly, "You have got to be kidding"

"Come on, we have a good hour left. Back to work."

At the end of the session, Marie packed her music away. "I must run. My husband is collecting me. See you tomorrow. I think we have two sessions, before and after lunch, so we can eat in the canteen together. If you would like that."

\*\*\*

Arabella waited for Marie in the studio. *If she wears that pencil skirt again, I'm done for.*

Today, she was dressed in a pair of comfortable well-tailored slacks, low heels and a top with jacket. Gorgeous, but not quite so incendiary. They worked for two hours, before breaking for lunch. As they walked over to the canteen, Marie turned to her.

"My treat for you being available like this for me."

"But I'm on the call sheet. It's my job."

"Yes, but you could be coaching something more interesting."

Arabella looked at her. "I can't think of anything I would rather be doing."

"You're sweet. But don't you have another concert coming up soon?"

How did she know? Had Arabella mentioned it herself? She couldn't remember. They had barely spoken after the Laura incident. "Middle of October. I start rehearsing in ten days from now."

"Maybe I can come to a rehearsal. I have a recital in Cologne that night."

*Does she know the date? How?* "Would you really?" Arabella couldn't believe what she heard.

"I'd love to." They piled up their salad plates and sat at the far end of the room. They had to share the table. It was a full break, and there were choristers and dancers filling the canteen. Only the orchestra was missing, which was a godsend.

"Arabella, have you seen yourself in Gala?" A chorister brought the magazine to the table. There was a picture from the *Rheingold* party. It was the one with the giants. She was relieved to see it was flattering for all of them.

"And look, Miss Nyman, you are on the same page." It was a shot taken at a film premiere the previous week, of Marie and Nicholas. They held hands. Marie grimaced.

"It was a terrible film. I'm thankful the photo was taken before and not afterwards."

"Is your husband in the film?"

"Yes, unfortunately. It's nothing to be proud of."

"Isn't it funny that you are sitting here at a table and are both on the same page of Gala."

Marie smiled at the chorister. "I suppose I'll have to buy a copy."

"Would you autograph this one for me."

Marie obliged, and they were left in peace to finish their salads. Arabella leapt up to fetch two coffees, as Marie, true to her word, had paid for their lunch.

The afternoon session was productive. As they packed their bags, Marie said softly. "Going to the tube?"

"No, we have our weekly music staff meeting."

"Don't say nasty things about me."

Arabella grinned.

As they left the room, Marie ruffled her hair. "I'm sorry, I don't know why I just love doing that to your hair. It's such a thick…what do you call it… mop. Tell me to stop."

Arabella blushed. "Please be my guest."

At the bottom of the stairs, they went their separate ways. On her way home later, Arabella stopped at the supermarket and bought the last two copies of Gala. She would send one to her grandmother. She texted her mother in Cardiff to buy one. Neither would know what a thrill it gave her to see herself and Marie on the same page. Figuratively speaking, they now seemed to be.

\*\*\*

The next morning Marie rushed in, several minutes late. This time the pencil skirt and matching suit jacket were black, the silk top and four-inch stilettos a deep burgundy. Her hair was in a chignon. She looked like the CEO of a major bank. She wore sunglasses, and as she threw her bag on a chair, pushed them back onto her head, breathing heavily.

"Shit, I shouldn't have done that. Force of habit. My hair!" She carefully pulled off the glasses. "I only have an hour. Interview."

It was not a good session. Marie was distracted, finding it hard to concentrate, and Arabella found it even harder not to fumble the keys every time she looked up and saw those long legs perched on a high stool. The tight skirt rode up Marie's thighs. All Arabella could think about was pushing it even higher.

"Sorry about this morning, Arabella. It was a waste of your time."

*No it wasn't.* "No problem. Have a good interview and enjoy your weekend." She knew from Matilda that Marie had not asked for coaching again until Monday.

"You too, my love. I hope you have some free time. See you on Monday."

She waved. For a second, Arabella thought she was going to blow her a kiss, but her hand went back to her bag, and she was gone. She craned her neck out of the window from where she could just see the stage door. There stood the black Audi parked on a double line. She resisted the temptation to continue looking, fearing she might be seen. She wandered over to the canteen for lunch. She had a session with Sir James all afternoon, and she wanted to ask him if they could work on her concert pieces.

\*\*\*

Matilda gave Andrew the coaching sessions on Monday and Friday. Arabella had Tuesday to Thursday. On Tuesday, they worked both sides of the lunch break and went to the canteen. They shared a large table with the cast from *Norma*.

The Swedish mezzo-soprano in the production was a friend of Marie's and they sat together speaking their own language. Arabella perched further down the table with two company members and tried not to look at Marie. Once or twice, their eyes did meet, and locked for a few seconds.

*I must be careful. If anyone saw those looks, they would be suspicious.* Luckily, most singers were so self-obsessed they wouldn't notice.

Arabella got up first, and they didn't return to the studio together. She called into Matilda's office.

"Has Miss Nyman told you she wants to work at home tomorrow?"

"No."

"Don't you talk to each other? Does she expect you to read it on the call-sheet? Is she really an Ice Queen?"

"She certainly can be." Arabella took this as a golden opportunity to put Matilda off the scent.

"I've put you down for two to five at her house in Richmond Lock. Here's the address in case she forgets to give it to you. Can you do an hour and a half with Peter Clapton here first, then take the tube down there."

"You are a real friend,"

"Don't be sarcastic now."

"Sorry about that," said Marie as she came back to the studio. "I wanted to ask you over lunch if it would be possible for you to come to my house tomorrow. Sir William said it would be OK sometimes. I'm finding fitting everything into my schedule a bit too much on some days. What do you think?" She looked apologetic. Arabella decided not to let on that she knew.

"No problem at all. Where, and at what time?"

"Here's the address." She handed over a visiting card. Their fingers touched. Arabella shivered. "All afternoon if that's possible."

"I'll be there."

\*\*\*

She looked up on the map how to get to Marie's house. She would need at least an hour, changing from the Piccadilly line to the District line, followed by a brisk fifteen-minute walk over Richmond footbridge. She just had time for a sandwich after Peter Clapton's coaching, before she set off. Although she pretended to Matilda that it was a bit of a chore, she was looking forward to seeing where and how Marie lived.

As she approached the house, she didn't even have to look for the number seventeen. Parked in front of the double garage was the black sport Audi and next to it a slightly shorter, but wider, black Audi SUV. *Do they breed them*? She took in the lovely house, built of honey coloured brick.

She remembered the Instagram photo. It was taken here, probably in the back garden. She rang the bell. Expecting Marie, she was taken aback when Nicholas Miller opened the door, a scowl on his face.

"Marie, it's the piano player."

*Phew, that was rude.* Marie came to the door, her eyes apologetic.

"Thanks, Nick. Come in Arabella. Let me take your jacket. The Steinway is in here." Nicholas disappeared into a room to the left where Arabella just caught Beyoncé's *Diva* at a penetratingly loud volume. She snorted. *Figures. But him or her?*

Marie led her to a room diagonally across from her husband's, on the other side of the spacious hallway. It faced the garden, and was obviously soundproofed, with a triple glazed picture window looking onto the not overly large, but beautifully kept garden. There was a terrace to the left with a pergola under which stood a long table and chairs. This was where the photo was taken. At the far corner of the high walled garden was a designer greenhouse.

In the room stood a Steinway baby grand. The walls were lined to the ceiling with shelves, and they were filled largely with CD's and musical scores. One section contained music theory literature written in Swedish, German and English as far as Arabella could see. In front of the piano was a long suede couch.

Next to the instrument sat a small rectangular table and upright chair. On it the *Rosenkavalier* score stood open. Marie gestured to the piano.

Arabella took in her appearance for the first time. She wore a charcoal grey pencil skirt, and rather incongruously a soft, sloppy sweater and Ugg-like slippers. Her hair was loose to just below her shoulders. It was the first time Arabella had seen Marie with her hair not tied up in some way. It made her look several years younger. She longed to push her hands through it.

"I'm sorry about my husband just now. He is rather stressed, waiting to hear about a film role. But that's no excuse." She added softly. "I hope you like the instrument. Steinway came to tune it this morning."

"Oh…you didn't have to do that." She blushed and played an arpeggio to cover what she hoped were only slightly rosy cheeks, and not full-on scarlet. "It's fabulous. The rehearsal instruments get so knocked about, and although they are tuned regularly, they all sound rather awful, and are sometimes hell to play."

They worked hard, taking just a ten-minute break to drink some water. At four thirty, Nicholas opened the door without knocking.

"Don't forget we have to go at five thirty sharp." He left without waiting for a reply. Marie pursed her lips. *If this was a happy marriage, then she was Lady Gaga.*

"We have twenty minutes, if that's alright with you."

"Sure. I'm on the clock until five."

There was no sign of Nicholas when Marie took her to the front door and stood waving until she was out of sight.

The call sheet for Thursday gave her another three-hour session in Richmond, after a morning coaching with Penelope, who was going to sing the comic role of Annina in *Der Rosenkavalier*.

As she approached the Richmond house, it began to rain. She dashed to the front door. The Audi sport was not there, but she supposed it could have been in the garage.

Marie opened the front door. "Oh, Arabella, you're wet."

A sharp pang hit her clit. *Oh my god, she doesn't know how right she is.*

"No, look, I just made it in time."

Marie wore faded blue jeans, and a tank top with thin straps under an outsize sweater, which slipped down her arms. She had on the same Ugg slippers, and her hair was tied back in a messy ponytail. The wetness in Arabella's pants increased.

"It's a big day today. I'm going to try the first few scenes, up until the arrival of Baron Ochs, off the book."

She closed her score and prepared to sing from memory. Arabella sang in the role of Oktavian, her young lover, written for a mezzo-soprano, and perfectly within her voice range. Marie needed very little prompting, and they came to the end of the scene triumphantly.

"Marie, that was really great."

"You weren't bad yourself. Pity you aren't a singer. I would love to sing the Marschallin to your Oktavian." Arabella stared at her, and Marie looked away embarrassed. After all, the scene they had just rehearsed took place largely in the Marschallin's bed after a night of sex.

Marie cleared her throat. "Coffee?"

"Yes, please."

They took a break, and turned to the scene with Baron Ochs, which was rhythmically difficult. Although Ochs had the most to sing, the Marschallin's interjections were tricky. Marie would need the score for a while. The text was fiendishly difficult to learn.

Just after five o'clock, Marie closed her score. "Are you hungry? I'm going to make myself an omelette."

"I am a little. I didn't have time for lunch."

"Oh, Arabella, I'm so sorry. That's my fault. Come on. If you have time, of course."

"I'm free now. I don't have to go back to the theatre."

Marie pulled her from the piano bench, and they walked through a large sitting/dining area into a state-of-the-art kitchen. Marie still held her hand, and let it go only after guiding her to sit at a high stool at the breakfast bar.

"Is an herb omelette OK? Do you want cheese in it?"

"Just French herbs would be lovely. I always eat my omelettes like that."

"Me too. Nick likes cheese with a small amount of omelette." She shuddered. *Are they in any way compatible?*

Marie took green salad out of the fridge. "Tomatoes?"

"God, no." It was Arabella's turn to shudder. "I like tomatoes well enough, but not in green salad."

Marie leaned over her side of the bar, arms at her sides on the counter, so that her breasts squashed together. Arabella was less than a foot away from a deep cleavage. How she managed to suppress an appreciative moan was beyond her understanding. But it only got worse. Marie drew her forefinger from Arabella's forehead, across her nose, and over the lips to her chin.

"You and I have a lot in common." They locked eyes and were so close Arabella thought she would have to kiss her. The phone rang, and they both started backwards, Arabella clutching wildly at the seat of her stool to stop herself from falling.

Marie answered. "Nick, yes, OK. No problem, I'm just eating something with Arabella anyway. See you later." She hung up. The moment was gone. Marie took four eggs out of a cupboard and beat them, adding a little cream, herbs, salt and pepper. She also mixed a vinaigrette dressing, then took a large skillet and made the omelette, which she split down the middle and served on to two plates.

Arabella watched her hands at work. She was deft and fast in the kitchen and seemed to be a good cook. Marie pulled a half-full bottle of Chablis out of the fridge and poured two glasses. She came around the bar, and they sat next to each other. The food was wonderful, the salad dressing perfectly balanced, and the omelette so fluffy, it practically floated away.

"Is this good," she mumbled between mouthfuls. "Do you always cook like this? Can I stay?" *Damn, that was stupid*, but Marie laughed.

"You would probably appreciate my cooking more than my husband does. Now tell me more about yourself. I know what it says on your homepage…" She paused, then continued. There was no way back. *She has searched my website.*

"But tell me more about how you grew up, and why music, and why conducting, and so on."

Arabella filled her in, spoke about her grandmother and her parents. About her grandmother's encouragement of her musical abilities, and how she overrode her parents' preference for an academic career, although she did have her music bachelor's degree. She also told her about her house and her platonic arrangement with James and Ian. Marie visibly relaxed. They finished their wine, and Arabella stood to leave. She did not want to overstay her welcome, and she didn't want to be there when Nick returned. It had long ago stopped raining.

At the door, Marie took her into a hug, and said softly into her ear, "I'm glad you're here for me, and I'm glad we cleared up that misunderstanding."

This time she didn't stand at the door waving, but as Arabella turned the corner and saw the house in her peripheral vision, she noticed a shadow in the hall window.

In bed later, she reviewed the afternoon, found herself soaking wet again, and came fast, hard and long.

***

As much as Arabella wanted to see Marie again, and as soon as possible, she was grateful for a free weekend ahead. On Friday, after a morning coaching, she had a two-hour session with Sir James, and managed to avoid the worst of the rush hour getting home.

She took herself to bed early with her concert scores, and worked until she felt herself getting sleepy, earlier than she hoped.

Saturday morning was filled with weekly grocery shopping with James and Ian, followed by stripping paint off the stair banisters. They took the evening off, and she baked a lasagne. They drank two bottles of wine and watched TV. It was unusual for both men to be home on a Saturday night, but they enjoyed the effortlessness of just being together.

On Sunday, she concentrated hard on her music. She was not nearly as nervous about the forthcoming concert as she had been in May, but she wanted this one to be even better than the first one, so her subjective pressure was just as intense.

She was early as usual in Golders Green and was surprised not to see Chloe. Admittedly, she hadn't thought much about her in the intervening months and couldn't decide if she was relieved or not when she saw her seat was taken by a young man. At the break she said as casually as possible to the manager, "Where's Chloe?"

"She's in Leeds, at Opera North for six months. She's substituting for a colleague off having a baby."

"Good for her." Arabella was relieved after all. She did not want to analyse exactly why, but deep down knew she had been 'faithful' to Marie since they first met. She also knew this was ridiculous and determined to do something about it as soon as her heavy autumn work schedule eased up, which wouldn't be until after Christmas. That made her feel better. Christmas was a long way off.

On Tuesday, she worked with Marie all afternoon in the opera house. She had obviously been memorising over the weekend. She tried the Ochs scene off the book. It was not as secure as the first scene, but it was coming on.

Nonetheless, Marie was not pleased with herself and surprisingly grumpy. Arabella was as gentle as possible, but the singer left in a bad mood.

At the second concert rehearsal the following day, she worked on the Samuel Barber *Adagio for Strings*. It was not difficult to play, but required a lush string sound, and that was difficult for the young players. But they made good progress.

On Thursday, she went to Richmond for the afternoon. The black Audi sport was missing again, and she hoped Marie would be in a better mood. She was. They tried the Baron Ochs scene, and this time it was almost perfect.

Just before the session ended, there was a flash of lightening, and the heavens opened. Standing together at the window they watched the deluge.

"You can't go out in this. I'll drive you to the station."

"I'm sure it will stop soon." But it didn't, and they made a dash for the SUV. Marie's hand went to the sat-nav.

"Where do you live?"

"No way, Marie. The station will be fine."

"Oh, come on, I fancy some fresh air after that session." Arabella unwillingly gave her the address and she punched it in. It gave a journey time of twenty minutes.

"But that's fantastic. I was dreading you saying you lived on the Isle of Dogs or somewhere. We're virtually neighbours."

The drive did take a little longer through the torrential rain, but the SUV made light work of the conditions. By the time they arrived and slid into a parking spot right outside the house door, it had slowed down to a drizzle.

Arabella put her hand on the door handle.

"Aren't you going to ask me in for a cup of tea? I must admit I am curious to see how Arabella Cooper lives."

"Yes…please come in. The house is still like a builders' back yard, but I can just about push through the rubble to get to the kettle."

Marie looked uncertain. Arabella laughed. "I'm joking, well sort of. Come with me."

They walked up the four steps to the front door and into the narrow hallway.

"This is the living room which was originally two rooms. We knocked them through." The room stretched the entire length of the house and with windows at both ends it was warm and sunny. They went back into the hall.

"Up there on the half landing is Ian's rather small room, above him the bathroom, and on the top floor two bedrooms, mine and James'. And when we go down the stairs, there at the front, in the half basement, is our office and where my piano will stand. Only an upright of course. At the end of the corridor, on the right, is the dining room, with French windows to the garden. Straight ahead is the kitchen. You cannot believe the state this house was in when we bought it. The bath was in the kitchen. The family put an old wooden door on it and used it as a table, when they weren't bathing in it, which I doubt was very often. The room had no window, so we knocked a large picture window into the far wall, which looks out onto the garden. But as you see, there is still a huge amount to do, though I have at last finally finished tiling the kitchen and bathroom."

"You did the tiling yourself? With your pianist's hands?"

"Gloves. Would you like to take a seat in the dining room, which is probably the most finished room in the house. I'll make us tea." Marie didn't sit, but studied the bookshelves, occasionally taking a book out and looking at it. Arabella made two mugs and joined her.

"Eclectic taste in books."

"Ian is an IT nerd, James works in an office, but studied chemistry, and me music."

"You know, Arabella, I'm really impressed with your house, and I have to admit envious."

"Envious?" Arabella almost choked on her tea. "You have the most gorgeous house I have ever seen in my life."

"Yes, but I bought it as you see it. Even most of the furniture came in the asking price. It suited me, because with all my, or our, travelling, there was, and is no time for interior decorating. But your house reflects your personalities, and I can see the love that has gone into it."

They finished their teas and went back up the stairs. They stood for a moment rather awkwardly at the front door.

"You can show me your bedroom another time." Her voice was husky. She placed a gentle kiss on Arabella's mouth and let herself out. "See you next week…I hope."

Arabella waited until she drove off. She closed the door, and leaned against the stairs, her lips burning despite the gentleness of the kiss. *Bedroom. Another time.* What did that mean? She heard a key in the lock, and James came in.

"I just saw my dream car pull out. Anything to do with you?"

"That was Marie Nyman. Superstar soprano. She owns a three-million-pound house in Richmond and is married to Nicholas Miller. James, I don't know what to do. I'm crazy about her."

"How about a cup of tea, and you can tell me all about it."

"No more tea. Didn't I see a new bottle of gin?"

\*\*\*

On Friday, the orchestra read though the Brahms works, and on Monday they worked on details of the Britten and Barber. When she needed her, Matilda was a true friend. Arabella was scheduled for coaching only on the mornings of her evening concert rehearsals, and for afternoon sessions in Richmond on Tuesday and Thursday.

"How come Andrew and Paul have never been to the witch's lair? Only you are invited down there. Does she have a cauldron boiling in the kitchen?"

"I don't think so, but I noticed a book of spells in the downstairs cloakroom, and there's a rather elegant long black cape hanging on the coat rack." They were eating a thick bacon sandwich in Matilda's office. The fat oozed into the bread. They both needed the calories. "How's Sam?"

Matilda lost interest in Marie, which was the intention. She sighed.

"The sex is wonderful, but I don't know. He wants to get divorced, but he doesn't. He uses the kids as an excuse, but I think he has been spoilt for so many years, he doesn't want to have to look for a new apartment, and furnish it, and generally lose his creature comforts. He wants his home…and me for sex. Quite frankly, I feel a bit used, but I can't give him up. Do you think a woman would behave like that. I mean, having your cake and eating it."

"I don't know. I doubt it." She suddenly had a vision of Marie and Nick, and her and Marie. Nothing had happened yet, but if it did, was she getting herself into a similar situation. No, it wasn't going to happen. She said that phrase in her head at least twice a day.

*\*\*\**

Only the SUV was visible as she turned the corner after her walk over the bridge. *Good.* The atmosphere was entirely different when they were alone. For example, the way Marie dressed. When alone she wore low cut, comfortable jeans, a sloppy sweater and her Ugg slippers. When Nick was around, it was either a skirt and top, or well-cut slacks. Arabella liked whatever she wore, but they were more relaxed with each other when they were alone, and Marie's choice of clothing was a good barometer.

"Are you ready for a run of the last scene of act one off the book?"

"I did that yesterday with Andrew. It went OK. He's not the Oktavian of my dreams though." Arabella was disappointed. It was the heartrending scene where the Marschallin realises she is ageing, and reluctantly sends her young lover away. She had been looking forward to singing that with Marie.

"It's on to the last act today. Don't forget I am away all next week, and after that there is just a week left before rehearsals begin."

"Where are you going?"

"I have a recital in Cologne on Sunday, then two performances in Hamburg on Wednesday and Saturday. *Cosi fan tutte.*"

They worked the customary three-hour session.

"Do you have a moment?"

"Yes of course."

"I would like to brush up an encore for the recital." She reached for some sheet music and gave it to Arabella, who gawped.

"Marvin Hamlisch?"

Marie laughed. "You know, after a stuffy recital, it's nice sometimes to send the public off with something light. Everyone does it, but they sing a light classical song. I like to go a step further."

Arabella started playing *The Way We Were.* She nearly had to stop. Marie sang with a totally different vocal technique, bringing her chest voice up much higher, like musical singers do. It was sensational.

"Once more, and you join me in the last verse, singing the harmony."

They sang together *So it's the laughter, we will remember, whenever we remember, the way we were.*

"That was fun. Something else?" Marie rifled through a stack of songs on one of the shelves. "Did you see the film?" She put Lady Gaga's *Shallow* on the piano. Arabella played, taking Bradley Cooper's lines. Marie changed *Tell me something boy* to *girl*, and Arabella pressed her thighs together, feeling a strong pull in her core.

"Here's something you are much too young for." She replaced *Shallow* with the music for *Hush Little Baby*.

"You are so wrong, lady. My Oma had an unhealthy obsession with Dusty Springfield, and I heard her songs day and night."

"You sing the melody and I'll improvise around you." They launched into *Mockingbird*. It wasn't perfect, and they finished out of breath and flushed, but grinned at each other like teenagers. The door opened and Nick came in. For once he was smiling.

"What on earth is going on here? Have you nearly finished? We have tickets for the Aldwych, don't forget."

"We are done," said Marie regretfully. Nick left. "I would much rather stay here and sing some more, but we'll have to take a rain check."

"Is it really alright for your voice, singing like that?"

"I'm careful, don't worry. I wouldn't do it a couple of hours before a concert, but I learnt how to *belt* when I was at university. I used to sing in a bar to make some money. But talking of concerts, is your dress rehearsal still on Friday evening? Can I come to see it?"

"I will be so nervous. The orchestra is young. You would hate it."

"Don't be idiotic. You can give me the details on Thursday. I think I have to hurry now."

Arabella stuffed her things into her bag and left. As she shut the door, Marie was already dashing up the stairs.

\*\*\*

Their Thursday session took place in the opera house as Marie had arranged an interview in central London beforehand. Arabella gave her details for the dress rehearsal and arranged to meet her at the artist's entrance ten minutes before the beginning of the rehearsal.

Marie was already waiting for her.

"I'm so nervous."

"Not on my account, please. I'll just sit quietly at the back. Don't worry about me. I'll see myself out at the end of the rehearsal. You will be busy."

Marie was right. She was caught up in the drama of the first viola having to be replaced, after the other one fell sick. The new player was excellent, but Arabella had to go through points with him in the interval and at the end. Marie walked down to the stage, and put both thumbs up, smiling.

"I'll be in touch," she mouthed.

The orchestra manager gave her a lift home. "So, tell, what was the great Marie Nyman doing at our rehearsal, and how do you know her so well?"

"I don't know her that well. She has to learn the Marschallin for our new production, and we have been coaching her. Three of us pianists, almost daily. We take it in turns. It was sweet of her to come tonight."

"You are getting quite the fan club. There's another 'great' coming to the concert."

Arabella went pale. "Who? No, don't tell me. I won't sleep at all tonight."

"No, I won't tell you, but it's an honour for the orchestra as well."

Arabella's mobile beeped. * 'Darling girl, you are a natural and will go far. I'll be thinking of you tomorrow. Have a good week. Looking forward to our last week of coaching—Help! Marie.'

\*\*\*

The concert was a triumph for Arabella and the orchestra. The audience stood and cheered after the Brahms *Hungarian Dance*, and she took at least half a dozen bows. It was Sir James Staples who had made the effort to come, despite his arthritis, and Arabella burst into tears when he told her how well she had done, and how proud he was.

There was an excellent review in the Guardian, which Arabella was tempted to send Marie, but she thought better of it. Marie Nyman had had hundreds of good reviews in her life and was probably sitting on a pile of them in Cologne and Hamburg. She was a tiny bit disappointed not to have received a text but shrugged it off. She must be busy, and probably had dozens of friends in both cities. Nick wasn't with her she knew that. Marie had told her he was filming in Edinburgh until the middle of November. She hoped the last week of sessions would be in Richmond, and not in the opera house. They would be alone.

She was in Matilda's office on Friday, after an intensive week of coaching the smaller roles for *Rosenkavalier*.

"I'll let you off the hook with the witch next week. Paul hasn't done his share, and Sir James wants to work with you every afternoon except Wednesday."

"Let me at least do Wednesday then. I want to see how far she has learnt it. I am the assistant conductor after all."

"That makes sense. Let me see, Wednesday is a Richmond day. Sorry about that."

"It's not a problem if I can go home afterwards. As Marie said, we are practically neighbours. It only takes twenty minutes."

"How, pray tell, does she know where you live?" *Shit!*

"She took me home on her broom once during an electric storm. It was a wild ride. You should have heard her cackle."

"Whatever turns you on." *If only you knew.* "You can have Wednesday morning off if you work with Peter Clapton on Monday and Tuesday."

"I. Hate. You."

Wednesday turned out to be a gorgeous, autumnal day. There was a chill in the air, but Arabella felt full of energy, and decided to cycle. She dressed in her black leather jeans, a pink sweater and her black leather jacket, which would protect her from the wind. She put a hint of kohl under her eyes and some lip-gloss to protect her lips from chapping.

No car stood outside the house, and for a panicked second, Arabella wondered if Marie was home, and there had been a mistake. It must have been in the garage, because the door opened as soon as she rang the bell.

"I've missed you. Paul is no…" Marie stopped, and her mouth opened wide. She raked her eyes up Arabella's body and stared at her. Then she slowly pulled her inside and closed the door. She was wearing a linen button-down dress and stilettos, so they were the same height. Arabella had on flat ankle boots for cycling.

Marie pushed her roughly against the door and took her face in her hands. Their mouths moved together. The kiss was wild. Arabella moaned and opened her lips and Marie thrust her tongue in, then bit her under-lip. She was immediately drenched and moved her hips to meet Marie's, who ground into her.

Marie pulled the leather jacket off and threw it in the direction of the coat rack. After taking her hand and pulling her to the music room, she slammed the door behind them. She shoved Arabella onto the couch and lay on top of her. Their mouths met again in a frenzy.

Marie pushed her hand under Arabella's sweater and fondled her right breast. The nipple was instantly erect. Then she moved to the left one and pinched the nipple hard. Arabella cried out, but Marie's darkened eyes glinted, and she pinched harder. Arabella started to writhe and moved her hips upwards to meet Marie's.

She thought she would explode. She felt the button of her leather jeans pop and the zipper pulled down. Marie's hand tried to slip down under her thong, but the jeans were too tight. With a growl of frustration, she sat up and pulled the jeans down past Arabella's hips.

Then she was back on top, and their mouths met again. Marie's hand pushed the thong to one side and stroked her soaking wet folds. She entered her with two fingers. Her nails were long, and it hurt a little, but it was agonisingly good. She whimpered.

"You like that?" Arabella reached up to Marie's breast and groaned in frustration at the material in her way. With her other hand, Marie undid the top buttons of her dress and Arabella took a full breast in her hand, kneading the nipple, which was already rock hard. Now Marie groaned and manoeuvred herself so that she was riding Arabella's right leg.

Arabella could hear how slick she was and pulled her knee up to give Marie better purchase. She thrust deeply and Arabella knew she couldn't last long.

Marie's rhythm increased, and she was panting. "I'm going to come." She pressed her thumb against Arabella's clit, which tipped her over the edge, just as Marie cried out, "Bella," and went rigid. It had lasted no more than five minutes, and was practically rape, but it was the most fantastic orgasm Arabella had ever had.

Her walls still throbbed on Marie's hand, as she continued to twitch on Arabella's leg. Then she collapsed and buried her head against Arabella's shoulder. She softly pulled her fingers out, leaving her hand on Arabella's stomach.

"I'm so sorry. My nails. Did I hurt you?"

Arabella had trouble speaking she was so overcome with emotion.

"No, you didn't hurt me."

Marie sat up and buttoned her dress. She got up and walked to the window with her back to Arabella, who now felt cold, and shivered.

"It won't happen again. I don't know what's wrong with me."

"It's not your first time with a woman, is it?"

"No. I... I don't think I can work this afternoon. Do you mind?"

Arabella did. She wanted to run over and take Marie in her arms, and do it all over again, but she knew she would not be welcome. Without saying a word, she got up, running her hand down over the juices covering her right leg.

She tidied herself. She heard Marie's intake of breath as she pulled up her zipper. She opened the door. Marie had not turned from the window. She picked up her jacket and bag and left, closing the front door softly.

\*\*\*

How were they going to face each other on Monday? Arabella contemplated getting a migraine, but that would only delay the agony.

She dressed in roll neck sweater and slacks, instinctively covering and disguising as much of her body as possible. The morning rehearsal was a musical one for the first act protagonists. Arabella took the lift to the music director's suite. Marie was in the anteroom talking to Suzanne Weigl.

Andrew and Paul were already there. The door opened and Johannes invited them into his large room, in which stood a Bösendorfer grand piano.

"Sit everyone. Welcome. I'm so happy you are here, Suzanne. And, Marie, how can we thank you enough for rescuing us, and in a way we couldn't have dreamt about when the cancellation came in September."

"Johannes, it is my pleasure, and I just want to thank the three people who have made it possible. Suzanne, in case you don't know them, this is Andrew and Paul, and...Arabella."

Marie looked at her for the first time. She saw a flash of insecurity, and something else, impossible to fathom in those grey eyes, before she looked away. *Oh, ok we are back to Ice Queen. What did you expect? She got what she wanted at that moment. But I did too.* The memory of them climaxing together made her face hot.

"Andrew, will you play please. Let's go from the top. Arabella, please watch me carefully and try to memorise my tempi. You will be conducting rehearsals on some days."

Later Marie and Suzanne left to go to lunch together, probably to the Bistro across the road. The lunch break was an hour and a half today, as Johannes finished early. The pianists went to the canteen.

Paul and Arabella were early on the rehearsal stage that afternoon. Everyone was nervous on the first day of rehearsals. They did not know the director, who was a famous New Zealand film director called Terry Te Awa. He was of Maori descent and didn't speak a lot of German.

Considering the amount of text in *Rosenkavalier*, this was controversial, but they had been assured he was well prepared. He was already there with his set designer, and they were talking over some points with Janet, about the way the set had been marked up on the rehearsal floor. He grinned at them and waved. He stopped talking when Marie and Suzanne walked in and went over to them.

"Suzanne, great to see you. How's Beth?" Arabella thought it an odd question, until she remembered Suzanne's wife was a New Zealander.

"She's fine. Thanks. Terry, this is Marie Nyman."

"I'm so happy to meet you and get to work with you. It's a dream come true for me."

"Well, I can't think why," *typical Marie*, "but the pleasure is mutual."

They gathered around the detailed model of the set, and he explained what he was aiming for in his direction. Arabella noticed that his German pronunciation left much to be desired. He called a ten-minute break, and Marie beckoned Arabella over to where she was talking to Suzanne and Terry.

"Terry, if you need some help with German words, and Suzanne isn't here, ask Arabella. Her mother is German, and she is bilingual. And Suzanne, if you get stuck for words with Terry the same applies."

"*Es ist mir ein Vergnugung. Wie schön Sie sind.*" She looked at Arabella appreciatively, but there was no flirting in her big brown eyes. She was a striking woman, her dark shoulder length gently curling hair made exotic by a white strand sprouting from her forehead. Marie's look hardened but she seemed satisfied with what she saw.

"*Außerdem ist mein Englisch seit zehn Jahren sehr viel besser geworden.*" Arabella and Marie both laughed. Terry looked nonplussed until Suzanne translated that her English was much better since she married Beth.

They began blocking the first scene. The overture to the opera described a night of sex. The orgasm was plain to hear in the music. After several bars of gentle post coital tristesse, the curtain rises on the Marschallin and her young lover Oktavian von Rofrano, in whatever position the director wants to put them into. Terry wanted them coming out of a deep kiss.

Both singers were professional and good actresses, and they were not embarrassed to be asked to do this. Arabella felt her cheeks burn. The pictures from last week seared her retina, but Marie seemed cool and unmoved. They locked gazes once, and Arabella felt the electricity. She thought Suzanne had seen it too but couldn't be sure. In any case, she didn't react.

For the rest of the week, they worked hard to block the first act, as Marie had a previous commitment during the second week of November, for performances at the Vienna State Opera. As she wasn't in the second act this worked out perfectly. The cast and staff ate in the canteen, and usually managed to get a large table to themselves. Arabella made sure to let the stars sit at one end, while she sat at the other end with some ensemble singers.

Once Matilda joined them. "Nyman and Weigl seem very close. Is there something going on between them?"

"Sure, we all watch them making love every morning." Matilda's mouth fell open. "You don't know *Rosenkavalier* very well, do you? And no, I don't think there is anything between them other than friendship. Suzanne's every second word is Beth, who she misses dreadfully. It's very sweet."

On Thursday, Marie managed to manoeuvre sitting next to Arabella, who had great difficulties swallowing her salad. She noticed Marie had trimmed her nails but was distracted from what this could mean by Marie pressing their thighs together, while blithely carrying on a conversation with Terry sitting on her other side.

"I'm going to get a coffee round. What does everyone want? Arabella would you please come and help me."

They stood in line at the counter. Marie whispered. "I need to see you. We must talk. Can you come to Richmond tomorrow evening?" Arabella nodded, and they brought the coffees back to the table.

\*\*\*

*I can't do this.* Arabella walked over the bridge. *What does she want? I can't be alone with her. She's a married woman, deeply in the closet, even if she is at the very least bisexual, and she is going to break my heart. If I leave now, it's only cracked.* But her feet didn't listen, and she pushed the bell.

"Bella, please let me hug you. I didn't think I would get through the week. It is hell being in the same room with you, do you know that." Arabella let herself be hugged but kept her body stiff and willed herself not to respond. It took all her strength.

"My darling, I'm sorry, so sorry. I treated you abysmally."

"You didn't even send a text."

Marie hung her head. "I know. I couldn't find the right words, and as each day passed, it just got worse."

Arabella pulled herself out of the hug. "Marie, it's no good. You're a married woman. I don't do things like this. I don't do relationships either."

"May I show you something," gently she took Arabella's hand and guided her up the stairs. She opened the first door. It was a master bedroom suite, with a king size bed and adjoining bathroom.

"Marie, I repeat. I don't do this."

"Shhh… This is Nick's." She shut the door and continued down the hall to the farthest room. She opened the door and pushed Arabella in gently. "And this is mine. It has never been any different."

"But why…"

"It's complicated, and… I'm a coward. Bella, I agree there are many reasons why we can't be together openly, but my husband isn't one of them. Now may I take you into my bed…please?" Marie kissed her softly, then their tongues clashed, and their breathing became ragged.

"I want to see you properly." Marie pulled Arabella's sweater over her head and unclasped her bra in one easy movement. *Oh yes, she had done this before.* Her lips moved down to Arabella's breasts, and she sucked on her hard nipples.

"Heaven. You are the most beautiful woman I have ever seen."

Arabella pushed her away before reaching out to unbutton her shirt, slipping it over her shoulders. Marie wore no bra, and she gasped. The voluptuous breasts were high and firm, and more gorgeous than any she had ever set eyes on. But she would worship them later.

She opened the zip on Marie's jeans and pulled them down her legs. Her black lacy pants followed. Marie stood completely naked and breath-taking was an understatement.

"You owe me this."

"I know."

Arabella shrugged off her own jeans and thong, and Marie pushed her backwards onto the bed, lying on top of her.

"Oh, no, you don't," Arabella flipped her easily. "I'm just as much a top as you are."

They kissed deeply, and Arabella pinched a nipple. Marie groaned and tried to get at Arabella's breasts.

Arabella pulled Marie's arms above her head and pinioned them with her left hand.

"It's my turn." She kissed her way down the long neck, sucking gently on her collarbone. Then she worshipped both breasts, nibbling on the erect nipples and butterfly kissing down over the soft flat stomach. It took all her strength to stay on top of Marie's gyrating hips.

"Bella, you are killing me."

She grinned and returned to Marie's face, kissing her deeply, then softly.

"Please, I can't hold on much longer."

She took pity, and slid down the bed, keeping one hand on Marie's right breast. She kissed along her inner thighs, still teasing, then swiped up her glistening folds with her tongue. Marie uttered a deep groan.

She slipped two fingers into her and started thrusting, every now and then curling the ends of her fingers. Marie was panting hard, and Arabella knew she was past the point of no return. She sucked on her swollen clit, and Marie came with a wail pressing her hands over her mouth. She felt the contractions for long seconds.

She slid back up the bed. Marie had tears running down her cheeks. She kissed her gently. Marie clung to her.

"Stay inside me."

"I'd like that. Don't cry. Don't be unhappy."

"I'm not unhappy, Bella. I'm scared…but it's like coming home." She sighed, and gently pulled Arabella's hand up to her mouth, kissing her fingers and tasting her own musky scent. She reached up to Arabella's lips, running her fingers over them.

Then she leaned in for a kiss and flipped her over. Her hand went down to Arabella's stomach, down the trimmed hair and gently raked her folds from bottom to top.

"You are so wet, my love. All for me?" Arabella could only nod, as she raised her hips to meet Marie's hand. "I've cut my nails, so I won't hurt you this time."

She pushed in deeply, and brought her head down to Arabella's nipple, which she bit gently, then harder, as she increased the speed of her thrusts, adding a third finger.

She rode Arabella's leg, her juices slipping on the smooth skin. Marie slowed her thrusting for a moment, and Arabella lifted her hips wanting more.

"Hold on just a second, my darling. I'm a selfish singer and I want to come again… with you…together." Arabella bit her lips with the strain as Marie increased her rhythm on her thigh until she was panting.

"Yes, yes, now, my love, come for me." She thrust deeply into Arabella, brushing her thumb on her clit. They exploded together. Arabella saw nothing but a white film in front of her eyes, as she threw her head back.

Marie collapsed on her side, pulling her into her arms. They lay panting until their breathing slowed, and Marie pulled a cover over them both.

"Come with me to Vienna."

Arabella giggled. "What would people think? You can't be serious. And anyway, I'm conducting rehearsals all next week because Johannes is away somewhere. We have to block the second act. *Rosenkavalier*…remember."

"Are you working next Saturday?"

"No, I don't think so. Tomorrow morning, yes, but not next week."

"So, you could get a flight on Friday, and we can fly back together on Sunday."

"Are you serious?"

"Ice Queens don't have a sense of humour, you know that. Yes, I am. I'll book you a flight as soon as you can tell me what time you finish on Friday. I know there is an evening one at seven o'clock."

Arabella stared at her. "Well…I suppose I could. But I will book my own flight, if you tell me which one you are returning on." She smiled. "I'm not a kept woman."

Marie kissed her softly. "You are rather wonderful, you know."

"I think I had better be going. The rehearsal tomorrow is at ten, and I promised I would run through her music with a very nervous Penelope before we begin."

Marie smothered a yawn, "I'll drive you home."

"No, you won't. You stay right here and get some sleep. You have a flight tomorrow morning I think." Marie nodded. "Early?"

Marie nodded again. "I fly out at nine o'clock."

"That means getting up at six."

Marie shrugged. Arabella slipped out of bed and pulled on her clothes. She found her taxi app and ordered one. Five minutes. They kissed, both moaning as their tongues collided.

"You better go before I wake up again, which is very tempting."

She let herself out and closed the door softly.

In the taxi, her mobile pinged: * 'I'll be counting the hours until Friday. Sleep well, my lovely Bella.'

\*\*\*

Marie texted her on Saturday evening. She had arrived for the rehearsal and as usual in Vienna, there was almost nobody else there. It had been a short session as she knew the production, and it was only important to go through her music with the conductor, to get to know his tempi.

She had performances on Sunday, Wednesday and Saturday. Arabella sent a good luck text on Sunday.

She was both dreading and longing for the rehearsal on Monday. She would be conducting this week, which she was looking forward to, but Gemma would be there. Her role of Sophie, the young girl Oktavian falls in love with, wasn't in the first act, but she was onstage for the greater part of act two.

Arabella went first to the pianist's room, hoping to find Paul who was to play the rehearsal. He was just leaving so they were able to go together. That didn't stop Gemma greeting her with a kiss on the mouth. She blushed, and she saw Suzanne raise her eyebrows. As Gemma turned to greet someone, she shrugged her shoulders and gave a rueful smile, mouthing, "*es ist nicht was du denkst.*" (It isn't what you think.)

The second act of *Rosenkavalier* is much busier than the first act, which is suffused with melancholy, and basically involves only three characters. There are many more in act two, and the chorus is onstage for the first time. It was typical of Johannes to give her a baptism by fire by being away, but Arabella had learnt the score backwards and forwards, and she rarely needed to look at the music.

She could make eye contact and give cues to all the singers individually. Under her baton the musical side of the rehearsal week went smoothly. Suzanne congratulated her. "You are very good, Arabella. I hope you get an opportunity to stand in front of an orchestra."

"I'm so lucky to have a young chamber orchestra who engage me, but of course opera is another world, and it is difficult to break into. And I'm a woman…"

"If I can ever be of assistance, let me know." She was kind and Arabella warmed to her even more.

Things on the Gemma front were not so positive. Arabella did her best to avoid her, but she took every chance to get close. She started making silly mistakes, so that Arabella would have to call her over to her music stand in order to correct her. In the canteen, she somehow managed to sit beside her, and once she put her hand on Arabella's leg.

Towards the end of the week, it happened again, and Gemma moved her hand up to Arabella's crotch. Suzanne was watching them and took Arabella aside before the afternoon rehearsal began.

"I think you need some help Liebling. Just take my lead and follow me. I'll tell Beth everything, and you can explain to Marie." Arabella jerked her head in astonishment, and Suzanne winked. "Don't worry, no one else has noticed anything, but there are a thousand volts sizzling between you two."

"Oh. Please, no…"

"I'll only tell Beth, and we are the most discreet people in the business. Here comes Gemma." Suzanne put her arm around Arabella and whispered in her ear. "She's watching us…now act."

Arabella gazed into Suzanne's eyes. Suzanne kissed her softly on the cheek. "Tell her you are involved with someone," she whispered. Gemma's mouth hung open, and she threw Arabella dirty looks all afternoon.

At the end of the rehearsal, Suzanne gestured to her, and they left together arms around each other.

On Friday morning, Gemma cornered her. "What's going on?" She demanded. "The woman is without her wife for a couple of weeks, and her hands are all over you."

*That's the pot calling the kettle black…* Arabella shrugged enigmatically. "She is the opera world's lesbian icon after all, can you blame me?"

Gemma stomped off. The plan worked and she was left alone at the lunch table.

Suzanne grinned. "We'll have to keep it up for a bit next week, so don't forget to warn Marie."

Arabella was not sure she wanted to have that conversation.

At the end of the afternoon session, which thankfully Terry shortened by a good half hour, she ran to the tube, praying there would be no delays. There weren't, but she still cut it fine for her flight to Vienna. Marie had given her the name of the hotel, so she came out of baggage control and made to follow the sign for taxis, not resisting a smirk at the Brits haven't to queue up with all the other non-Europeans.

*That's Brexit for you.* She had dual citizenship and used her EU passport.

"Bella." Marie was in the crowd waiting, wearing a casual, if expensive jacket, and a beanie completely covering her blonde hair. In her jeans and sneakers, she looked about twenty-five, and was unrecognisable. They hugged, and Marie took a nip at her ear, as she breathed, "I can't wait."

In the taxi they were careful. Vienna was renowned. It was said that every taxi driver knew the evening performance at the State Opera, and most could tell you who was in the cast. And as for the gossip! The city really did revolve around its cultural institutions.

However, their driver gave no sign of recognising Marie and dropped them off in front of the hotel. Marie used a card to open the lift, not needing to go through reception. She opened the door to a small suite, with kitchenette.

"Are you hungry? I have some antipasti."

"Maybe, but could I have a shower first? It was a long day, with full chorus, then the rush to the airport, and I feel a bit grungy."

"Of course. The hotel is shabby, but they have a state-of-the-art shower. You go on in, and I'll open a bottle of wine."

Arabella stripped off quickly in the bedroom and ran the shower. As promised it was very modern, running along the length of the far wall, with a rainbow head, and a plain glass wall into the room. She slipped in and stood under the shower. She didn't notice Marie come in until a hand full of shampoo soaped her back.

"Mmmmm, that's nice." Marie turned her around to face the bathroom door, which she had closed. There was a full-length mirror on the door. She stood behind her and looked over her shoulder.

"Look at me in the mirror." Their eyes locked, as Marie reached around and soaped her breasts, turning the nipples instantly hard. Her breath caught as

Marie's hand continued down over her stomach, which trembled, and further to her hips. She made a detour and bent down, soaping her legs, and then up the inside of her thighs, making eye contact again.

Her eyes were dark. Arabella opened her legs, and Marie slipped inside her.

"Don't shut your eyes. I want to see them when you come." Arabella felt herself gush and moaned. Marie quickened her pace, and her thumb pressed against her clit. Her eyes widened and she came hard, slumping against Marie, who held her in strong arms.

"It's been a long week without you."

They finished showering and wrapped large fleecy towels around each other, rubbing themselves dry.

"Now, food."

"No way. Come here." Arabella pulled her to the bed and flopped down with Marie on top of her.

"Insatiable are we."

"Yes, but that's not what I want now." Arabella pulled Marie's knees up, so that she knelt either side of her head. She brought her down to her mouth and raked her tongue up Marie's folds. She groaned and supported herself on the bedhead as her hips started moving with Arabella's rhythm.

Arabella found her entrance and used her tongue to tease it, then moved back to her clit, which was visibly swelling and hardening.

"That is so good. More." Marie's voice was an octave lower than usual. Arabella increased her speed, then, as she felt Marie nearing her climax, she concentrated on her clit, sucking and licking, sending Marie over the edge. Marie ground down on her tongue, twitching, until she slid down her body, and they kissed passionately.

"Where did you learn that? No, don't tell me, I don't want to know. I am becoming a very jealous person."

Their breathing slowed, and they lay in each other's arms.

"But I do need a glass of wine right now." They got up, putting on hotel robes, and nibbled on antipasti, drank wine and talked, never taking their eyes off each other.

"How was the week?"

"I conducted the whole time. That was great."

"You were, I know."

"I was what?"

"Great. Suzanne sent me a text singing your praises."

"Did she mention anything else?"

"No, why? Did something happen?"

"No, not really." It felt too sordid to tell her about Gemma, so she put off the moment.

"I have a ticket for you tomorrow, if you would like to come. But I understand if you don't. You've had a hard week."

"I'll be there with the greatest of pleasure. And talking of coming…"

They didn't sleep until the early hours, but were not wakened by alarms, or noises outside. It was midday.

"Breakfast."

"Isn't it a bit late."

Marie laughed. "This hotel caters for singers. You can order breakfast twenty-four hours a day." She called down to reception with a breakfast order and pulled on a robe. "Stay where you are. I'll get it." So, Marie didn't want her to be seen. Well, it was understandable. But it niggled.

They ate a healthy breakfast and went back to bed. Marie needed a nap before her performance, as was customary with singers. Arabella watched her sleeping. She had never seen anything so beautiful.

Marie's long eyelashes brushed her high cheekbones. Her full lips were slightly parted. Arabella itched to touch her, and she felt herself get wet again, but she had a sense of responsibility, and knew Marie needed all her strength for the performance, although she assured her that Donna Elvira in Mozart's opera, *Don Giovanni* was one of her least strenuous roles. When she woke, she reached up to pull Arabella's mouth to hers.

"I'd better go. The opera will be out looking for me. You have your ticket. I think it's better if you come straight back here after the performance. Autographs can take ages in Vienna. There's a second room card next to your ticket."

She got up and dressed in elegant trousers with a silk blouse and the fur-lined trench coat she wore when Arabella first saw her. Arabella got out of bed and kissed her gently. "Toi-toi-toi. Until later."

"Mmmmmmm. You bet."

The performance was typical for the Vienna State Opera. Playing in the pit was arguably the best orchestra in the world, but as usual, the actual Vienna Philharmonic made up only half the players… if that. The rest were substitutes, paid for by the orchestra members, so they could pursue more lucrative or more interesting engagements.

It meant there was brilliance combined with run of the mill, and the conductor, who Arabella watched closely from her eighth-row seat, and who of course had not rehearsed with the orchestra, had his hands full.

Marie sang gloriously. Arabella blushed to think how she could do it after everything that had happened between them the night before, the thought of which turned her on and she squirmed in her seat. The ache hurt.

The applause at the end was mixed, but Marie was greeted by an ovation, which she acknowledged humbly, leaving the stage before her applause died down, to allow the other cast members to come on to take theirs. But neither the Don Giovanni nor the Donna Anna's applause matched Marie's. The poor tenor got a few boos, which was unfair, although typical for Vienna. It probably didn't even reflect on his singing. The notorious standees had their favourites, and if you weren't one, you got the bird.

The applause continued for round after round, again typical for Vienna. The audience thinned, leaving only the diehard fans who seemed determined to get their money's worth, even if it meant endangering the health of the singers as their sweaty costumes became clammy on their rapidly cooling bodies. The main cast stopped taking solo bows, and now came on each time in a line-up. Marie surreptitiously waved her hand to signal Arabella should leave.

She did, and as she entered the foyer, she heard the applause end at last. She sauntered back to the hotel, realised she was very hungry, and hoped Marie would want to go out for a quick meal.

Half an hour later, she came in, clutching some flower bouquets, which she dropped unceremoniously on the table. "Can you do me a favour, my love. There are vases under the sink. Could you dump the flowers in with some water. I'm just going to change. I'm sure you're hungry." She came out quickly in her jeans and jacket, tucking her hair under her beanie.

"The restaurants around here are so full after a performance. I have a better idea." She drew her into a hungry embrace, her hips grinding against Arabella's.

"And besides, I want to be as quick as possible." They walked past the back of the opera house to a simple snack stand where a queue stood waiting to be served.

"I know you think I'm crazy, but they have the best sausages you have ever tasted." Which turned out to be the case. They walked back slowly under the dark portals of the opera house, as the fat from the sausage oozed down Arabella's fingers. Marie stopped, looked around, and licked her hand.

It was incredibly sensual especially as someone could see them at any moment. They couldn't wait to get back into the room, and frantically pulled each other's clothes off as soon as they arrived.

Arabella uttered a series of guttural groans as she felt her orgasm welling from deep inside her. Marie put her hand over her mouth. "Shhh. The hotel is discreet, but…" When she herself had a shuddering orgasm soon afterwards, she put a pillow over her head.

They lay wrapped in each other's arms. Marie stroked Arabella's hair.

"Back to reality tomorrow. Nick will be home, and I must go to Edinburgh with him on Monday and Tuesday for some PR. I know I'm not needed for rehearsals until Wednesday."

Arabella broke the ensuing silence. "I know it's none of my business, but you made it clear that your relationship is not what people think it is. You want to tell me?"

"Bella, nobody knows we are anything other than that loving golden couple, adored by the press. But I agree you do have the right to know. I told you I worked in a bar to help me pay my way while I was at university in Stockholm. I met a woman there, ten years older than me, and she made me realise that I am bisexual. I was so happy and felt free for the first time in my life. I wanted my parents to share in my joy, but they put up a wall, and simply refused to acknowledge anything I had to say."

"But I thought Sweden was one of the most tolerant societies to be found anywhere."

"It is, but it doesn't apply to everyone. My parents are catholic, which is rare in Sweden. I was brought up as one, and my parent's disapproval made me question myself, and I withdrew from Kerstin. She couldn't believe the reason was religion, she was naturally the other type of Swede, and she was so furious that she left me. And then I studied in Hamburg and kept myself to myself. I was so busy and so happy singing rather than being a biology teacher, which is what my parents expected of me, that I needed nobody. To avoid suspicion, I can't help my looks and men fall for me, I had to flirt a bit with some male students, but I never let it be anything more than a one-night stand, and even that didn't happen often. I was much more interested in some of the girls, but none of them came on to me, so that was that. Then I won the prize at the Cardiff Singer of the

World representing Sweden, and was taken up by an agent, who found me so much work, I didn't have time anyway. I moved to London to be close to my agency."

"And Nick?"

"I was doing a sponsorship gala in Paris. He speaks French, and he was compering it. We got talking during the rehearsals. I liked him, but mostly I liked his looks. We were photographed a few times, and then the rumours about a romance started in the magazines. We met up back in London. His agent set up a photographer to catch us having dinner. The press coverage escalated. One evening Nick came to my apartment. He asked me how I felt about a business arrangement, which would benefit us both. He was right. The publicity had my offers of work quadruple.

What did I have to lose? I wasn't interested in anybody. I didn't dare to look for the relationship I would really like to have, so I agreed. He said it meant marriage in order to get the most out of the whole thing. My parents were visiting from Stockholm, and met him, and were ecstatic. At least my mother was. I caught my father's sceptical look a couple of times, but when Ulrike Nyman gets the bit between her teeth, there is no stopping her. I was too overworked to argue so we got married six years ago. I bought the Richmond house, and we moved in."

"And you never had sex with him?"

Marie hesitated. "A couple of times, on our honeymoon. Not since then. He thinks I'm asexual, or at best frigid."

"And you have never told him about your feelings for women?"

"No. Nick is a bit of a gossip, especially when he has had a few. He would never talk about our own lack of a physical relationship, it would make him look bad, but I don't trust him not to blab if he knew about my attraction to women."

"And would it be so terrible if it came out?"

"Yes...yes it would. I couldn't cope with the unravelling of our tangle of lies."

"But it's no big deal these days to love your own sex, especially in the theatre world. Look at Suzanne."

Marie sighed impatiently. "Suzanne is the opera world's leading gay icon. She is untouchable. But you wouldn't believe some of the snide comments I've heard behind her back. Often caused by envy I've no doubt. I just can't face the thought. And then there are still my parents, or at least my mother, who asks once a week when they can expect grandchildren. And she idolises Nick, without knowing him of course. You have seen his other side. I told you I'm a coward. Maybe it would all be different if I had a grandmother like yours, but I have no support system. I will have to continue in the closet."

She turned to take Arabella's face in her hands. "It's not fair on you, but I must be truthful. It can't be any other way between us."

"OK. Let's make the most of tonight then." Arabella rolled over on top of her and they took their time, revelling in each other's bodies, until they fell asleep.

\*\*\*

They packed. Marie asked Arabella to take the luggage directly out to the waiting taxi, while she paid the bill at the reception. This was the way it was going to be. Arabella sighed, but she couldn't say she hadn't been warned. At the airport, it was clear that Arabella was in economy class, while Marie was in business class, and she reconciled herself to the idea.

But Marie hurried off to the British Airways desk and upgraded her ticket. Business class was almost empty on a Sunday late morning, so nobody could hear them talking, and they were served breakfast. Both were hungry.

"Tell me, what your dreams are for the future. Do you want to stay at Covent Garden for ever?"

"That's difficult to answer. I'm very happy there, and I have a commitment to the house, but of course my conducting this year makes me think there might be a chance of more. Not at Covent Garden of course. I would have to leave and get a job in a small house in Austria or Germany. Who knows where I would live."

"And where would you like to live, if the fairy godmother waved her wand?"

"I went on a boat trip with my Oma to Lake Starnberg in the summer. There are wonderful houses on the lake, and you are right in the foothills of the Alps. Clara would like that as I would be closer to her, but it really is a dream, and will remain one. I would quite like to live in Munich. I grew up there. It's my second home."

The plane landed and they took a taxi. Marie wore her incognito clothes, so there was no chance she would be recognised, although both women turned heads.

As Nick was at home in Richmond, they went the long way back, and Arabella was dropped off first. Marie waved off her attempt to pay. She kissed her on both cheeks and briefly on her mouth, and Arabella jumped out. The taxi rounded the corner, and Arabella felt bereft.

\*\*\*

Johannes was back at work, so Arabella sat near him watching the rehearsal, taking notes, and occasionally relieving Andrew and Paul at the piano. Neither Gemma nor Marie was in the beginning of the third act. It was the most burlesque part of the opera with Oktavian, a woman playing a man, dressing as a woman to dupe Baron Ochs.

After the first morning session, Suzanne said. "Beth's arrived. Have lunch with us in the canteen."

"Great. I'll meet you there. I just must sort something out in the company office."

Matilda looked at her when she walked in. "You've had sex this weekend. Who?"

Arabella's stomach dropped. How could it be so obvious? And had anybody else noticed. No, she didn't think so. And no one could possibly guess she had been in Vienna.

"Who? You're not leaving the office till you tell me."

"Just a pickup, from a bar." She crossed her fingers behind her back.

"Are you going to see her again?"

"I don't know. She is certainly hot."

"Go for it, girl. It's about time. You've been working so hard for weeks, because of the witch." *If only you knew.*

"I must dash. Suzanne wants to introduce me to her wife."

"Then it can't be Suzanne, despite what Gemma's been spreading around."

"She hasn't! Why can soubrettes be such bitches? No, I swear on Greta Garbo and Marlene Dietrich's graves that it isn't Suzanne."

"What nostalgia. You know there are at least two generations who have never heard of those two, let alone know rumours about their sexuality. You. Are. Getting. Old."

Suzanne was sitting in the canteen next to a tall woman with long hair, tied back in a low ponytail with a black silk clip. She couldn't have been much older than Arabella, but her hair was snow white.

"Beth, *mein Schatz*, this is Arabella."

"I've heard a lot about you. If I didn't know better, I would be jealous."

"Suzanne helped me out with a problem last week. It would be most unfortunate if you got to hear about it."

"Don't forget to warn Marie on Wednesday, that's if you haven't already." Suzanne studied her closely.

"No, I haven't yet." Terry joining them saved her. "Beth…at last. Wonderful to see you."

"Will you come to dinner this week. I can cook you Kiwi bird stew or something."

"Mmmm, my favourite. Do you use fresh or frozen Kiwi?"

\*\*\*

Arabella heard nothing from Marie, but by now she was used to it. She reconciled her disappointment. It had to do with Marie's intense need for privacy, and not wanting to commit herself in writing. Hence no social media. She snorted. How ironical, considering she was splashed across some magazine or other at least once a week. But that had nothing to do with reality or the real Marie. It was a fantasy world she inhabited with Nick.

So, she wasn't upset, just happy to see her at the rehearsal on Wednesday afternoon, where they would stage the entrance of the Marschallin. Gemma had been onstage in the morning, and sulked when she saw Suzanne and Arabella in an intimate conversation she couldn't hear.

"Have you told Marie yet?"

"How? I haven't seen her, and she isn't the greatest communicator."

"I thought maybe over the weekend." Arabella blushed but didn't answer. Suzanne was either too astute, or she was hazarding a guess. But she couldn't know anything. No one had seen them together in Vienna. Marie had made sure of that.

"We must continue the charade this afternoon. I hope there won't be a problem."

Arabella was playing the piano. Marie didn't come over to her but gave her a little wave. She was introduced to Gemma, who was immediately all over her. Marie pulled her head back as if Gemma had bad breath.

"I hope we will be friends. It's lonely for me after all that's going on between them." She jerked her head in Arabella's direction, just as Suzanne put her arm around her shoulders. Marie froze.

"Oh shit!"

"I warned you. We'll let her know in the break." She gave Arabella a squeeze. Marie turned and walked to the back wall from where she would make her grand entrance. Her hands were clenched. Suzanne gave a low giggle.

"I'm not sure it's very funny."

The Marschallin was pure Ice Queen in this scene, and Marie had no difficulty with that. Suzanne was being evil and came over to Arabella at every opportunity. Gemma, standing next to Marie, ticked in disgust. "Obviously lesbian marriage isn't taken as seriously as heterosexual ones are. We don't treat our husbands like that, do we?"

Marie grunted and walked away from her. At the break, she disappeared, returning only as the rehearsal began. At the end she flew out of the door. Arabella was distraught. "What now?"

"Yes, that didn't pan out so well. I'm going to call her tonight to explain. I sense you don't want to."

"I don't think she would answer the phone to me."

"Probably me neither. I'll call her on Beth's phone."

"Could you let me know what happens." She gave Suzanne her mobile number.

She was restless all evening, and in desperation nearly picked up the phone several times. Then an unknown number called.

"That was not easy. She wasn't best pleased that Gemma has been chasing you. *Not another soprano*, she said. I gather you have a history."

"I don't Suzanne. It was only once, and a while ago, but unfortunately Marie witnessed an embarrassing moment."

"You must tell me sometime. Anyway, she accepted that it is Gemma doing all the pursuing, but then kept asking me why I was ringing her to talk about you anyway. Why should she care what you do etc. Then she asked if I had told you something. I admit to being a bit evil there and playing the innocent by asking what you were supposed to have told me. Eventually I took pity and said that you had told me absolutely nothing, but that I could see the electricity between you both. She went very quiet. I assured her that Beth and I are discretion itself, and no one had noticed anything, but they would if she continued to look daggers at you across the rehearsal room. I told her to act as naturally as she could with you, and that you are both to come to dinner with us on Saturday, and then you can act unnaturally." She laughed, obviously pleased with herself.

"Suzanne, I don't know how to thank you. And I would love to come to dinner."

Suzanne rang off, and Arabella collapsed onto her bed. Her phone pinged: * 'You have the most terribly taste in women, apart from me of course. And Suzanne. But I will kill you if you go down that road, if Beth doesn't get to you first. See you tomorrow. Baci.'

Arabella sent her a kiss emoji.

***

Beth and Suzanne stayed in an apartment near Neal's Yard. Arabella arrived before Marie, bringing with her a cheese speciality she bought from a German delicatessen.

"Mmmm, we love that."

The doorbell chimed, and Marie came in cursing the lack of parking space in London.

"You can't drink."

"A glass of wine is fine. I felt like being on wheels." She looked across at Arabella.

"You can kiss her you know. We are not going to die of shock."

Marie took her face in both hands and kissed her on the mouth, deepening the kiss and running her tongue over her bottom lip. Arabella's legs felt wobbly.

It was a great step for Marie, and she pulled back to wink at Suzanne and Beth, who then kissed each other. "Let's eat," said Beth, and they all giggled. "I mean dinner."

Beth was an accomplished cook. Though she kept it light that evening. Watercress soup was followed by a perfectly baked salmon, cheese and a fruit salad of raspberries and strawberries, with double cream for choice. Marie brought with her an expensive bottle of Montrachet, but they decided it would be a shame to drink it after it had been shaken up in the car.

Beth offered a cold Pouilly-Fumé, and it was deliciously crisp. They chatted about the rehearsals, colleagues and their world in general, alternating easily between German and English. Then they moved to the small living area for coffee. Two little sofas faced each other across a low table.

Each couple took a sofa, and Marie rested her head on Arabella's shoulder, a small, contented sigh escaping from her slightly parted lips. Arabella squeezed her shoulders and kissed the top of her head.

"Was I really so obvious?"

Suzanne answered Marie. "No, but Beth and I know what it's like to have chemistry across a crowded room, and you two really exude it."

"How did you meet? I presume Marie already knows."

"I took modern languages and economics at University in Auckland, always with the intention of coming to live in Europe. But I was also deeply interested in music and theatre, and when a large bank, with headquarters in Frankfurt, offered me a job, I leapt at it."

"I'm sure you didn't work in a bulletproof glass cube, doling out money."

"No." She laughed. "The big banks often support arts institutions. It's a mighty tax dodge of course, but it makes them look philanthropic. I got a job in the sponsorship department, and we were behind a big Aids gala in Frankfurt. Suzanne was one of the singers donating her services. After the gala, we sponsored a party, and we sat at the same table. That's when the chemistry came in. Of course, I knew of the great gay icon, but had only worshipped her from afar." She coughed. "Actually, maybe the seating plan did cross my desk for approval, and maybe I did tweak it a bit." Suzanne kissed her. "I asked her for her phone number, as we were planning another gala in Berlin. Instead of going through her agency, you understand." She winked.

"And I gave it to her willingly because my agent at the time couldn't even book me a flight without getting the day wrong. She sent me her number too. But then a month went by, and I heard nothing, so…"

Beth interrupted. "I wanted to, but I had no concrete plans for Berlin, and I was too shy just to call."

"So…I called her. The rest is history. We knew we were meant to be together. Beth got a transfer to Berlin, and she moved into my apartment. But she is a New Zealander, and she needs space and greenery, so we bought a house together on one of the lakes. I love it too. It is an oasis after all the travelling I have to do."

"And Beth can still do her bank job and travel with you as much as she does?"

"No, that wouldn't work. After about a year of me screaming at my agent about wrong hotel bookings, money not being reclaimed for work done, and one near catastrophe when they gave me a wrong performance date, Beth couldn't stand it any longer. By then, she had picked up a lot of knowledge about the opera business, and I missed her unbearably if we were apart for twenty-four hours, and I still do, so she left the bank to manage me. I pay her of course, and as I no longer have to pay an agent between ten and twenty-five per cent every time I open my mouth, she is a rich woman."

Beth hit her gently on the arm. "It has worked out well. As I travel so much, I now do some consultancy work for a few opera houses. I watch a lot of performances and hear and see a lot of young artists."

"A talent scout. Might I interest you in a young conductor, who is not only very good at her job, but oozes charisma and is hot as hell."

"Don't worry, I have my eye on her."

Marie bristled, and they laughed at her, which was a sign for them to get up and leave. There had been an increasing aura of sexual tension between both couples from the moment they sat in the living area.

They walked to the garage where Marie was parked.

Once inside and with the heater on full blast as the walk had chilled them, Marie turned to Arabella, and put her hand on her face. "I didn't say anything before, because it wasn't definite, but Nick has gone up to Manchester to see a show. Can you come home with me…and stay the night?"

"How fast can this car travel?"

***

It was wonderful to have time for each other. They showered together, before indulging in long, slow sex, exploring each other's bodies and learning what each one wanted and needed.

As they lay together, sated and sleepy, Arabella gently stroked Marie's hair: "Are you freaking out about Suzanne and Beth knowing about us? I mean, you don't seem to be, but what's really going on in that beautiful head of yours?"

"I must admit I didn't like the thought at first. I wasn't very nice to Suzanne on the phone that night, but I'm fine with it now. I trust them both implicitly. For all her bravado, I think Suzanne had a hard time coming out when she did, and I presume Beth wanted to leave New Zealand because it is easier to be gay in Europe. They won't ever tell anyone about us."

"I wouldn't care if they did."

Marie stiffened. "I know you wouldn't, and I have a guilty conscience about that, but I made myself clear. I am not prepared to come out. Please understand, and don't pressure me."

"Shhh…I know, and I won't."

"But I will admit, it was rather wonderful to be able to kiss you in front of them. Do you think they are having sex too?"

"You bet. Beth had difficulty controlling her hips as Suzanne stroked her neck on the sofa."

Marie laughed and yawned. "I think my eyelids are winning the battle. Come here." She pulled Arabella backwards into a spoon, and they got comfortable, and very soon dropped off to sleep.

It was just beginning to get light when Arabella woke to find Marie's hand, slowly stroking her folds. What's more, she was extremely wet. She groaned.

"What are you doing to me?"

"I couldn't wait any longer. I want you so much. And if you could just bring your strong pianist's fingers behind your back, I would be immensely grateful." Arabella had such strength in her arms that it was not a problem.

Marie lifted her leg over Arabella's thigh to give her full access, and they fucked each other until both screamed as they came hard. When their breathing calmed, but they were still spooning, Marie whispered.

"Mmmm, Bella, can I ask you something." She was hesitant and sounded almost embarrassed. "Do you have… um… toys?"

"A few."

"You know…a strap on?"

"I think I might have. At the back of a drawer somewhere."

"It would be my Christmas and birthday present combined…"

"That solves a problem then. I have no idea what to get the woman who has everything."

"Now you know."

They slept again and woke late. After a leisurely breakfast, Arabella said she should be off, and Marie didn't hold her back. She had been a little tense for the last hour or so. It was obvious that Nick could arrive at any time.

"I'll drive you home."

"No, you won't. We go on to the main stage tomorrow and you need to rest up today."

"You too. We didn't get that much sleep last night. I have to say I feel my muscles a bit. They haven't had so much exercise for years."

"But you work out regularly or else you would not have your sensational body."

"These are muscles untouched by the workout bike."

Marie ordered a taxi, and they kissed until it arrived. Arabella climbed in quickly. As the cab turned onto the main road, she saw the black Audi sport coming towards her. *That was close.*

\*\*\*

The week of stage rehearsals came and went. The conductor and pianist were in the pit, so had little contact with the singers. Terry began to get nervous. What had worked on the rehearsal stage sometimes didn't when it transferred on to the main stage.

It is the mark of a good director, if he or she can identify why something isn't right, and moreover know how to fix the problem. Terry was good, and did, but it took time away from what he would prefer to have done, which was to work on detailing fine points and emotions. The cast also became more single minded, and there was tension in the air.

Marie was contracted to sing a recital in Bonn on Wednesday. She groaned about it, but said she couldn't cancel, as she had already done so the previous year after going down with bronchitis. She left on Tuesday lunchtime and would take a crack of dawn flight out from Dusseldorf on Thursday morning to get her back for the ten o'clock rehearsal. They texted each other.

Late on Wednesday night, Arabella heard a ping: * 'I sang The Way Were just for you. They loved it. I can't wait to see you (if I can open my eyes) in the morning. Küssi.'

Arabella conducted a few rehearsals when Johannes was with the orchestra preparing them. They would occupy the pit the following week, by which time Arabella's hard work was as good as done.

The tension racked up another notch when the singers stood above the orchestra for the first time. The score was huge and luscious and often too loud. Arabella had sometimes to tactfully point out to the conductor that he needed to reduce the decibels. It was frustrating for both Johannes and the orchestra and was the part of the assistant conductor job Arabella liked the least. She sat behind Johannes, taking his notes, and delivering them to the singers in the break. They occupied their dressing rooms when they were not on stage. Going into Marie's, she found herself pushed up against the door, and a hot demanding tongue explored her mouth.

"I'm going insane, but Nick is having a home week, and is being super nice ferrying me back and forth. I want time with you, but I can't find a minute."

Arabella reassured her. "It's fine. You must concentrate now until the premiere. I'm glad he's doing this for you."

"He thinks there will be huge publicity for the production, and probably hopes photographers will be hanging around the stage door."

The third act was scheduled for Friday and on her way in she got a text from Matilda. *'Johannes is sick. You are on this morning.'

Her stomach dropped. *Such short notice.* She had only ever stood in front of a chamber orchestra. Now it was Richard Strauss waiting for her. Why couldn't her first time have been *Magic Flute* or something easier. And the third act was much harder than the first. Sod's law he had to get sick this morning.

She collected her full score and ran to the pit. Some members of the orchestra were already practising. The harps were tuning.

She spotted the first violinist sitting in the front row turning his pages and making notes. She was thankful it was the nicest of the three holding the position.

"I heard. Don't worry, Arabella, you will be fine. I'll help as much as I can."

"Thanks. I'll do my best to keep everyone together."

"And Arabella, if you hear something you think we could do better, please stop and tell us what you think."

It was incredibly generous of him. Usually if this situation occurred, and it sometimes did, the assistant conductor was expected to play through the act, and not make corrections. An orchestra did not deem them worthy to criticise.

Arabella decided to let them play through to the Marschallin's entrance, and then go back to correct if necessary.

There were some things she felt justified in pointing out, both to the singers and the orchestra. Everyone was good about it. She got a few raised eyebrows from the brass section and the rear desks of the violins, but she would not have expected anything else. She sent them off for the break and tried to relax her shoulders. Marie and Suzanne came into the stalls behind her, and Suzanne massaged her shoulders.

"You are doing great, kid."

Marie stroked and squeezed her left bicep, one of her favourite pastimes under other circumstances.

The orchestra began to drift back. Janet came down to the edge of the stage. "Miss Nyman, Miss Weigl, onstage if you would be so kind. Miss Cooper, back in the pit please, and well done so far." That was praise indeed from Janet.

Arabella had timed her rehearsal well, and she had a good half hour left, when her baton signalled the beginning of the Trio, surely the most sublime piece of music ever written for three females' voices and guaranteed to have every lesbian peeing in her pants.

"*Marie Therese*" sang Suzanne in her low mezzo-soprano voice, and Marie's angel voice soared above it singing, "*hab' mir's gelobt, Ihn lieb zu haben in der richtigen Weis'.*" (I made a vow to love him in the way a woman should). Arabella didn't have to look at the score, she could watch the three singers every second, and control the orchestra with her hands, keeping just the right sound balance. The final duet between Oktavian and Sophie followed and at the very end the little servant came on searching for, and finding, Sophie's handkerchief.

As the last note played and she brought it off with a flourish, the cast burst into applause, and the orchestra tapped their bows enthusiastically.

"Ladies and gentlemen, thank you very much…Thank you for your patience. Now we have eight minutes left and there are a couple of things we should do again." Everyone laughed, and she made corrections until one o'clock on the dot.

Suzanne called out to her. "Canteen? Lunch?"

She realised she was ravenous. She nodded.

Suzanne and Marie were already occupying a table when she walked in, and Marie gestured to a salad and a large tuna sandwich.

"She knows what you like already I see," Suzanne smirked. Both Marie and Arabella looked down at their food.

"I'm so proud of you, Bella."

"It's not my work though. Johannes has rehearsed the orchestra and they know what to do. I just wave my stick and beat time."

"Modesty will get you everywhere. No, seriously, I know Beth will want to hear about this morning. She can put out some feelers."

"That would be wonderful."

They talked about other things. Arabella knew Marie's parents were coming over from Stockholm for the premiere, but she was disappointed to hear they were arriving the following day. She was secretly hoping for time with Marie over the weekend. She couldn't hide her reaction.

"I'm sorry, I told them to come next Friday, just in time for the premiere, but they wanted to be in London this week. They promise to keep out of my hair, but of course they won't."

"They will want to see you and be with you, especially before Christmas."

"But I promised to go back to Sweden for Christmas. I'm really pissed."

This was news too, and Arabella's heart sank. Suzanne looked at her sympathetically, and put her hand over hers, just as Gemma passed their table.

"Do marriage vows count for anything these days?"

Suzanne turned and gave her a look which would have cowed Sir William. "Indeed, Gemma, my dear, *do* they? Does your husband know what you get up to? Does he like to watch perhaps?"

Gemma paled visibly and hurried out of the canteen. "And I have to walk off into the sunset with her at every performance… It's tough at the top."

"I'd better be off. Nick will be waiting," she sighed. "I suspect he is behind my parents arriving early."

Under the table her hand moved up Arabella's thigh and settled for a second in her crotch, pressing hard. She drew in a breath. Suzanne winked.

"Sometimes I don't know why they call you the Ice Queen. You seem to be able to melt Arabella very effectively," she whispered.

\*\*\*

Monday was the day of the piano dress rehearsal. There was no performance that evening, because the rehearsal would stretch over more than eight hours. It began at two o'clock, and the cast were in their dressing rooms by twelve, busy with make-up, wigs and costumes.

Arabella was in by midday, but she knew better than to disturb Marie, who would be surrounded by wig masters and costume designers and in the constant presence of her dresser.

She went to a studio and practised Donizetti's *Don Pasquale* for an hour and a half. It was the next production, and she would be playing for the rehearsals. She was rarely scheduled for Italian opera, but she accepted the fact she needed to improve her Italian, and she was happy about this one. The opera was an absolute jewel, and the conductor really excited her.

He was a bright new star on the conducting firmament, an alumnus of the famous El Sistema system from Venezuela. Arabella would ask Matilda to schedule her for the orchestra rehearsals where she could observe Raoul working with them. She ate a sandwich in the canteen, and on impulse picked up another one and a banana, taking them to Marie in her room.

"You can read my mind. You are an angel, isn't she, Betty?" Unfortunately, Marie was not alone. She sat at the mirror, in her dressing gown, fully made up and wearing her wig, which was a dark brown in colour. It changed her appearance but made her grey eyes even more luminous. "Which act are you playing?"

"The first and third."

"I will come out front and watch the second act. Please sit with me and give me notes on the first act." Arabella glanced at Betty, who obviously saw nothing out of the ordinary in this request. And it wasn't. It was so easy to be paranoid. And nobody suspected anything in any case. Gemma had seen to it that the rumours were about her and Suzanne. She had a hard time explaining the whole ruse to get Gemma off her back to a sceptical Matilda, but eventually she was believed.

There were constant interruptions to the rehearsal, and the Levee scene in the middle of the act took nearly an hour. Arabella popped her head over the stage to see a long-suffering Marie, who sang nothing in this scene, but had to have her wig dressed. She was smiling serenely. Arabella could think of a few star singers who would have thrown a tantrum by now.

Johannes was bored and she feared he would ask her to conduct the second act while he disappeared somewhere, but luckily Sir William came to watch the rehearsal and he thought better of it, so after changing places with Paul, she took her score and sat in the rear half of the stalls. Nobody was behind her. Marie came in wearing her robe with a pair of soft jogging leggings underneath. They pretended to be working, but soon stopped. It was dark and no one could see them.

Marie whispered, "Sir William came to see me in the break. There is some sort of sponsor or supporter's gala on January the sixth, and he asked me if I would consider singing something as a contribution. He said it was fun and light-hearted, and the Royal Ballet did most of the work, but singers were also involved, and it would be a great honour etc. I said I thought it would be possible. Do you think we could perform a few songs, like we did at my house in October?"

"Would you really do that? The audience will be ecstatic."

"Why not? Let's think about it. I'll say yes to Sir William, and we can rehearse after the premiere. Tell Matilda you will need to come down to Richmond for a couple of gala rehearsals. My parents will be there, but they are banned from my room when I'm working, and it's soundproof."

She moved her hand seductively up Arabella's jeans. Arabella parted her legs slightly so that Marie could nestle her hand in her crotch. Arabella's hips jerked. Marie was in the same place because she sighed and pressed her own thighs firmly together. How could desire be so painful?

Luckily, or unluckily, there was a huge problem on the stage, and the house lights came on while it was fixed. Johannes had now had enough. He called Arabella to conduct the rest of the act and left the pit. Marie moaned softly, but maybe it was for the best. They couldn't keep their hands off each other and were very near the point of no return. Who knows what would have happened.

*** 

Tuesday was a free day for the *Rosenkavalier* cast, though not for Arabella who had a full day of coaching sessions.

Before the pre-general rehearsal began on Wednesday morning, she knocked on Marie's dressing room door with a mug of black coffee.

"Lifesaver!"

"It's black. I know that milk isn't good for some singers before they sing. It can clog up the mucus membranes. Maybe it doesn't affect you, but just in case."

"It can, so I always drink it black when I'm singing. I'm not going to ask which soprano told you about the problem." She was teasing, but there was an edge to her voice.

"Don't be crazy. It's the sort of thing you hear every day in the canteen, along with the colour of a singer's phlegm when they have a cold."

Marie made a face. "Been there, heard that. It's usually the basses. Ugh! By the way, my parents wanted to come, so I've planted them in the stalls, just in case you wonder who they are. I asked Terry and Johannes and it's no problem. I didn't catch Janet though. Could I ask you a big favour and if you see her, let her know it's officially approved that they are there. By the way, you look scrumptiously stunning. Get out of here before Betty gets back and finds us with my tongue down your throat."

Arabella was wearing a sloppy sweater with a tank top underneath and slim jeans with knee length brown riding boots. Marie's eyes were dark as she raked her eyes over her body.

She left reluctantly but couldn't find Janet on the stage. As she entered the stalls, she saw her talking to a couple of people she didn't know. She ran over.

"Janet, I was looking for you. This, I think, is Mr and Mrs Nyman, Marie's parents. Johannes and Terry have both given their permission."

"Fine. Then enjoy the rehearsal." Janet left.

"Thank you very much. What a terrifying woman…" Marie's mother spoke English, but Arabella sensed her unease.

"I speak German. Would that be easier?"

"*Gott sei Dank. Das wäre für mich viel leichter. Mein Mann kann besser Englisch als ich.*"

Arabella introduced herself as the assistant conductor on the production.

"Are you a friend of Marie's?"

Alarm bells clanged. "Together with my colleagues, I helped Marie learn the role in a hurry. Excuse me, I must take my place. We begin any minute."

The rehearsal got under way. Johannes was frustrated. The singers were generally holding back, marking their roles. After all, they had a dress rehearsal and the first night to sing, all within the next five days. As the act ended, and the curtain fell, he kept the orchestra back and called for the curtain to reopen.

"Nobody leaves the stage please. I understand, and I sympathise, but I can't get any feeling for the balance if you all stand up there, looking like fish in an aquarium." The orchestra howled their approval. There is nothing more like a lynch mob than an orchestra in full cry.

"Arabella, please take over. I'm going to the back of the stalls. I want to hear the first five minutes, the Levee, and the four footmen's entrance at the end of the act. And please everybody, sing out with full voice."

There was a groan from the stage. Arabella climbed over the parapet and dropped on to the rostrum below. She was greeted with a 'Way to go, Arabella', from an American trumpet player.

During the second act, Arabella was aware of Marie sitting with her parents. She guessed she was being looked at but resisted the temptation to turn around.

Johannes did the same thing at the end of the second act. As Arabella climbed lithely over the orchestra parapet back into the front row, and the orchestra went into their break, Marie left her parents and came to her.

"One day, you are going to conduct this opera and I am going to sing this role in those performances."

"Pigs can fly."

"Your best friend, Matilda, calls me the witch. I will weave a spell to make it happen," she whispered in Arabella's ear.

"How did you know that?"

"Because I really am a witch." Arabella laughed. Marie turned to her parents and gave them a little wave. Her father smiled adoringly at his daughter. Mrs Nyman had a frown on her face.

\*\*\*

The dress rehearsal was full of the *Friends of the Opera House Society,* patrons who paid a yearly subscription to get early ticket booking and for perks such as sitting in on a limited number of dress rehearsals per season. Nobody was very happy about it. It put pressure on the singers to give a full performance, instead of being able to coast a little, either vocally or by not playing the role with full emotion. But this morning they couldn't afford to. Although, these people were termed *friends*, everyone knew there were some who couldn't wait to get on a blog and give their opinion, usually negative, about the rehearsal and the cast. Arabella understood fully why Marie so hated social media.

The first six rows of the stalls were cordoned off for the team, but the rest of the house was packed. Arabella sat in the front row and concentrated on taking Johannes' notes, refraining from turning around. She had no idea if Marie's parents were in the rehearsal.

There was no stopping to correct mistakes, as the rehearsal ran as a performance. The applause at the end was more than generous. Sometimes there was only a smattering at the end of these rehearsals. The cast took a quick *tutti* line up. Individual calls were reserved for performances.

Arabella knew there was no point in going anywhere near Marie's dressing room. There was activity everywhere. The stage-staff were frantically changing the set for a ballet performance that evening, after the nearly five-hour rehearsal.

*Rosenkavalier* was a long opera. The dressers would be flinging costumes on rails, and the make-up staff tearing off wigs.

The dressing rooms had to be cleaned before the dancers came in to get ready. There was not much time for the turnaround. She sent Marie a quick text * 'A lot of sobbing in the stalls at the end. Me too. Have a good rest tomorrow. Saturday can't come quickly enough. *Küsschen.*'

\*\*\*

As expected, the premiere was a triumph. The sometimes-sedate London audience screamed their approval, and there was a standing ovation almost as soon as the final curtain fell. It was hard to say who had the most applause, Suzanne or Marie. From where she stood at the side of the stage, Arabella thought Marie had the edge, but it was difficult to tell through the heavy curtain.

She hoped it was neck and neck. They both deserved it. She stood with the team after the applause died down, and the emotional hugging began.

"You'll be at the party I hope," Marie whispered. She nodded and went back to the pianist's room for a while. Then she and Andrew and Paul walked over to the Floral Hall. Some of the smaller roles were there, but as yet none of the principals.

The buffet was devastated as usual. Beth saw Arabella and came over to her. They grabbed a glass of wine and stood talking.

"Why does it always take them so long? It's something I will never get used to. But at least we two can stick together this evening." Arabella saw Nick and the Nymans across the room.

Nick was holding court with some sponsors hanging on his lips. Mr Nyman looked a little dazed. Mrs Nyman saw Arabella and nodded her head slightly in greeting. She didn't smile. Then there was a commotion as Marie and Suzanne came in together. The room broke into applause, some of the younger singers stamping and whistling. Cameras flashed.

Beth sighed. "This is going to take a while. Let's wait here."

The two stars were surrounded by people congratulating them. Both had seen Beth and Arabella, and occasionally one or the other rolled their eyes in their direction. At last, they came over, and Suzanne kissed Beth tenderly on the mouth. Cameras flashed and for a brief second Marie shrank back, before taking a breath and kissing Beth on the cheek.

"I have to get over to Nick and my parents, but I want a photo." She put her arms around Suzanne and Arabella, with Beth next to Suzanne, and the four of them stood in a group and smiled as the cameras flashed. She squeezed Arabella's bicep and unhurriedly walked over to Nick and her parents.

Shutters clicked again, and she could see the photographers asking for close ups of her and Nick. They obliged, smiling at each other.

"That's a bit tough to watch, *mein Schatz*," said Suzanne sympathetically. "Come with us. I'm hungry." She stared at Beth who wore an immaculately cut velvet suit, her white hair piled on her head. "Yes, that kind of hungry too."

Arabella stayed with them until photographers wanted more and more photos of Suzanne, so she left and circulated, talking to her friends in the ensemble. The larger-than-life Gunter Schmidt, who sang Baron Ochs, smothered her in a bear hug and lifted her off the ground. More flashes at that. He kept his arm around her for a while, but it was a fatherly hug.

She saw Marie watching with narrowed eyes, just as Suzanne and Beth joined her. Suzanne made a play of blocking her view. Nick said something and she turned away. Arabella knew they could have no more contact that evening, and she left shortly afterwards.

She sent a text: * 'Brilliant, just brilliant. No words. Please take care, and rest, and let me know when you want to work on the songs.'

Later, much later, her mobile pinged: * 'Half my success is your success. I will be forever grateful. And don't let me catch you with Gunter again. There is a moment in the first act where I could knee him, and if necessary, I will.'

Arabella sent back a green jealousy emoji, and a large kiss.

***

The next performance was on Wednesday, the one after that on Saturday, and then it was Christmas.

Matilda called her on Monday morning.

"Hecate wants you to go to Richmond tomorrow afternoon to work on the Friends Gala. Is that OK?"

"She knows you call her that."

"You are kidding! How?"

"I really don't know how. She wouldn't tell me."

"How mortifying. Especially as it isn't true. She is rather lovely. Don't you agree?"

Arabella was careful. "Yeah, she's fine. Don't worry, I think she's amused."

"I'll put you down on the call sheet. I presume Sir William will turn a blind eye, if he even notices. The Richmond trips were an exception in the *Rosenkavalier* time."

"I'm sure it will be OK. The Friends Gala is a freebie after all. He can't say anything."

"It doesn't change the fact you have two coaching sessions here in the morning."

"Sadist."

"We can have an early lunch together before you go down." Arabella felt a twinge in her core. There won't be any *going down* unfortunately, with a house full of parents.

\*\*\*

She dressed in a skirt, and boots, and a demure polo neck sweater. Her instinct was to look as feminine as possible. Marie let her in with a smile.

"You are so clever. Normally, I would think your outfit to be anything but sexy. But I know why you have done it, and I'm grateful. They are out for a walk but won't be long. You didn't run into them over the bridge I presume?"

"No. Where's Nick?"

"In his study, learning lines."

They moved to the music room, and Marie shut the door. It didn't have a lock unfortunately, but that would look suspicious. Marie took her into her arms and kissed her deeply.

"I've missed you so much. It's unbearable. I go to bed thinking of you and am wet immediately. I must admit I take care of myself almost every night. I went for years without sex. Now I have a dull ache practically all the time. I want to fuck you twenty-four hours straight through."

"Stop. Don't start what you can't carry through."

"How long do you think it would take?" Marie nibbled on her ear.

"Not long, but what if…" At that moment there was a noise outside. Arabella dived for the piano stool. Marie rummaged in a pile of music on her small table. There was a knock.

*"Snälla kom in."*

"I just wanted to say we are back. Hello. Arabella, isn't it?" *You know exactly who I am. Don't be passive/aggressive Mother Nyman.* Arabella moved across the room and shook hands. Mrs Nyman looked her up and down and seemed satisfied with what she saw. "We will be next door in the living room." She left, leaving the door slightly ajar. After a moment's hesitation, Marie reached over and closed it.

"Your mother seems to have a strong gaydar."

Marie laughed. "You are so beautiful; she suspects you are irresistible to me. And she's right."

"What do you do about bedrooms? Isn't she suspicious about you and Nick not sleeping together?"

"Their room is on the third floor, and they go up early. They haven't asked, but if they did, I would say that during rehearsals I need my complete rest and must sleep on my own. So… what are we going to give the gala public? Have you had some thoughts?"

Arabella had, and they tried out a selection of songs, eventually settling on a programme of four numbers and an encore. Marie marked down an octave as they practised. She had the second performance the next day. They left the room. Mrs Nyman was instantly in the hallway.

"I really need to sing them with full voice. Can you manage Thursday afternoon, which gives me Friday for complete vocal rest before the third performance on Saturday."

"It should be fine. I'll let Matilda know."

"Oh, if Arabella will be here again on Thursday, why doesn't she stay for dinner. I promised I would cook something. Nick will be out rehearsing I think."

"How kind. If that's OK with Marie, I could stay." Anything for a few more hours together, even if it would probably not be a fun evening. Marie nodded.

*\*\*\**

They rehearsed the songs, Marie singing out, not at full power, but enough so that they could get the harmonies right. Arabella would duet on two numbers and the encore, if the public wanted to hear it. She had sung in college to avoid having to learn the clarinet, and she had only the rudiments of technique. She could never match Marie in power.

But they were going to use microphones and the sound engineer could turn her up to get a good balance. She had a much lower voice than Marie and was a natural alto. Their voices contrasted and blended simultaneously.

They left the room fanning themselves, their eyes sparkling. Nick was on the point of leaving.

"Ah, the piano player." But this time he was much friendlier and waved to them both as he shut the door. They wandered into the kitchen/dining area where Mrs Nyman was laying the table. Something smelt good.

"Your father is having a nap. Could you call him? Perhaps Arabella needs the cloakroom." She did. She nearly followed Marie up the stairs but stopped just in time as she realised Mrs Nyman was watching her.

"I'm sure you know where the downstairs cloakroom is?" Arabella nodded and veered to her right. She splashed some water on her hot face. She again wore a skirt and boots, and now she took off her sweater. Underneath she had on a black tight-fitting button-down shirt. She undid a button, revealing her cleavage, and a hint of black lace.

Marie and her father were already in the dining area. Marie's eyes went straight to Arabella's chest, and her breath hitched. They sat down, Mrs Nyman sitting directly opposite her, Mr Nyman and Marie on her left and right.

They ate *frestelse,* a creamy potato and anchovy casserole. It was delicious. "I thought this would be appropriate. It's named after an opera singer you know."

Dessert was fresh fruit salad. "I would have prepared something more typically Swedish, but Marie would not have eaten it. She is very conscious of her figure. Nick loves her for it."

Arabella very nearly, but didn't quite, choke on a piece of orange. Rather huskily she said. "Things have changed in the opera world. With so much being filmed and streamed, the public nowadays have a hard time with fat singers. I think we lose out on some great voices, but there it is."

"Surely you think my daughter has a great voice?"

"Of course, but there are others who fall by the wayside."

"Tell me about yourself, my dear. You seem to live in the opera house day and night. Don't you have a home life? A partner?" Arabella felt herself go cold, but Marie jumped in easily.

"Arabella has bought a house in Battersea with her friend James." Thank god, she wouldn't have been that quick.

"How lovely." Mrs Nyman beamed at her for the first time. "How long have you been…cohabiting?"

"Six years it is now. We bought the house the year before last and are slowly doing it up ourselves, with the help of a friend."

"Marie and Nick have been married for six years too. Blissfully. But of course, they have no need to indulge in home decorating. What a talented young woman, isn't she, darling?" She turned to her husband, who had barely said a word.

"Arabella, my name is Anders. Please call me that." Mrs Nyman pursed her lips and refrained from offering the same informality. Marie looked thunderous.

"Don't feel you have to stay, Arabella. I'm sure you have better things to do." She could see Marie was spoiling for a fight with her mother.

"Yes, you are right. I do have to practice. I'll be off. It was a delicious meal, Mrs Nyman. Anders."

"I'll see you to the door. Mother, can you load the machine. I'll help you when I get back."

Arabella put on her pullover, and coat. Marie pulled her into the corner of the hall where they couldn't be seen. "I am going to kill her."

"Sshhhh. It's alright. Why should she be on first name terms with your rehearsal pianist? That was a brainwave about James and the house."

"She won't know what's hit her tomorrow. Now I'm going to scream at her, and tomorrow I am not going to say a single word, claiming I need vocal rest." She looked round quickly, and kissed Arabella softly on the lips, pressing her hand on her breast and kneading it gently.

Arabella staggered out of the door, needing the cold walk to the station to cool down.

*\*\*\**

The third performance regained the momentum that the second one had lost. Second performances were notorious. The first night pressure was off, and everyone was a little tired. But now they began to get into a rhythm, which would continue hopefully until the end of the run.

Arabella didn't have great hopes of seeing much of Marie that night. She suspected her parents would be at the performance. She had a little Christmas gift, which she wanted to give Marie, so when the second act was running, she knocked on her dressing room, hoping she would be alone. She was.

"My love, I was so hoping you would visit me. I have my car tonight, and I want to drive you home. I can't be that late. Mother will be staring out of the window waiting, but at least we can have a few minutes together. It's in the garage on the second level. Can you meet me there? That's of course if you don't have something else to do. I know this is the last performance before the Christmas break. Perhaps you have a party to go to?"

Arabella laughed. "We only have three days off. Everyone will be dashing away to parental homes out of London if they haven't already left. I collect a hire car tomorrow morning and drive down to Wales."

"Yes, and we fly to Stockholm in the morning. I have three days at home, then I have to be in Vienna for *Die Fledermaus* performances over the New Year. At least, they are with Suzanne. Being alone over New Year is awful. Sleep is out of the question because of the fireworks exploding all night long. We could utilise the time so well, but I know you must work."

Arabella left her present in her pocket. She would be able to give it to her later. She grinned as she left the room, almost colliding with Betty the dresser.

It was cold waiting in the garage, and it was at least twenty minutes before Marie came running in.

"I'm so sorry. Fans and autographs. I just couldn't be any quicker. Get in."

She put the heater on full blast and rubbed Arabella's hands. She drove fast to Battersea and parked near the front door. There were lights on in the house.

"Come in for a few minutes?" Arabella knew she wouldn't.

Marie shook her head. "I really would like to meet James and Ian, but not like this, not when I'm in such a rush. And it's a little more private here I think." They were parked some distance from a streetlamp, and it was dark.

The Audi had smoked windows. "Let's get in the back for a minute."

Marie took Arabella in her arms and kissed her hungrily. "I won't see you for two weeks. I will miss you terribly." She pushed her hand under Arabella's sweater and rubbed her nipples, which were hard from the cold. She moaned. "I'm much too old for this, but will you please straddle me."

Both were wearing skirts, and both were wet for each other within seconds. They continued kissing as their hands reached into each other's briefs and rubbed hard. Their hips ground together. Arabella came first, and Marie followed her seconds later.

They collapsed, and held each other tightly, not willing or able to let go. Marie sighed. "Darling, that was just too much, but I must get going. Come back into the front for a second. I have something for you."

She reached into her bag, and gave Arabella a beautifully wrapped present, about the size of an average book, but thinner. It was sealed with a little silver rose. Arabella shyly handed her own gift, which was smaller and lighter.

"I want us to open them at the same time. On the twenty-fifth at twelve o'clock your time, which is one o'clock my time."

Arabella nodded, close to tears. She leaned over the wide middle console, and they kissed gently.

"Good night, sweet one. Drive carefully and send me a text when you arrive in Cardiff. I worry."

Marie waited until Arabella opened the front door and went inside before she drove off.

***

Arabella was restless all morning, but at last it was nearly twelve o'clock. She left her mother in the kitchen basting the turkey and went to her room. She rubbed her hand over the beautiful wrapping paper and undid the ribbon carefully.

Inside, wrapped in a layer of tissue paper was a silver frame, containing an original signed photograph of Richard Strauss. A card read, 'I can't thank you enough for being in my life. Forever, M.'

She pressed the frame to her heart and felt a lump in her throat.

She reached for her mobile to send a thank you text when it pinged. *'My dear, you hit the bullseye. And the leather is so soft and such a beautiful colour, and the best thing is, I will think of you every time I use my phone. I'm just counting the hours.'

Arabella noticed Marie didn't have a cover for her mobile, and had dropped it several times, without the glass breaking. But it would only be a matter of time before it splintered. She found an elegant soft leather smart phone cover in a beautiful rich burgundy colour. She texted back: * 'I'm sitting here speechless. Strauss will go with me everywhere and will always take pride of place on my dressing room table at every concert I conduct. Until soon…'

\*\*\*

Working the week after Christmas was a chore. Nobody felt like learning music, but they were called in for coaching anyway. A revival of the tired old production of *Die Fledermaus* was thrown on with a second-rate cast. It was always sold out on New Year's Eve and again on January the second.

Arabella had to conduct the tenor when he sang offstage in the first and third acts, so she was forced to hang around throughout the few rehearsals, as well as the performances.

Ian collected her after the New Year's Eve performance. It was not a good idea to take a tube or to walk anywhere on that night. They arrived home just before eleven, and she was in the kitchen opening a bottle to bring up to Ian in the living room as a thank you, when her smart phone rang.

It was Suzanne. "I know it isn't midnight yet in Brexitland, but it is here. Beth and I send you hugs and kisses and hope your every wish be fulfilled next year. And here is, I have no doubt, one of those wishes."

Marie took the phone, laughing. "I think Suzanne just drank a large glass of champagne a little too fast, and if I'm not mistaken that was the real stuff onstage, she was quaffing at the end. I echo Suzanne and Beth's wishes for you of course. Are you home? I was worried about you wandering around London alone or being at a party with colleagues. I admit that would worry me too, but for other reasons. We are in the hotel, in Suzanne and Beth's room. The fireworks outside are terribly loud. Take care."

"We love you," chorused Beth and Suzanne in the background, which was great to hear, but she ached to hear those words from Marie too. They hadn't been said yet, and neither had she the courage, though she had known for weeks that it was the case. The line went dead.

At midnight, Arabella and Ian toasted each other. Her phone rang again. She thought it would be Matilda, but it was Marie. She said goodnight to Ian and went to her room.

"I'm in my own room now, and I just wanted to wish you a happy new year your time. I can't wait for next week. I know you will be playing for *Don Pasquale*, but we should have another rehearsal before the Gala, and Nick will be away for a couple of days. I'll text you when I know for certain. Perhaps you can forewarn Matilda. Please, please make it work…All I can think about is the last time I was in Vienna, here with you." She paused and Arabella thought the connection had been broken. Then came a soft voice. "I'm just getting into bed. Where are you, and what are you wearing?"

"Well, I was wearing black jeans and a black jacket because I had performance duty, but I'm now sitting on my bed in a black lacy bra and a thong."

"Then please lie down and get under the covers."

"And what are you wearing?" Her own voice was low, and she heard Marie gasp.

"Nothing. Pull your bra down and pinch your nipples."

Arabella could hear the cotton sheets on Marie's bed rustle as she moved her legs.

"I've opened my legs wide, and my hand is moving down my stomach to my mound. I am so wet for you, Bella. Are your nipples hard? Mine are. Rock hard."

Arabella found herself gushing and whimpered.

"Push your thong aside and rub your fingers up and down your folds, like I am. Does it feel good?"

"Oh yes," breathed Arabella. "It's your hand, and your fingers."

"I'm circling my clit, and it's your clit. It's hard and swollen, and so sensitive."

That was too much for Arabella. "Marie, I'm going to come."

"So am I, my darling." She let out a low moan. Arabella pushed her head into her pillow to stifle the sounds of her wail.

They both breathed hard, still connected but quiet.

"Was that good?"

"I can't believe we just had telephone sex."

"I'm glad we did. Goodnight, sweet princess."

*What a way to start the New Year.*

***

* 'He will be away on Friday and most of Saturday. Can you come to Richmond to work on Friday afternoon, and then stay the night?'

Matilda didn't find it an odd request to schedule her for another Richmond visit. Instead of going straight to Marie's house after playing the morning rehearsal, she went home to collect her overnight things. She texted: * 'Running a bit late. Be there in half an hour.'

* 'Hurry.'

She took a taxi. Her black leather jeans were tight, and she didn't feel like walking from the station. Marie watched from the window next to the front door and opened it immediately.

"Oh my god." She took in the leather and the kohl-rimmed eyes and slammed the door. Arabella put her arms around her and pulled her in tightly. She ground their hips together. Marie gasped and cried out.

"Work or bed first?"

"Bed."

Marie pulled her up the stairs and into her bedroom. She made a grab for Arabella, who pushed her back.

"We do this my way." Marie nodded. Arabella undressed her slowly, pulling her top over her head, unclasping her bra and worshipping the heavy perfect breasts. Marie moaned softly but kept her arms at her side. Arabella kissed her down to her stomach, her tongue tip circling her navel and dipping inside it.

Marie shivered. She popped her jeans button and pulled down the zip, then slipped jeans and briefs down the long shapely legs. She pushed her back on to the bed and parted her legs. Her sex glistened with moisture and Arabella groaned appreciatively.

Marie tried to keep her hips still, but she seemed to find it difficult. Her pupils were huge as she looked at Arabella, who removed her black sweater. She had no bra on. Then she took a small bottle out of her pocket and put it on the bedside table, before undoing her jeans and slowly pulling them down, being careful to hold the leather strap-on in position. Marie whimpered.

"Bella, please."

"It's your birthday present. As promised." She knelt between her legs and reached for the bottle. "Give me your hand." She poured lube into Marie's cupped hand and placed it around the dildo. "Coat it."

"I don't think I need to. I am so wet for you."

"I know, but I don't want to hurt you."

She knelt over her and kissed her deeply and unhurriedly. Marie responded urgently, her teeth nipping on Arabella's bottom lip. She kissed down her neck, and her breasts, biting first gently, then harder on her nipples.

Marie let out a guttural moan. "You are killing me."

She took pity and moved downwards, swiping her tongue the full length of her slit. She really was dripping wet. After circling her clit and sucking once gently, she placed her hand on the dildo and moved it into position at Marie's entrance. She went in gently, and Marie's hips rose to meet her.

"More, deeper."

She pushed in forcefully, as Marie's arms came around to grab her butt. She started thrusting. Marie's legs circled Arabella's back and they moved together. The pressure on Arabella's clit from the base of the dildo was doing its work and she started panting.

"Marie, I can't hold back." Marie groaned louder and pushed her hips up even higher. Arabella found her clit and rubbed it.

"Bella." She screamed as she orgasmed. Arabella continued to thrust as her own walls clenched and unclenched, and her juices ran down the shaft of the dildo, entering Marie's vagina. Marie clutched her as a second climax rolled through her.

They both twitched as after waves pulsed through them.

"You would be pregnant if I were a man. You are full of my come."

"I…I would like that."

Marie hugged her tightly, moaning softly as Arabella withdrew, pulling the cover over them both, and sucking on her neck.

"Don't mark me."

"Scared of Nick?"

"No, Betty, my dresser."

Arabella undid the buckles and slipped out of the harness. They lay together, not an inch between their skins.

"Do you feel well fucked?"

"I have never had orgasms like that in my life, although my best has been with you anyway. I could die happy."

"No, you won't. And shouldn't we do some work?"

They got up slowly. Neither wanted to get back into wet clothes. Arabella collected her overnight bag, and they both put on comfortable jogging outfits.

"I feel I don't have bones in my legs." Marie sagged against her.

They went arm in arm downstairs and into the music room.

Later, Marie quickly and efficiently grilled two chicken breasts and Arabella made a salad. They worked well together in the kitchen.

"I have another bottle of the Montrachet we didn't drink with Susanne and Beth. Would you like some?"

"I admit I have never tasted it."

Marie opened the bottle and poured two glasses.

"No wonder it's so expensive. It's like nectar. Honey, lemon and I don't know what else."

"I know something which tastes just as good."

They ate the perfectly cooked chicken and took the rest of the wine into the living room, where Marie lit a fire, and they curled up together on the wide comfortable couch. Arabella was nearly asleep when Marie sighed.

"I am going to the USA for four months after *Rosenkavalier* ends."

"I know. I'm trying not to think about it."

"Let's just live hour by hour until then."

"Marie, please come back to my house for dinner after the Gala. I want you to meet James and Ian."

Marie stiffened slightly.

"I…don't…" Then she let out a sigh. "Yes, I will. You have every right, and I do want to get to know them. I can't stay long, but Nick won't think anything's odd if I'm back by ten."

They made love that night. Arabella knew it was love. But she didn't say so, and neither did Marie.

\*\*\*

The alarm woke her at six o'clock. She groaned. It was Sunday, and it was unseemly, but she had a lot to do, so she got up, and without washing, threw on her jogging leggings and a big shirt.

She crept downstairs hoping not to wake the men, made herself a coffee and got to work peeling vegetables and preparing the bacon and meat. She had only time to use the pressure cooker method, but she wouldn't be admitting it, and if she was being honest, had never personally been able to tell the difference. She closed the kitchen door and opened the window wide.

Nobody padded into the kitchen, so they were still sleeping. The last thing she did was to prepare buttered mushrooms, before adding them to the finished Boeuf Bourguignon, and leaving it all to cool. It tasted pretty good, even at eight o'clock in the morning.

She ironed her conductor's suit. She had had new very slim pants made in the same material, with a wide silk stripe down the sides. She was very pleased with the result.

Then she showered and dressed in low-slung jeans and a black roll neck sweater. It was time to go. She ordered a taxi to the opera house.

There was chaos on the stage. The sponsor's gala had to be rehearsed in only three hours, before the public was allowed in for curtain-up at three o'clock, hopefully to enjoy a programme scheduled to last for around two hours without an interval. The Royal Ballet bore the brunt of the performance, and dancers were all over the stage, trying to find an inch of space to rehearse the individual numbers.

Arabella spoke to a harassed Janet, and went through their needs, already submitted the previous week; consisting of the Steinway grand piano with the lid closed, and two stand microphones. The lighting was to be as intimate as possible in a pool from around the piano to the front of the stage. Janet ticked her list, and Arabella went to the dressing room she shared with Marie. She sat gazing into the mirror.

"I'm just a tiny bit nervous."

"Me too, but we are well rehearsed."

"What if they don't like us?"

"They adore you. They don't know me. You could recite the telephone book and get a standing ovation."

They waited for the call to the stage. Everything was running late. Their place in the programme was second to last immediately before the big ballet finale. They were summoned at ten to two, which left them just enough time to check the lighting, and the microphones. For the beginning of their routine, the mikes were to be out of sight behind the piano.

They dressed and made up, helping each other where necessary. Marie made up conventionally, except for a deep burgundy lipstick. Arabella was heavy on the kohl. The gala had begun a while ago, and they could hear its progress over the relay system.

Between dance numbers, Sam and Gunter sang the patter duet from *Don Pasquale*, and three of the young ensemble girls performed what was obviously a highly suggestive version of Gilbert and Sullivan's *Three Little Girls from School*. They could hear the catcalls and whistling.

They were called to the stage and waited while two ballet principals danced a very funny choreography to Taylor Swift's *Willow*.

"Oh god, I can't go on after that," Marie's breathing was shallow.

Arabella gripped her hand tightly as the Steinway was wheeled quickly onto the stage, and Sir William, who was compering, introduced them. They walked on, to huge applause. Marie wore a full-length black velvet coat. Her burgundy stilettoes were barely visible. Arabella spread her music on the piano.

Marie looked at her to begin, and Arabella played the introduction to Grieg's *Ein Traum.* There was a very slight murmur of disappointment, then the audience settled and listened attentively. The applause at the end was not ecstatic but generous. Marie held up her hand to stop them. One did not clap individual songs during a recital.

She pulled open her coat and threw it to the side. She was wearing a short leather skirt and bustier. The audience gasped. At the same moment, Arabella took off her coat and sat in her pants, and her waistcoat, with her bare arms adorned with rows of silver bangles kept up by her biceps. On her wrists she had black leather straps with buckles.

They pulled their mikes into position and launched into *Mockingbird.* Arabella could see the first three rows and every single person had their mouth hanging open.

The applause was difficult to stop, but Marie quieted them with an extremely sexy version of *You Don't Own Me.* The significance of the words was not lost on Arabella. If only Marie would practice what she preached. Then they duetted on Gaga's *Shallow,* for the last verse Marie taking her mike off its stand and leaning over the piano with her head close to Arabella's.

She changed 'boy' to 'girl' which they hadn't agreed on. The applause was deafening. People stood and screamed. It was like a pop concert. Marie put up her hand.

"We started with something Scandinavian, and we can finish with a song from my homeland. If you want to hear it."

A roar went up and they duetted again on Abba's *Happy New Year.* They took half a dozen bows, before Sir William stopped the audience.

"Ladies and Gentlemen, I am as surprised as you are. Only the Royal Ballet can follow that with our grand finale, though quite frankly I don't envy them."

They went back to their dressing room.

"Told you so."

"God, you're sexy." Marie grasped her biceps and groaned. They changed back into street clothes.

There was a knock on the door, and the other singers were waiting outside.

Sam spoke for them all. "Is this the Ice Queen I see before me? Girls, you were something else. And you know it's all on film, don't you. We each get a copy of our individual acts, though personally I'm quite willing to exchange."

Gunter whispered something in Marie's ear, and for a moment she tensed and shook her head.

They left. Marie was subdued.

"What's wrong?"

"Oh nothing. I'm just coming down from a high. And I'm starving. Let's go."

They tried to leave, but there were autographs to sign. Arabella at first stood to one side, but the fans wanted hers too.

They reached Marie's car. Arabella sent a quick text.

"You want to drive?"

"May I?"

"Of course."

She drove around the garage for a moment to get the feeling of the large vehicle, but soon felt confident, and they were on their way. Marie was nervous, she could tell. She parked with the help of the integrated park assistance. They went inside. Marie held Arabella's hand in a tight grip.

"We're home." They walked into the living room. James and Ian were reading a pile of Sunday newspapers. They both stood.

"James…Ian…this is Marie." They shook hands.

"Please don't let me interrupt."

"Would you like a drink?"

"I think I would die for a beer."

"James, did you put the pot in the oven?"

"Yes, ma'am." There was a heavenly smell wafting up from downstairs.

"Marie, come and help me. There's beer in the kitchen. I'll call you both down in twenty minutes or so."

They went down, and Arabella poured four glasses of beer.

"I'll just take them up."

"No, let me. You have things to do down here."

"Are you sure? Are you OK alone with them?"

Marie laughed and took the tray with three glasses. As Arabella put together the salad, and warmed up baguette, she heard laughter from upstairs. She hadn't expected that, and she was relieved, relaxing just a little.

James, or Ian, had laid the table. She quickly tasted her casserole, and adjusted the seasoning, put everything on the table, including a red wine she had decanted earlier. She called up the stairs.

They came down, James carrying the tray with empty glasses.

They sat and Arabella served. The ice had been broken upstairs. Perhaps it was better she hadn't been there. "Mmmm, Bella, did you cook this? It's great, and I'm so hungry."

They all ate a second serving. The conversation was wide ranging. James and Marie were deep in conversation about developments in biochemistry as Ian helped Arabella to clear the table.

They went upstairs with coffee or tea and chatted for a little longer. Marie said she had to go, and the men went downstairs to wash up.

"I really enjoyed that. They are nice, both of them. It was a great change to be able to exercise my rusty old brain with topics outside theatre and opera." She pulled Arabella into a hug and kissed her deeply.

"I wish I could stay, although I'm too full to do anything but sleep." She kissed her again, and ran her fingers lightly down Arabella's neck, obviously revelling in the velvety skin. She pressed their hips together.

"What do you do to me?" She breathed huskily. "I guess I won't see you until the tenth. You have *Pasquale* rehearsals, and I have some interviews. But I'll text you."

She called goodnight down the stairs to Ian and James. They kissed again at the door. Arabella watched her until the Audi turned the corner. She went downstairs.

"Thanks, guys."

"She is sensational," said James.

"I think I'm in love," sighed Ian.

"Don't let her go. She's perfect for you, and you for her."

"I wish, but there is the small matter of a husband, catholic parents, and an international career, and she has no intention of coming out of the closet, ever."

\*\*\*

Arabella forgot to turn her phone back on until she woke in the middle of the night. It pinged and pinged with messages. The latest was from Marie.

* 'And you can cook too. Is there no end to your talents? Think of me as I will think of you. Always.'

The rest were amazed messages about the gala. No colleagues, other than those you took part, had been there, but word had got around. Matilda was beside herself and ordered Arabella to come to her office first thing in the morning. She got in early, although she was tired.

"Look what's on Facebook."

"Ugh, I hate Facebook. You know that." It was a wobbly recording of *Mockingbird.*

"Sweetie, that cannot be the witch. It's a clone. She is damn sexy, and you are not bad yourself. What did Sir William say?"

"I think he was OK about it. The Ballet weren't best pleased having to follow us. The funniest part was the reaction of the audience as Marie sang the Grieg song totally seriously. A resigned sigh went up," she giggled. "And then we sort of stripped, and they freaked. As far as I know it was all filmed, and some of it will go onto the house website."

Her week was busy, and she counted down the days until Thursday. Marie sent a loving text on Monday, but nothing after that. It wasn't unusual, but Arabella was uneasy. She had a meeting with the music staff and missed the first act of the *Rosenkavalier* performance.

When the second act started, she made her way to Marie's dressing room. There was a *no entry* sign on the door. She was just about to ignore it, and knock softly, when Betty came down the corridor.

"I'm sorry, Arabella, but she doesn't want to be disturbed by anyone."

"What's wrong?"

"She's not feeling well." Betty stood and waited.

"OK. Tell her I wanted to say hi, and to get better soon."

She felt nauseous and suddenly terribly tired. She decided to go home. She sent a text: * 'I'm so worried. Please tell me what's wrong.'

Much later there was a reply: * 'Don't worry. I have a bad period and was struggling with the performance. I'll be OK for the next one, but I think it's better if you don't come to my dressing room. We might have gone too far at the gala. I'll explain one day.'

*One day!* What did that mean. She was in a daze. It must be Nick. He must have found out something. But what did he really care, unless it affected his precious career.

Arabella knew Marie by now, and though she was desperate to contact her, she held back. She didn't want to be on the receiving end of an even colder shoulder. She would grit her teeth and not bother her. She wouldn't even go to the next performance.

As it happened, she didn't have the option.

She played *Pasquale* rehearsals all morning. She felt as if she was under water, with a heavy lead weight on her chest, but she was always professional. If nobody looked into her dull eyes, they could not guess the turmoil plaguing her inner organs. Luckily, apart from Sam, the rest of the cast were Italian or South American, knew each other well, and jabbered away to each other in their own languages. There was no need to make small talk.

She had the afternoon free and decided to go home. She couldn't face being in the theatre knowing Marie was there and did not want to see her.

On the tube, her phone rang.

It was Matilda. "Where are you?"

"Nearly home, what's the problem?"

"Then get there, pack your suit, and take a cab back here as quickly as possible. Johannes has a kidney colic, and can't leave his bathroom, and you're on tonight."

"No way. They can find someone who has conducted it before."

"Nobody available, and anyway, look at the time, girl. The performance starts at six o'clock, and it's now nearly three."

"I can't."

"You can. Please, Arabella. The orchestra and the cast will be with you. It's an emergency."

"Not the whole cast."

"What's that supposed to mean? Oh, never mind. Please, I must start informing everybody. See you very soon."

She knew there was no alternative. A sold-out auditorium full of patrons paying top prices for their tickets could not be sent home. And she could do it. Of course she could. She knew the score inside out. She had been at all the rehearsals. She knew what the orchestra and singers expected.

She sprinted home, collected what she needed, and was back an hour and a half before curtain-up. She locked herself in the guest conductor's room and studied the score. There were several knocks on the door, but she ignored them, narrowing her vision so that she concentrated only on the music.

She changed and made up, including her trademark kohl rimmed eyes. She decided on the long skirt version of her suit. Her name was called over the intercom system at ten to six, and she went to the prompt corner where Janet was waiting for her.

"I will send you down to the pit in five minutes. Give your score to the orchestra manager. He will put it on the desk. Sir William will make an announcement of course."

Sir William arrived at that moment and shook her hand.

"I have every faith in you, Arabella."

Suzanne and Marie hurried up. Suzanne hugged her tightly. Marie whispered, "I knocked on your door, but you didn't answer."

"Yeah, well...you know now how it feels."

Marie shut her eyes in pain. "You'll be fabulous. I knew you would conduct me in this role, but I didn't think it would be so soon."

"Miss Cooper, please go down now. Sir William, here is your microphone. Houselights dim in two minutes. Get ready to open the curtain for Sir William."

She heard the slight groan as Sir William announced the change of conductor. It didn't upset her. After all Johannes was the music director, and some of the audience was there to see and hear him. She clasped her baton tightly, then loosened her grip and walked to her desk.

There was friendly applause as she gestured for the orchestra to stand and turned to face the public over the edge of the parapet. The first violin looked at her and smiled. That helped. She raised her baton and gave the downbeat.

She hypnotised the orchestra into playing the introduction faster than they ever had before, and the orgasm in the music crashed louder than it ever had, after which she slowed them. They played beautifully, as she made eye contact with one orchestra member after the next, willing them to follow her. The curtain went up.

She had her eyes on the singers the whole time, automatically turning the pages of her score, but not needing to look at it. At the end of the act, the first violinist played a perfect solo. The lights went down on Marie looking pensively at a wildflower Suzanne had brought her when she came on for their tragic farewell scene. The curtain fell and there was a long silence, eventually punctuated by a loud 'Bravi.'

The second act was a different kind of tour de force with so many characters on the stage, but again Arabella conducted from memory.

The audience always honour conductor and orchestra at the beginning of the last act, and as she reached her desk, an ovation sounded. She was almost knocked backwards by the force. The rest went by in a dream, and the final curtain fell to thunderous applause. The orchestra tapped their bows and their feet.

The first violin helped her down from the desk and escorted her to the door in the pit from where the orchestra manager brought her up to the stage. She was in a daze as she joined the cast behind the curtain. The smaller roles were already taking their solo bows. Janet was sending the singers through the gap in the curtain in order of importance.

Sir William hugged her this time, as did the singers as they came back through the curtain. She was aware of Marie waiting, and then going through. As the singer singing the title role, Suzanne took her solo bow last, and she returned grinning. Janet pushed Arabella gently through the curtain. She was blinded by the light but could see most of the stalls standing and clapping wildly.

She gestured to the orchestra to rise and take their applause, bowed again herself, and quickly gestured for the cast to come back in front of the curtain in a line up. She was at the end of the row, until Marie walked out of her position and brought her back into the middle to stand between herself and Suzanne. The applause increased in volume once again.

Eventually the audience got tired, and the curtain fell for the last time. Behind the curtain was laughter and clapping. Arabella had only one instinct, and that was to throw herself at Marie, but as she got near, Marie took a step back, and she faltered. Marie reached out and held her at arm's length, kissing her on both cheeks.

She was disorientated and felt dizzy, but was saved from falling by Suzanne, who took her into a gigantic hug, trying to spin her around. Gunter stepped in and lifted her off the ground. Out of the corner of her eye she saw Nick in the wings talking to Beth. Marie walked slowly over to her husband, and they left the stage.

Suzanne walked Arabella over to Beth, holding her tightly. "She's coming home with us."

Beth nodded. "Do you need any help getting out of your suit? I'll come with you."

Arabella stood with bowed head, then lead the way to her room. She said nothing until Beth had helped her pack her bag.

"Why?"

"I think Suzanne knows something. She'll tell you." They went back to Suzanne's dressing room. Marie had already left hers. The door stood open, and Betty was hanging her costume on a rack.

Suzanne took her hand and hauled her down to the stage door. They signed autographs. Arabella managed to smile and talk to the fans. She felt numb as they walked back to the Neal's Yard apartment.

"I think we all need a drink. How about that bottle of Montrachet Marie brought with her?"

"No, please, not that. Do you have a beer?"

"Arabella, we should be toasting you in champagne. You should be the happiest young woman alive. You were fantastic."

She shrugged. "Beth says you know why she is behaving like this. It's so out of the blue. Everything was wonderful. The gala was a success, we had a lovely meal at my house where she got on fantastically well with my men, and now it's as if we have hardly met."

"She is freaking out."

"Why, what's happened?"

"Several things, I think. Gunter told her after the gala, with a smirk, that you make the ideal couple, and that she should join your team."

"I remember that moment. She was quiet after he spoke to her. But so what? Gunter probably likes watching girls together."

"There have been some strange blog articles about the gala and you two being the hottest number in town."

"I didn't know. I never read that stuff."

"But the worst was a husband-and-wife interview where Nick was asked if he minded the girlfriend in their marriage. Nick was totally floored, but when the interviewer said your name, he laughed it off with…*you mean, the piano player. Arabella is Marie's coach…* Of course, he questioned her afterwards, and she denied everything, which is why she has pulled right back into her shell. She can't let Nick see you together."

"I see. She could have told me at least."

"She is in such a panic; she isn't seeing straight. I don't know what it means for you both, but I know she is going to keep her distance. She feels she must. She is terrified of her well-ordered world collapsing."

Arabella caught a sob in her throat, which was so tight she could hardly swallow.

"I suppose that's it then. It was just one of those production romances." The tears coursed down her cheeks. Beth wrapped her arms around her.

"I must go. James and Ian will be up waiting to hear what happened."

"I'll call a cab."

"Yes please."

She was thankful when she arrived home and the lights were out. There was a note. 'Tell us tomorrow. I'm sure it was a huge success. Love, James.'

She washed and put on thick warm pyjamas, curled into a ball and sobbed herself to sleep.

\*\*\*

The next day was the worst of her life, though it should have been one of the best. She tried to hide herself away, but every person she met congratulated her, and she had to smile and make small talk as if she had not a care in the world. Fortunately, the *Don Pasquale* rehearsals were now on the main stage, so she could hide in the pit.

She enjoyed watching Raoul conduct and was glad she could look forward to attending his sessions with the orchestra for the rest of the week. When she returned to the pianist's room at lunchtime, the theatre postman had left an envelope with a DVD copy of the gala. That meant Marie would have one waiting for her at the next performance. *What will she do with it?*

She turned on the office computer to check if excerpts had been uploaded onto the website. They had. There were sections of *Mockingbird* and *You Don't Own Me*. They were not incriminating. She was grateful they hadn't put up the last verse of *Shallow* when Marie leant over the Steinway, and they looked into each other's eyes. It would be embarrassing to ask the video department to remove it. Thankful for the smallest of mercies she went to the company office to see what was planned for the last two *Rosenkavalier* performances.

"Sweetie, you look ghastly. Did you celebrate all night?"

"Yeah, well you know how it is." She realised everyone put her red eyes down to partying.

"Last two *Rosenkavalier's* coming up. Pity you can't conduct them, but Johannes seems to have recovered quickly." She winked. "He won't have liked hearing about your great success. Anyway, you have orchestra keyboard duty for both."

"Must I? I don't really want to confront him for exactly that reason." It sounded convincing, even to herself.

"Can't be helped. Both Andrew and Paul asked for the evenings off ages ago, before you were catapulted to stardom."

Arabella snorted. "Whatever."

\*\*\*

For the rest of the week, she went to the *Pasquale* sessions, and enjoyed watching and learning. Raoul made what could be a very pedestrian orchestral accompaniment sound fresh and interesting. She lost herself in the music and forgot about Marie, at least for minutes at a time.

She was dreading the next performance but got through it without either bumping into Marie or catching Johannes' eye. Marie did not sound at her best, and for the first time the solo applause for Suzanne far exceeded hers. It didn't make Arabella feel any better.

At the final performance, she had to go onto the stage at the end. It would have looked very odd if she hadn't said goodbye to the cast. There was a large crowd.

"Ladies and gentlemen, the stage crew are on a tight changeover tonight. Could I ask you to take your farewells down to the canteen." When Janet commanded, even Sir William acceded.

They trooped the short distance to the canteen.

"The drinks are on the *Rosenkavalier*," shouted Suzanne above the noise. It was a nice gesture. They wouldn't stay long as the dressers were waiting. Most of the cast took a beer.

Arabella was cornered by Gemma. "I'm glad this is over. You know, perhaps we can go back to the way things were before Suzanne arrived."

Arabella stared at her.

"Gemma, could I borrow Arabella for a second, then you can have her back." She couldn't believe Marie said that. She was still jealous, in spite of everything. They moved to a corner away from the others.

"I must see you alone. I'm flying to New York on Monday. May I come to your house on Saturday afternoon? Please."

Arabella let out a breath and nodded. It would be better for them both to have closure on this, though it would be hell to be alone with her.

"What time?"

"Whenever you want to. I'll be home working on the house."

"Thank you." There had been no physical contact between them. Arabella turned and left the canteen, signalling to Beth that she would be in touch.

***

She wasn't going to dress up for her, and anyway, they really were working on the house. She had on an ancient short button-down denim skirt and tight black t-shirt. She was barefoot when the doorbell rang. Ian and James were working downstairs in the office, stripping once lurid old paper off the walls.

Marie wore grey slacks and a sweater. Her hair was in its chignon, and she wore dark glasses. They stared at each other. The electricity was undeniable. *Will it be like this forever?*

"Come in. Let's go to my room. We don't want to be disturbed. Can I get you something to drink?"

"No, thanks."

Arabella gestured to a low antique chair in the corner, and Marie sat. She perched on her bed. They looked at each other.

"I couldn't go without trying to explain."

"No need… Suzanne told me. I understand your position, but it would have been nice to hear it from you."

Marie hung her head. "I was like a deer in the headlights. I couldn't believe that interviewer's question. She said *girlfriend*."

Arabella snorted. "Well, we know I'm not that, don't we."

Marie looked at her. She had dark rings under her eyes and appeared to have lost weight. Her breath came out as a shudder.

"I can't come out. I've been fighting with myself for the last two weeks. I just can't. But I can't give you up either. I'm away now for four months, then back here for four performances of *Figaro*. Nick will be filming a lot. You can come to Richmond, or I can come here. It can be like it was, if we are discreet."

Arabella's anger surged. "So, I'm to be your dirty little secret, am I? At your beck and call when you feel the need for a good humping. No, Marie, I'm not going there, and you have no right to ask me to."

Marie got up quickly and pushed Arabella backwards onto the bed, but she was stronger, and flipped her over, slamming her down hard. She mounted her and ground their centres together. Marie's hips rose to meet hers and they desperately pushed on each other. Arabella slipped under her sweater and pinched her nipples with no consideration for the pain she caused.

Marie groaned and bucked her hips harder. Arabella growled and yanked her slacks down below her knees, pushed her briefs aside and entered her hard. Marie bit back a cry and tried to pull her face down to kiss her, but Arabella locked her outstretched left arm and kept out of reach. She rode Marie's leg, her arousal slick. Both were panting. She thrust harder.

She could feel them both on the brink and as her own orgasm surged, she pressed Marie's clit with her thumb and pushed her over the edge. They continued to twitch for a minute or longer. Arabella maintained her position, not lowering her face to be kissed, though Marie was desperate to pull her down.

"We always were the best at coming together. Déjà vu." She climbed off her and walked to the window, watching the road outside.

"You can see yourself out."

Marie let out a shocked sob. She said nothing. After a long moment, Arabella heard her dressing herself, and sitting up. Marie was trying to cry soundlessly. She wanted to turn round and take her in her arms and apologise, but instead pressed her fists hard onto the windowsill, her arm muscles taut.

Marie ran down the stairs, leaving through the front door. Arabella watched as she pulled the car door open and fell into the driver's seat. She looked up at the window, but Arabella suspected she couldn't be seen through the double glass. The early evening sun was hitting it with full force. Marie drove away. Arabella sat in the chair, pulled her knees up to her chin and whimpered like an injured animal.

***

For the next few weeks, she found it difficult to eat. She solved the problem by over exercising on the rowing machine. That made her so hungry she was forced to feed herself. But she noticed that her shoulder muscles and biceps were growing harder, and that was not good for a pianist, and she didn't want to look like a body builder either, so she slowed down, and went for long cycle rides whenever possible through thick traffic. She had either to concentrate or be killed.

She worked conscientiously. The only joy was preparing Penelope and Peter for her next concert with the chamber orchestra. Even though she did not like Peter's voice, his secure top notes were ideal for the work she had suggested. Mahler's great song cycle *The Song of the Earth* was her idea, and the orchestra readily agreed.

It gave individual members of the orchestra a chance to shine as soloists within the fabric of the orchestration. The last of the six songs was the breathtakingly moving *Abschied—Farewell*. It took all her strength not to cry when Penelope's beautiful deep voice sang the words.

She worked regularly with Sir James.

When Beth called her from Berlin, three weeks had passed. "How are you? Is that a good question or a silly one?"

"The latter I'm afraid." She heard Suzanne in the background.

"Suzanne wants to know if Marie has contacted you?"

"No."

*"Diese dumme Frau. Ich werde sie nächste Woche töten."*

"I imagine you heard that."

"Difficult not to. Why will she see her next week?"

"We fly to New York. The Met. Marie is rehearsing Donna Elvira in *Don Giovanni*, and Suzanne will sing Dorabella to her Fiordiligi in *Cosi fan Tutte*, the next revival there."

"Sorry, I hadn't followed what she is singing."

"I understand. Look, I've been putting my feelers out for you in smaller houses in Germany and Austria. There is definite interest, though there are no vacancies for the moment, but some theatres want to hear you in an informative audition. I think it would be very good for you to do some, for the experience. I know they are awful, but you learn a lot."

"Thanks, Beth. That would be great."

"I'm going to New York with Suzanne, but I will continue to do business via email. I'll let you know as soon as I have definite news. You would do well to go to Sir William and ask him for permission and leave of absence when necessary. Ours is a small world, and he might not like to hear from somewhere that you are looking for a new job. You are his protégée, after all."

"I'm not sure he sees me like that, but yes I will go and ask him."

"Don't underestimate yourself, Arabella. And don't sell yourself short."

"*Tschüss mein Schatz,*" came from the background, as Beth ended the call.

*\*\*\**

She asked for an appointment with Sir William and explained what Beth had said.

"Arabella, I'm thrilled for you. It's exactly what should be happening in your career. I can't give you your own production here. Apart from the fact that we have contracts with conductors for the next three years, you are still too inexperienced. But if you gain that experience in Europe, you can be sure I'll be knocking on your door in the years to come. Of course, you still must honour your commitments here, but any request you put in for leave, I will try my best to accommodate."

She went to the company office after her appointment and told Matilda.

"Why are you so sad, sweetie? You miss her so much I know, but she's married."

"What? What are you talking about?"

"You've been moping about ever since *Rosenkavalier* ended, don't think I haven't noticed. But she won't ever leave Beth."

Arabella laughed. "She's married all right, but it's not Suzanne."

"Oh no, not Gemma again. That will come to grief."

"It has already come to grief, but it's not Gemma. Are you crazy? Gemma?"

Matilda looked at her, suddenly enlightened. "It's Marie, isn't it?"

"Was."

"You were very careful. I don't think anyone noticed."

"Unfortunately, a few started to put two and two together after the Friend's Gala. But it is now well and truly over."

"Why? I know the distance thing is a bitch, but she'll be back at the end of the season."

"Because she most definitely won't ever leave her husband, or more to the point, come out of the closet. And I won't hide away for her. It's too sordid. We can never have a future. Matilda…She's broken my heart after just six months. Imagine how it would be for me after six years."

Matilda looked at her, before hugging her.

"Please don't tell Sam. It's over, so nobody needs to know."

"I promise. Come with me, we're going to have a couple in the Nags. Maybe Gemma will be there."

"I really do hate you, you know," but she managed to laugh for the first time in weeks.

\*\*\*

The concert was again a great success and was reviewed favourably in three papers. And Chloe was back playing in the orchestra. This time she went out with her after the concert. After too many drinks, she went back to Chloe's apartment. But as soon as she got in the door, she knew she didn't want anything to happen.

They sat on the sofa. Out of pity, Arabella kissed her, and Chloe pulled her down on top, opening her legs wide, and pushing her hips up to meet Arabella's.

"Fuck me please. I've been dreaming about this moment ever since I saw you in October."

But October held quite different memories for Arabella, and she sat up.

"I'm sorry, I can't. It's too soon."

"There's someone else, isn't there?"

"No… not anymore. But I'm not ready yet. I'll call you."

She left feeling guilty, but about who or what, she wasn't prepared to analyse.

\*\*\*

As a result of the good reviews, her agent was contacted by a choral society in Manchester who had a sick conductor, and she jumped in for a *Messiah*. It was a new experience keeping together an orchestra, soloists and a chorus of well over a hundred. Thrilling.

Beth rang from New York.

"I have an audition for you next month in Würzburg and another in Kassel. I repeat; only informative for the moment but who knows what changes there might be during the next season. The performances are three days apart. Do you think you could get a week's leave?"

"I'll try. How's Suzanne?"

"It's a bit tense here. She is so furious with Marie; they are barely speaking to each other. Which is not great as they play sisters in *Cosi fan tutte*, and the cast has only six singers. They are thrown together all the time, and when they do have to speak, they bitch."

"And Marie? How is she?"

"Arabella, she is not doing at all well. She looks ten years older and has lost a lot of weight. And for the first time in her life, she has had indifferent reviews for her Donna Elvira, the role she usually triumphs in."

"I doubt it has anything to do with me though."

"Dear girl, you are so wrong. It has everything to do with you. We've tried talking to her, but she is too stubborn. She just doesn't have the courage to come out of the closet. She changes the subject whenever it's mentioned. But every time Suzanne says your name, and my wife can be evil, and does so frequently, she looks so sad, I want to muzzle Suzanne. It is plain sadistic."

"Is Nick with her?"

"Not anymore. He's run off to Hollywood. She's rudderless, and lonely. She has a concert in Los Angeles after the Met engagement ends and will join him. Suzanne and I are afraid of what she'll find there. We both know he has someone."

"Yeah, well she knows he has discreet affairs. It doesn't bother her."

"Suzanne is great friends with a film producer in Hollywood, and he says that Nick is no longer being discreet. If it breaks, there will be world magazine coverage, and I don't know how she will cope with the fall out. If only you could be here."

"She made her choice. I am no longer part of the equation."

"But how we wish you were."

"I love you both. I'll organise my trip to Würzburg and Kassel. Can you tell me as soon as possible which pieces I will conduct. It's a terrifying thought. I hope I know the operas."

\*\*\*

Arabella was restless after her call with Beth. She couldn't help herself and she searched for reviews of the Metropolitan Opera *Don Giovanni* production. No, they were not good. *Under par... listless... disappointing... unexpectedly uncharismatic*, were among the epithets.

At least there was nothing negative about her voice. But no wonder Nick had run out of town. He wasn't accustomed to his wife having bad press. That did not suit his image at all. She wondered if his apparent indiscretion in Los Angeles was a direct response to the unfriendly criticism. If it was the case, it would not be very supportive, despite the partnership being a sexless sham.

Lying next to her laptop was the gala DVD. She hadn't been able to watch it. What the hell, if she was having a Marie Nyman nostalgia hour, she might as well get it out of the way too.

She had to smile as one of the cameras panned the resigned faces during the Grieg song. Then they threw off their clothes. She had been too busy herself to appreciate Marie's performance. Hell, she was sexy. She oozed erotic in that leather outfit. When it came to *Shallow*, and she substituted *girl* for *boy*, and then leaned across the piano to look at Arabella, she saw love in both their eyes.

She knew she was in love, and had been for months, but who was Marie kidding to deny it. No wonder there were rumours after the event, although as far as she knew only she and Marie had a copy, excluding the master copy held by the video department. She hoped they would hold to the copyright. It could not be legally reproduced, but who knows what it might be worth.

Thankfully nothing had leaked yet, and most people had forgotten about it. She watched it again, and again.

***

Her agent called, so excited she could barely speak.

"The Birmingham Symphony Orchestra just called. Their conductor for next week has a frozen shoulder. Can you take over? They thought of you because of the Strauss, and it is an all-Strauss programme. *Metamorphosen* in the first half, then *the Four Last Songs,* and the *Rosenkavalier Waltz Suites* after the interval."

"I haven't conducted the songs, but I've played the piano version. The Waltz Suites I can busk. The notes are the same after all. Who is the soprano?"

She had a moment of hope, which was idiotic. Marie, who must sing them divinely, was in New York.

"Angela Masters."

"Fine, she's great. Well, if they want me, I can make myself free. Next week was only coaching anyway, and I don't think Sir William will stand in my way."

***

She hired a car to drive herself to Birmingham. Her scores were heavy, and she had her suit and other clothes for the week. She was getting quite well paid, and she felt she could treat herself. She kissed the Strauss autograph as she packed it carefully.

She had worked on the music for three days and nights and had a good three-hour session with Sir James. She felt confident about her preparation.

She could not face breakfast on the morning of her first rehearsal. It was all very well having rehearsed a chamber orchestra of young players, but now she was going to stand in front of England's arguably best regional orchestra, and she was going to ask seasoned, and probably jaded, older male players to do what she wanted.

But she knew that showing any nerves at all would be fatal. If she appeared weak, they would go for the jugular.

She got a reasonably warm welcome, despite some sceptical looks here and there. She took a major risk. Instead of beginning with the strings only relatively small *Metamorphosen,* which would have eased her into the rehearsals, she called the full orchestra for the *Suites.* It was a brave thing to do, but she suspected it earned her some points.

Arabella had very acute musical ears and perfect pitch, which predestined her for her job. She was not at all easy on the orchestra, and picked them up on their mistakes, even doing the odd sectional rehearsal where a group of players was exposed and had to play alone. Which they hated. It got results, and by the first break she sensed she had them convinced. The work after that was pure pleasure as she motivated them into playing with imagination, passion, and where required, with humour.

The press officer came to her and asked for some newspaper interviews. One was particularly urgent because they wanted it in print before the concert.

The journalist was nice enough, and none of the questions were unexpected or difficult to answer, with one exception.

"You are particularly associated with the soprano Marie Nyman?"

"Really?" she answered. "Well, I did coach her for *Rosenkavalier* which she had to learn very fast, and then we did a fun segment for the Covent Garden supporters gala, but everyone does daft things at that event."

"The website shows it was more sexy than daft. Are you married by the way?"

"Not yet. My friend and I have bought a house together in south London." She knew James would forgive her for bending the truth a little. "But, just out of interest, do you ask young male conductors about their relationships?"

He wasn't embarrassed. "Occasionally, but people are not especially interested. You are an attractive young woman, an exotic, and the readers will want to know about your private life."

"If you've got it, flaunt it, as my grandmother always says."

She hoped that was not going to backfire, but it didn't, and the juxtaposition of the questions diffused his innuendo about Marie entirely. A photographer was present at the interview and the photo was glamorous. Arabella now wore her hair longer, though still layered. It flew around her head when she conducted.

She maintained her kohl-rimmed eye look, and under her very slim fitting black jacket her biceps were visible. Marie would have salivated if they were still together. Maybe that decided her to mail through a copy of the interview to Beth and Suzanne in New York, with the comment: 'Phew that was close, but Miss Nyman's honour is intact.'

The concert was a triumph. She was glad she could debut with such a wonderful programme. The orchestra manager promised to be in touch with her agent soon. After having a fun drink in the pub with Angela Masters and some of the orchestra, she got in her car and drove back to London.

She had to be in the opera house the next morning at ten o'clock. There was a limit to how much free time she could be given, and she had her week in Germany coming up. Adrenalin kept her awake for the drive down, but she fell into bed exhausted, just about remembering to turn on her phone again.

\* 'Thank you for the interview. I really appreciate your discretion. I will be crossing fingers for your important concert. *Jag tänker på er.*'

\*\*\*

She was on tenterhooks waiting for Beth to call.

"I have the operas you will conduct, but first things first, have you and Marie been in contact?"

"She sent me a good luck text for the concert in Birmingham and thanked me for the interview."

"I hope that was alright. My conniving wife of course printed a copy and gave it to her."

"Yes, fine, I was half hoping she would."

"And did you reply?"

"No…look Beth, I'm just getting to the stage where I only think about her eight hours a day instead of eighteen. There is no point. Nothing is going to change. I'm trying to move on."

Beth sighed. "You are right of course, but anyway, something did click, and she was more or less back to her old Ice Queen self just in time for the premiere of *Cosi fan Tutte,* which she walked away with. Suzanne didn't mind playing second fiddle. She is just so happy to have her friend back."

"I'm glad. Maybe she has her eye on someone at the Met."

"No way. Suzanne's beagle nose would have smelt that out immediately. Anyway, here goes. You have *The Magic Flute* in Würzburg, and *Tosca* in Kassel."

She felt dizzy for a moment as the blood rushed from her head. *Tosca*!

"Beth," she wailed, "I can't conduct Puccini. He's much too difficult."

"Yes, you can. You have three weeks. Off you go. Learn it."

She ran to Sir James, who calmed her down.

"It's the first act, my dear. People only think of the highlights like the tenor aria and duet, but the difficulty is all that parlando with the sacristan, the children, and the Te Deum at the end. Come along, let's get down to it. I will work with you every day. Evenings as well if you are busy during the day."

She breathed only *Tosca* and the *Magic Flute*. She was sent DVDs of both productions, and she studied them avidly, memorising the singer's movements on the stage so she would know where to make contact and give them their cues if needed.

She was scheduled to play *Fidelio* rehearsals, but Paul was a dear and took over as much as he could, leaving her some additional free afternoons.

The day before her first performance she flew to Munich on the first flight. Clara and Mia were waiting at the airport, and she drove them all to Würzburg in Clara's car.

The audition system for conductors in Germany and Austria had to be about the most brutal part of the job. She was given only a three-hour rehearsal with the singers and a pianist on the evening before the performance. The cast were nice enough, except for the elderly bass singing Sarastro, who made it clear he wasn't about to be told anything by a young woman.

He wanted his arias to be painfully slow. Arabella gritted her teeth, and they came to a compromise about the tempi.

She went back to the hotel and had a quick dinner with Clara and Mia, although her stomach roiled.

She tried to sleep for as long as possible. She went down to breakfast, and ate as much as she could, as she had no intention of having lunch. She took two bananas from the buffet. Clara and Mia had gone out sightseeing. Her grandmother knew she needed no distractions.

She returned to her room and replayed the DVD. The Sarastro wasn't even good. She sighed. She packed her new outfit. Her suit was too formal for a repertory performance. She had been back to the wardrobe department and together they created a deceptively simple beautifully cut billowing black silk shirt and slim slacks tapering at her ankles. She would wear a thin leather tie, of which she had various colours, pulled half open, with the collar undone.

She walked into the pit that evening, never having met or worked with the musicians. She shook hands with the Konzertmeister, the German name for the principal violinist and orchestra leader. His hand was warm, and he smiled at her.

She conducted the overture without even opening her score. There were a few raised eyebrows, but she knew she now had them, and they followed her intentions. She had to look at the score after that because the dialogue is different in every opera house.

But she could keep her head up for the musical numbers and gave the singers their cues with her left hand, whether they needed it or not. Inevitably the Sarastro began his aria at a snail's pace, but she was not going to let him win. Either he would look an idiot, or she would. It was very easy for the conductor to look stupid in a situation like this, when the audience could hear that orchestra and singer were painfully out of sync.

She caught the Konzertmeister's eye, and he nodded. With the full support of the orchestra playing at her tempi, she managed to push the bass into following her. During the applause following the aria, the orchestra lightly tapped their bows, and she grinned happily at them.

She had survived the first performance. Clara and Mia were ecstatic.

"I am so proud of my granddaughter."

"It helped so much having you both here. But you can't be at the next one, and that is going to be a monster."

The performance in Kassel went far better than she could have dreamed, and much of the credit she knew went to Sir James.

Both the Scarpia and the Tosca hit on her at the rehearsal the evening before. The Scarpia was all too visibly disappointed and sulked when she sent him home after rehearsing the end of the second act; leaving the field clear for the Tosca.

But Arabella escaped to her hotel room. She spent the performance day much as she had in Würzburg, watching the DVD and studying her score.

There were a few rocky moments in the first act, but nothing that an audience would notice, and she managed, with the help of some signalling with her left hand, to steer everything back on course. The Te Deum at the end of the act was thrilling, and she revelled in the huge sound orchestra, organ, chorus and soloists made.

The applause at the end of the performance was loud and long. The Intendant, the theatre director, was complimentary, apologising that he had no vacancy, but promising to contact her agent as soon as he had something for her.

She dodged the baritone and went out to dinner with the soprano. They drank a bottle of wine and had a hot make out session in the car park of the restaurant. She was Hungarian, with generous breasts, and as Arabella felt herself getting wet, and Eva writhed under her as she pinched her nipples, she seriously considered taking her back to the hotel.

But like a bucket of cold water thrown in her face, she thought of Marie saying, "You have terrible taste in women." She apologised profusely, went back to the hotel, packed and checked out. She drove down to Munich, but it was too late to wake Clara, so she checked into an airport hotel, returned her hire car, and much to Matilda's delight, went home a full day earlier than planned. That afternoon she was back at the piano in the rehearsal room.

***

\* 'You don't know how much it helped me seeing your picture in that interview. You are more beautiful than ever. Beth told me about your auditions and how the feedback has been great. I am so happy for you. I am now going to Los Angeles for a concert and to be with Nick who is filming there. It was all arranged months ago and involves interviews and things. I would much rather fly home. I will be back in June for *Figaro*. I know you have cut me out of your life, and you have every right to do so, but I would love to see you again. It will be hard, but I want to be your friend. I miss you so much.' The text was entirely unexpected. Arabella read and reread it until she had it memorised. Could they just be friends? She doubted it, but it made her warm all over to know that Marie was missing her. Despite how busy she was, she always thought of her when she was alone in bed and had on many occasions taken those magazine photos out of her bedside table and looked at them.

They always turned her on, and it was images of Marie with her head thrown back in ecstasy saying her name, which made her climax as she rubbed hard on her clit to relieve the tension.

She began to hope. Suddenly her life seemed better again. She was happier.

"You are a totally different little chick this week." Matilda greeted her as she came whistling into the company office after a coaching. "Are you and the witch back on?"

"Shhhh. No, of course not. She's in Los Angeles doing the golden couple thing with her husband."

"Are you screwing someone else then?"

"No, but I had a weird experience in Kassel. You wouldn't believe that both Scarpia and Tosca tried to get into my pants."

"And did she succeed?"

"Nearly. But she is a Hungarian version of Laura Kandinsky, and I left her standing pressed up against her car, panting. It was not my finest moment, and I don't think I have made a friend for life there. But anyway, how are you and Sam?"

"His divorce is finally going through. Mine too. I think we will probably get married."

"That's fantastic news." Arabella felt guilty. She hadn't been there much for her best friend. She had been so caught up in her own problems.

"Come on, let's go to the Nags for a drink, and I'll treat you to a pasta, that's if you don't have plans with Sam."

"He's in Paris, singing a Mahler concert. Let me finish up here."

There was a group standing at the bar, including Gemma, thankfully with Pierre.

"Have you read the blog? What a bombshell."

Arabella shrugged. "I don't read the thing."

"And some people have too much work to do."

"I don't know how Sam puts up with sharing you with your office." Gemma was the biggest bitch in the business. Pierre looked at her adoringly.

"Whatever. So, what's the bombshell?"

"The golden couple is no more. The Ice Queen and her husband have split up, and they both have new partners."

Arabella felt lightheaded and gripped the bar railing to steady herself. Matilda leaned into her reassuringly.

"Do tell all, though who knows if it's true. The blog is sometimes way off."

"He has a Hollywood starlet, and she has found herself a tennis hunk, or at least an ex-tennis hunk. You remember Fredrik Rasmusson. He's now a trainer, but still a hunk."

Arabella was almost overcome with nausea. She stared at Gemma.

"Anything wrong, Arabella? You look as if you've seen a ghost."

She found her voice and mumbled. "Just the time of the month. Matilda, I think I had better eat something. Can we go?"

Matilda linked arms and they went down the street to the Italian restaurant, although Arabella couldn't face food.

"I'll order some antipasti and pizza bread. Perhaps you can just nibble. I think it would do you good."

"She wrote me a text, wanting to meet up again in June. Saying she missed me. That was ten days ago. How could she do this to me? I thought I knew her so well."

"Maybe it's not even true."

But it was. For the next few days, it was all people in the opera house could gossip about, and the following week it was all over the magazines, with photos of the four involved. Still Arabella thought it might be a mistake, as the photos were individual mug shots. She couldn't reconcile the situation with Marie's text. Then she saw a photo of Marie and Fredrik Magnusson arm in arm, smiling at each other.

She fell even harder than she had done in February. She had accepted Nick in Marie's life, but that she could find another man to hang on to was too much to bear. It was the ultimate betrayal of what they had had together, even if neither had admitted to being in love. And surely Fredrik would not accept a sexless relationship, which meant they were sleeping together. She imagined them, heard her cries of pleasure, heard him grunting as he thrust into her. It was too much.

She called Chloe and arranged to meet. Chloe invited her to her apartment. She didn't even accept the proffered drink, but dragged her into the bedroom, stripped her and spread-eagled her on the bed. Chloe was more than willing. She kissed her, their tongues mingling. Then she licked her way down her neck, not taking too much time over her small breasts, before she pushed into her. Chloe wrapped her legs around her hips and pushed frantically against her hand. Arabella thrust with all her strength and as deeply as she could, trying to banish the image of Marie and Fredrik she kept summoning up in her head. Chloe climaxed and collapsed back against the bed.

"Arabella, you are fantastic." Her breath slowed. "What do you want me to do to you?"

"I'm good, thanks. I came with you." It was a lie.

"Oh, I'm so glad. I think we are good together. Don't you?"

She hadn't even undressed. She rolled off Chloe and sat on the edge of the bed. She wanted to cry but fought against it.

"I had better be going." Chloe seemed to be perfectly satisfied. Arabella covered her with a blanket and was about to leave the room.

"When can you come here again? I have toys you know…"

"I'll let you know."

Despite her misgivings, she did go back. Chloe was a genuinely sweet person, and they had things to talk about outside of sex. She was a fine musician, and Arabella learnt a lot about orchestra mentality listening to her. They occasionally played cello/piano pieces together, revelling in Richard Strauss' Sonata, among other works. Marie's present of the composer's autograph remained on her bedside table, taunting her.

Only the sex was a chore. After using Chloe's collection of dildos on her, she became bored with how one sided it was. Chloe always asked but was perfectly happy when Arabella said she was taken care of. She bought a new strap-on.

Her old one was in a box at the back of her wardrobe. She thought back to her own juices running down the shaft and entering Marie. She would never again feel so at one with a lover.

Chloe was thrilled, and at least the friction from the base of the dildo did make her climax. She never stayed the night, and she never invited Chloe to her house.

***

Beth and Suzanne were back in Berlin, after completing a recital tour of Japan. They called Arabella, Suzanne as emotional as ever. "That's it with our friendship. I really can't face her, and I'm so relieved our schedules don't coincide for another eighteen months. I was terrified we would both be doing the Vienna *Fledermaus* over New Year, but she is singing in the Munich one."

"Hasn't she contacted you?"

"She did try after it all broke in the press, but we were already in Japan, and it was easy to avoid her calls. Beth wants to hear what she has to say, but I've lost all patience. What is she trying to prove? A tennis hunk! What a cliché. She's as gay as I am for fucks sake."

"She would most definitely deny it."

Suzanne snorted and continued. "And she loves you."

"I…I'm seeing somebody else."

"*Ist das eine Trotzreaktion?*"

"No, it's not an act of defiance. Well, maybe a little." Suzanne was no fool. "She's sweet. A cellist, a good one as it happens."

"And the sex?" Beth, in the background, protested at the question.

"Um… She's a pillow princess. She really needs a big butch for a partner. I now wear skirts and dresses all the time to prove to myself that I'm not one."

Suzanne howled with laughter. "Well, *Liebling*, that's not going to last, is it? You and Marie were so perfectly balanced." She sighed. "I still haven't given up hope, but I admit there isn't more than a flicker of light at the end of a very long tunnel."

"She blew out the candle when Mr Rasmusson came on the scene."

Suzanne sighed. "Here's Beth. She's champing at the bit. She has some important news for you."

"Hello, darling. I heard news that the Gärtnerplatz Theatre in Munich is looking for a Zweite Kapellmeister. That is usually combined with duties as a pianist/coach, but in this case, it is an exclusively conducting position. I thought you would have to get a combination job in a smaller house first to get more experience, but I put your name forward anyway, and yes, they want you to audition. News travels, and that *Rosenkavalier* performance and the concert in Birmingham have made you a hot property. And it's not just one performance to audition with…It's a mini revival, with three rehearsals and five performances."

"When?"

"Rehearsals are the end of June with performances through until the end of July."

"That would be fantastic. We only have *Figaro* then, and I would do anything not to be here for it. Sir William will almost definitely let me go. What's the catch? Is it Rossini, which I have no idea how to conduct, and have never worked on?"

"Not quite so bad. It's Donizetti. *Don Pasquale*."

Arabella whooped.

"Is that good or bad?"

"It's better than good. It's great. I studied the score with Raoul Fernandez this season and can't wait to try out my ideas. And I can, because I can rehearse with the orchestra."

"Don't go overboard. I think you get two rehearsals with them, and a dress rehearsal. But that's certainly better than nothing."

"It's the best news you could have given me. I can spend time with my Omi as well. I love the Gärtnerplatz. I saw masses of performances when I was growing up, and I believe since it's been renovated it's just gorgeous. I can't thank you enough, Beth. I love you both so much."

"The feeling's mutual. If you have time, come up to Berlin to visit us, and meet some of our friends. Don't fall over in a faint, but Suzanne is taking July and August off this year, and we will be at home on the lake."

\*\*\*

She had just under three weeks left of the season before her departure for Munich, and it was three weeks before the *Figaro* cast were due to return for their revival. There was no chance she would run into Marie. She received two short texts, saying that they needed to speak when she was in London, and would it be possible. She had to explain something important. Arabella did not reply. After reading them through a dozen times, she deleted them.

She asked Matilda to give her extra coaching before her departure. Her colleagues had helped her so much, and she wanted to assuage her conscience by giving them some time off, especially as the weather was warm and sunny.

She also worked more than her share in the house on the weekends, and cooked James and Ian the food they liked best. James had a girlfriend who now often stayed in the house. Arabella liked her very much and was delighted for him. Ian was an IT nerd, and rarely had his nose out of his laptop.

They as good as finished the office downstairs which meant that Ian could work in there and not have to clutter up his small bedroom with all his equipment. She had not seen much of Chloe, so on her last day before leaving, she made a date to meet at the stage door after her final coaching. She would take her somewhere nice for dinner, then they could have one more night of sex.

Arabella knew it would be their last night together. Her strap-on lived with Chloe, and she would give it to her as a farewell present. Not that she would tell her that. She didn't want a scene.

She was wearing a short denim skirt with a cut off matching waistcoat, and long cream coloured stiletto cavalier boots. On her bare arms, she wore the silver bracelets she had had on at the Friend's gala five months ago. She now always wore a light version of her make-up as she was often recognised. She checked in the mirror. She would do.

She was slightly late as she ran down the stairs and pushed open the internal door to the foyer, without looking at the group of people standing talking to the stage door keeper. Chloe was perched on the edge of a bench reading something on her smart phone. Arabella pulled her up and kissed her lightly on the lips.

"Sorry I'm late." She linked her arm in Chloe's and turned. Marie was watching them with an impassive expression. She felt the colour drain from her face. She found it hard to breathe. They stared at each other.

"Marie…I thought you weren't coming in until next week."

"Evidently." She was as elegant as ever. Full on Ice Queen mode with chignon, charcoal pencil skirt and jacket and a starched white dress shirt. Her burgundy stilettos completed the outfit. The light was diffuse, but Arabella thought she could see some fine lines around her eyes. They were new.

"Is this Sophie?"

Arabella gasped, the full significance of the question hitting her hard. Marie was of course referring to *Rosenkavalier*, by casting herself in the role of the Marschallin, Arabella as Oktavian, and Chloe as Sophie, the young girl Oktavian leaves the Marschallin for.

Chloe looked puzzled.

"Hello, no, I'm Chloe. I recognise you of course, Miss Nyman."

"*Weiß sie etwas?*"

"*Sie weiß gar nicht—gar nix.*" Arabella quoted from the opera.

"Thank you for that. Hello, Chloe."

Arabella let go of Chloe's arm.

"Chloe, could you run to the restaurant. I think we might lose our reservation. I just need five minutes with Miss Nyman."

Chloe again looked puzzled but said goodbye to Marie and left. "Let's go outside. It's too crowded in here." They walked to the end of Floral Street and stood in front of the main entrance to the opera house in Bow Street.

Marie lost something of the Ice Queen she had been at the stage door. Her gorgeous grey eyes were dull. Arabella searched her face. Yes, there were some new lines there. Suzanne was right. She looked older.

"Of course. I should have realised. I thought time would stand still. It doesn't. The Marschallin is right. She seems sweet. Your taste is improving." It was said with an edge.

Arabella growled softly. "Was that remark necessary, Marie. What should I say? After all, you're staying true to your taste… with another hunk."

"I…it's not…oh never mind."

"I presume this one demands sex. Have you got women out of your system for good?"

Marie clenched her hands. She had long fingernails again. So there really wasn't a girl in the background, for the time being anyway. Unless she was a masochist.

Arabella looked at the soft skin at her beautiful throat. Marie was trying to swallow back tears. For a split second, she wanted to throw herself in her arms and say yes, she would be there for her, whatever the personal cost. She took a hesitant step.

Then Marie held out her hand to shake. "Bella…Arabella, I wish you nothing but the best. I know you have a great future ahead of you. Perhaps we'll work together again at some point. I would like that. Please take care of yourself and…I…be happy."

She withdrew her hand, hailed a taxi, which had just stopped near where they were standing, got in and was gone.

\*\*\*

Arabella sat in the plane to Munich numbed. She had eaten dinner with Chloe in a daze, the expensive food tasting like straw. She pleaded the beginning of a migraine and left to go home, where she finished packing.

She groaned now as she leafed through the in-flight magazine. There was an interview with Marie and Fredrik. *They had known each other for years, and met again in Los Angeles where his protégée was playing in a tournament... Yes, she and Nick were getting divorced. He wanted to marry his girlfriend...*

*No, she and Fredrik had no definite plans. Their jobs meant that they would often be apart... But there was Wimbledon... Yes, there was Wimbledon... It was close to where she lived wasn't it? Quite close yes.*

She was as noncommittal as ever. Something made Arabella pack the gratis magazine in her bag. Omi liked to look at this type of publication.

She shook herself. She had much more important things on her mind. She knew this *Don Pasquale* audition could change her life. She just had to make a success of it.

She stayed with Clara, but things were different. Mia had at last moved into the apartment, and she had now to vacate the guest room for Arabella to use, and sleep in Clara's bed. It didn't seem to bother either of them. *Who are they kidding? After all these years.*

\*\*\*

There were two days of staging rehearsals with the singers and pianist. They had all sung the production before, and were at the end of a long season, so they rather listlessly walked through the moves. Arabella gritted her teeth. It was going to be hard work to deliver anything other than a routine performance.

At first, she didn't interfere, just subtly tried to introduce a few of her tempi ideas while conducting the rehearsals. When she worked with them the next day, she deepened her interpretation. Suddenly there was some enthusiasm for her ideas, and she and the cast began to establish a rapport.

Most of the singers were around the same age as she was. That helped. And they invited her to go for a pizza after the rehearsal, which was fun.

The first orchestra rehearsal began just as lacklustre, except for the solo cello, who smiled up at her and dug into her instrument. She remembered the baritone singing Malatesta had said his wife was a cellist in the orchestra. It was good to know he had given his wife positive feedback. It energised her.

"Ladies and gentlemen, I would like us to do a few things differently. I think you will find it more interesting to play, and I hope the audience will like it too."

By the end of the rehearsal and the end of the first act, she had them convinced. They were much more receptive for the second act rehearsal the following morning.

The dress rehearsal was hampered by technical problems. Arabella was not surprised. The revival was being thrown on, and the set had been pulled out of the storage warehouse and virtually dumped on the stage. She kept her cool.

She was experienced enough to know that miracles usually happen in the theatre world, and it did. The audience went along with her musical interpretation, seemed to understand that this was a little more than a routine revival and she was greeted with wild applause as she took her bow.

Curiously, and fortuitously there was a review in the evening paper, which was unusual after a bread-and-butter revival in a German theatre. She wondered if Beth managed to pull a few strings. Or more likely it was Suzanne, who was a living legend in Munich. The critic wrote that the performance had more the character of a premiere than an end of season revival, thanks to a most impressive debut from young conductor Arabella Cooper, and urged readers to see for themselves at the remaining four performances.

As she walked past the front of the theatre before the second performance, there was a long queue waiting for the evening box office to open.

Neither the Intendant nor the Music Director had been at the first performance, but they both sat in their respective boxes for this one. At the final curtain, they congratulated her, although neither said anything about a possible job. But she didn't expect that. They had other candidates to hear, and who knows if she wouldn't make a mess of the next three performances. Anything was possible.

\*\*\*

There was a gap of a week before the next *Don Pasquale*, and Arabella flew up to Berlin to stay with Suzanne and Beth. Their house was gorgeous, as she knew it would be. Suzanne loved gardening and there were extensive flowerbeds, planted with red, pink and white blooms and flowering shrubs.

The lawn ran down to the lake, where they owned an impressive boathouse. Inside floated a motorboat and a small yacht. Beth favoured sailing. She had done a lot of it in New Zealand. Arabella knew the basics, and they went out together on quite a windy afternoon.

It took all Arabella's strength and agility to keep the sails moving on the right side. They moored, and she collapsed onto the grass. Suzanne thought it was terribly funny but did go and get her some pain relief cream to rub into her aching muscles.

"Beth thinks sailing is better than sex."

Beth rolled her eyes. "I won't even deign to refute that. You're fishing for compliments." They kissed. The love in their eyes was so palpable. Arabella felt the ghost of Marie's lips on her own and fought back tears.

"But I do enjoy sailing, and it keeps me fit in the summer. Suzanne on the other hand, keeps fit by being evil, and plotting. You know she sent Marie a copy of your *Don Pasquale* review, with the message, 'see how well our girl is doing'."

"Well, I can tell you that she ripped it up without reading it. You remember your beacon of light at the end of a long tunnel? Not only has the light been snuffed out, the door has slammed shut with a resounding thud. We had a confrontation at the stage door the day before I left for Munich. She saw me with Chloe. It was not a good moment. I sent Chloe away, and we talked for five minutes. I said the vilest things…again. She wasn't much better. She flounced off in a taxi." That wasn't quite fair, but Beth and Suzanne weren't to know it.

"Sounds like a lovers' tiff to me."

"Suzanne you are the most optimistic person I know."

"That's a good lead in. We promised to introduce you to a few of our friends, so we are having a small dinner party tomorrow night. There is someone coming we would like you to meet."

***

Arabella expected a lesbian only dinner party, but it wasn't, and she was glad. She was not a man hating gay and lived very happily with James and Ian and had many other men as friends. She simply preferred women sexually. Beth and Suzanne seemed to think the same.

A Berlin theatre Intendant and his wife were guests, as were a well-known designer and her husband. There was a gay actor and his partner, and two singles, a male economist friend of Beth's and a surgeon from the famous Berlin Charité hospital.

If Suzanne's plotting didn't stoop to busting up her friend's relationships, then it must be the surgeon she was being set up with. She was in her mid-forties, with shoulder length lightly waved auburn hair and penetrating green eyes. She was about four inches shorter than Arabella, so she had to look up as they were introduced.

She had faint laughter lines around her eyes and on her forehead and seemed to be a warm and friendly person. She wore a lint green linen dress and designer sneakers. More of a contrast to Marie would be hard to find. Arabella liked her immediately, although there was no jolt when they shook hands. She wore her nails trimmed short, but that had probably more to do with her profession than her sexual orientation.

They were seated next to each other at the table. Beth's food was as scrumptious as ever. There were two vegetarians among the guests, so they were served the most delicious quiches Arabella had ever tasted, with crispy rosemary potatoes, and a green salad with a dressing to die for. It was followed by sorbet, a huge selection of cheeses, and summer pudding with cream. The wine was a fabulous, and no doubt expensive, white from the Moselle region.

They went outside for coffee and lounged on the terrace overlooking the lake. It was warm.

Arabella sat on a comfortable chunky wooden chair with a slightly extended footrest. Nadine, that was the doctor's name, had been helping Beth in the kitchen, and carried out a tray with coffee cups and two large French presses, one containing normal roast, the other a superior decaffeinated blend. Suzanne took over and poured the coffee. Nadine went around handing it out.

Arabella's decaf was the last and, after bringing it over, she stayed sitting on the broad wooden arm of Arabella's chair. That sent a pulse through her core. *Yes, she was still alive.*

Arabella was quiet during the meal. There had been much talk about the cultural scene in Berlin, and there was a lot she didn't know. When Beth came outside and took her seat on a padded double lounger next to Suzanne, she looked at Arabella.

"I'm sure you all don't realise it, but this young woman is going to be the biggest thing ever in the conducting world."

"Beth, please don't." Arabella blushed bright red, but it was now dark and probably wasn't too obvious in the candlelight.

"She's just had a sensational success in Munich at the Gärtnerplatz theatre."

Nadine looked down at her from her perch. "Are there more performances? I will be at a conference in Munich next week. I would love to see it."

"Yes, there are two next week," mumbled Arabella.

Nadine handed her a smart phone. "Here, type in your number, if that would be OK of course. I can contact you when I arrive. Perhaps you could get me a ticket. Or will that be difficult? I imagine the performances are a sell-out."

"Yes, they are, but I get two tickets for each show."

Arabella typed in her number. She looked up and saw Beth and Suzanne eyeballing each other. Suzanne was smirking. Beth shook her head slightly.

The guests left soon after coffee, and Arabella helped Beth load the dishwasher while Suzanne cleared up outside.

"Are you OK with Nadine? I'm a bit sceptical about this matchmaking. If I'm honest, I don't think she's your type."

"If we are being honest then, I don't think she is either. But don't worry, Beth, I'm a grown woman, and we haven't just got engaged. There's no harm in meeting her in Munich."

"Just as long as you don't do a rebound thing."

"I got that out of my system with Chloe."

"The pillow princess." Beth giggled. "She might be a better fit with Nadine."

\*\*\*

How Beth knew about Nadine's sexual preferences was not quite clear to Arabella, but she wasn't wrong. She gave her a ticket to the fourth performance, and of course they went out to dinner afterwards and inevitably landed in Nadine's luxurious suite in the Bayerischer Hof Hotel. Nadine was unrecognisable. She wore a tight leather skirt, stockings, stilettos and black satin shirt.

As soon as she closed the door, she pushed Arabella onto the sofa, and straddled her hips. She ground down into her, and leaned in to kiss her, her tongue dancing against Arabella's, then withdrawing it to bite her bottom lip. It was sexy, Arabella had drunk a lot of wine at dinner, and she was still on a high after the performance. Her hips responded and pushed back against Nadine's.

"That's my girl," her voice was husky, "but I think the bed might suit us better."

She climbed off and pulled Arabella up. She was surprisingly strong for a slight woman. They kissed all the way into the bedroom. Nadine began to undress her. Arabella reached for her but was stopped. When she was completely naked, Nadine locked eyes, and slowly took off her skirt and shirt.

She left on her black satin bra and thong and her hold up black stockings and stilettos. It was incredibly hot, and Arabella squirmed as she felt her own wetness. Nadine pushed her onto her back and looked at her, her green eyes now dark. The low light of the bedside lamp caught her auburn hair, and it looked as if her head was on fire. For a second, Arabella felt afraid, then reminded herself that the woman was an established surgeon. She doubted she was in a room with a serial sex killer.

"Open your legs and hold onto the headboard." Arabella felt exposed, the more so because she knew her excitement was more than visible. Her folds were coated. Nadine topped her and brought her mouth to her nipples, and she groaned as they hardened painfully. But it was nothing like the pain which coursed through her when Nadine bit down hard on first one then the other.

"I need this," she whispered. Arabella nodded. It hurt but it didn't stop her wetness which she was sure was now a pool on the sheet. She continued to bite her way down Arabella's stomach. Arabella writhed and pushed one hand through Nadine's hair.

"No... back on the headboard."

She bit up and down the soft skin of her inner thighs and breathed on her folds. Arabella whimpered, and thrust up her hips, but Nadine backed off. Suddenly she flipped her over and was back up at her neck, her breasts pressed against her back.

"Spread your arms wide on the pillows," she whispered in Arabella's ear, nipping the lobe. Nadine worked her way down her back, alternatively biting and licking, until she got down to her butt cheeks. Arabella yelped as she was slapped hard. Again, and again. Nadine was grunting with the effort and her own arousal.

Then she was turned around, and her legs spread wide. Nadine knelt between them and at last she felt the touch she so longed for swiping up her slick folds. She knew it wouldn't take long. Nadine was kneeling between her knees, and she spread her own legs.

Arabella saw her hand push her thong aside, and she started rubbing herself hard. She bent her head, her eyes narrowed and staring at Arabella's sex as she panted, and then groaned. She climaxed, throwing her head back, her legs shaking. Almost as an afterthought she bent down to Arabella and sucked on her clit. Her orgasm hit and she moaned, but it was over quickly and felt like an unsatisfactory hook-up. Nadine rode her leg, still twitching. It had obviously been better for her than for Arabella, who wanted to get out of the hotel room as quickly as possible. Nadine remained where she was.

"What a pity I have to go back to Berlin tomorrow. Are you staying in Germany after the last performance?"

The lie came easily. "No, I must get back to London."

"But your profession allows you to travel, doesn't it? I have some toys in Berlin I think you will enjoy." She slapped Arabella's leg.

"I have no Berlin engagements coming up, but who knows." She cursed having given her the phone number. "I'm sorry. I really must get going. I have a rehearsal early tomorrow morning and have to prepare for it." Another lie slipped out with ease.

Nadine let her get up. She dressed herself quickly, conscious of Nadine's narrowed eyes enjoying the view. She felt intensely uncomfortable.

When she was ready, she turned to say goodbye. Nadine still in bra, thong, stockings and stilettos, sat on the edge of the bed and opened her legs wide.

"Come back to me soon."

Arabella mumbled something unintelligible and left the room. In the lobby she thought everybody was watching her and knew what she had done. She smelt of sex and felt like a paid prostitute.

Back home in Clara's apartment, she stood for a long time under the shower. She had been unfaithful. It was ridiculous. She pictured Marie writhing under Fredrik, but it didn't make her feel any less guilty.

***

The curtain fell on the fifth and last performance of the series. It was so sold out that the maximum number of people had been let into the auditorium, and she could see many were standing. The applause was again loud and long. After the final curtain, everyone hugged her and even the chorus asked when she would be back.

She couldn't answer that, but it was nice to be asked. The soloists were going to have a drink and snack in the canteen and asked her to join them. Clara and Mia had her two seats, and she declined, but they insisted, and told her to bring her grandmother too. She collected them both from the stage door, and they were thrilled to sit with the cast.

Arabella had rarely seen Mia so animated, and Clara looked at her so lovingly that her heart ached. One day she wanted this too.

She stayed on another week in Munich. She had promised to take Clara and Mia to Salzburg on a day trip. They parked in the rather creepy multi-story garage burrowed deep into the mountain. It felt like a medieval dungeon. The exit was directly in front of the huge Festival Theatre artist's entrance, and it was only a short walk to the centre of the old town.

They took their time, sitting in the famous Tomaselli Café for a coffee and decadent cream cake, before wandering to the nearby *Sound of Music* fountain, where a scene from the film was shot. It was crowded with tourists snapping selfies. Almost all were American or British. The Austrians barely acknowledged the musical or the film. The Nazi content wasn't a comfortable memory. Younger Germans were not as sensitive, and Arabella had seen on the Gärtnerplatz website that they had a long running production in the repertory.

The three women sauntered towards the old town, which was a pedestrian precinct, although thousands of tourists made walking three-a-breast impossible. Clara and Mia were enjoying window-shopping. Arabella was a little bored and walked a few paces ahead. During the summer months the shops decorated their windows with festival related themes, and there were large pictures of star singers lurking incongruously between loaves of bread and sausages, or whatever else the store sold.

Seeing a bookstore, she wandered over and was confronted with Marie's official record company photo propped up between best-sellers. She knew the photo, but she hadn't expected to see it. The beautiful grey eyes seemed to look straight at her. She caught her breath. *She's not here, is she?*

It would be a disaster to run into each other. She quickly found the festival website on her phone and tapped in *Marie Nyman*. She would be singing the Strauss *Four Last Songs* in concert, but not for ten days. She would not be in Salzburg yet. No artist stayed longer than they had to during the height of the festival season. The town was cripplingly expensive. But Arabella wanted to leave immediately. Clara and Mia joined her as she stood staring at the photo. Fortunately, they were both tired.

"Tell you what. Let's not try to eat here, it's just too crowded. Let's drive back along the country roads and find a nice Gasthof." Her grandmother looked grateful, and they made their way back through the mountain to Clara's car.

It was a relief to get out of the town. The drive back through Berchtesgaden was beautiful, and enroute they found a private brewery with its own restaurant. They could sit outside in the sunshine shaded by a large umbrella. The beer and the food were fantastic. Arabella enjoyed the enthusiasm with which the older women attacked their roast duck, red cabbage and dumplings. It wasn't an everyday treat. During the return drive, her phone pinged with a text message, but she didn't look at it.

When she did, she found it was from Beth: * 'Call as soon as you can. You've got the job.'

*It can't be the Gärtnerplatz.* She knew they had more auditions lined up in the new season. She went to her room and punched in Beth's contact. Her fingers trembled.

"Darling girl, they want you, and immediately. They want you to start on October the first."

"Who wants me?"

"Don't be so obtuse. The Gärtnerplatz, of course."

"But they are still auditioning."

"I guess they've cancelled them. They are so impressed they can't see the point in waiting. Now, what about money? Do you want to do your own negotiation, or should your useless London agent, or shall I?"

"Beth, would you? I'll pay you the commission of course."

"Don't insult me. I don't want a share of your hard-earned salary. I won't be able to get millions. You are too inexperienced, and they will take advantage of that. And Munich is fiendishly expensive."

"I can live with Omi."

"That will help, but it'll cramp your style eventually. Talking of which, did Nadine come to a performance? Did you…you know…"

"Beth, I am not going to ask how you know about Nadine's tastes. I love Suzanne too much to think of what it could mean."

"Don't worry. It's not what you're thinking. Heaven forbid. I met her through a mutual friend in the banking world, who um…told me about her Dr Jekyll and

Mrs Hyde personality. But she is a good and loyal friend. You saw her in her dress and sneakers. That's how she is out of the bedroom. That's how we know her. But wait, she flew to Munich. Surely, she doesn't travel with all her…things."

"No, thank god. But her hands and teeth are weapons enough. I still have bruises. I wonder what her lovers look like after she has used her… equipment… on them. Do you think she takes them to hospital after sex, changes into her sneakers and sews them up?"

Beth couldn't stop giggling. "I'm so sorry. I didn't want to set you up, but Suzanne is very devious. She thought it would make you see what you are missing in Marie."

"She wasn't far wrong. You know, joking apart, I'm not crazy about Dr Jekyll having my phone number, but I've just thought of something. I'll need to get a German number. I think I will just let my English one go to the end of its contract, then kill it."

"That's a brilliant idea. You need to send around a change of number when you get it, then you can weed out the numbers which are no longer important. Nadine's among them. Your London agent too, if you want my advice."

"So please don't give her my new number."

She got a text later: * '*Liebling, es tut mir so leid.* I didn't think she was quite as bad as you described to Beth, though I did have to laugh about her stitching up her sex partners. I would never give your new number to anybody, except perhaps…no, not even to Marie. Bussi, Suzanne.'

***

She returned to London with her mind in a whirl. She had to tell her parents, James and Ian, and Sir William. She told James and Ian first, and they discussed the repercussions for the house. Ideally, she would like to continue paying the mortgage, just in case it didn't work out in Munich, but she would never be able to afford it.

Ian had recently received a big promotion at his workplace, and he was keen to buy her out. James's girlfriend had already moved in, and they would take over her bedroom, which was the largest. Ian would move up to James' room, leaving her the small guest bedroom for which they agreed she would pay a minimal rent. For the foreseeable future.

Ian set in motion two independent valuations of the house as it now stood. After all the work they had done, and the fact that the street value was on the rise, with any luck she would have quite a sum of money to help with her moving costs.

She took a train to Cardiff and told her parents. They had been following her successes and were proud of her. They understood and supported her. Her mother was very happy that she would be moving to Munich. Clara was not getting any younger, and it was a great weight off her mind to know Arabella would be on hand in case of a medical emergency.

She dreaded facing Sir William. She could only work at the Opera House for the next five weeks, and she was on three months' notice. It wasn't easy to find another pianist with repertoire experience, let alone one to replace her language capabilities. He had every right to refuse to let her go, until the end of the year.

But he was kindness itself and repeated what he had said to her earlier in the year. He was very proud of her, and even promised to release her earlier than the end of September if he found a replacement quickly. She didn't want that. She wanted to be with her friends and colleagues for as long as possible.

There were still three days left before everyone came back from holiday. She hadn't had any time off, except for the short week in Munich after *Don Pasquale* ended. She was restless and went for long cycle rides. Without thinking she cycled southwest in the direction of Twickenham, her mind occupied with upcoming plans.

She found herself at the street end of Marie's house. If she cut down it, she could go over the footbridge and back along the other side of the river.

The house looked dead. Both garage doors were closed, and no car stood outside. She couldn't be sure, but it looked as if nobody was there. Nick would have moved out anyway. And where was she? Singing somewhere? Not likely.

Theatres and festivals were closed for the summer holidays. She was probably in Sweden with hunk Fredrik. Arabella accelerated and sped down the road towards the bridge. She would never see that house again; of that she was certain.

***

She thought her last weeks in London would flash past, but it wasn't the case. Once she got past all the explanations, she sensed that her colleagues were already moving on. Matilda and Sam were upset of course, but both newly divorced, they were busy looking for a house together.

She conscientiously played rehearsals for *Die Walküre* but had less work to do than she had with *Rheingold*. The cast were all guest artists apart from the eight Valkyries. The director Helmut Kirsch was not as hysterical this year, and Johannes was friendly but distant. She knew she wasn't forgiven for that triumphant *Rosenkavalier* performance. He would be glad when she left.

She spent as much time as possible with Sir James Staples. She would miss him terribly. He promised to be on the end of a phone or a mail whenever she needed him. They both choked back tears when they said goodbye.

Matilda arranged a Nags Head send off, and the ensemble presented her with a new full score of *Rosenkavalier*, signed by them all. They were in the pub until after closing time when the stragglers were thrown out.

She hired a medium sized van for all her belongings, clothes, books, and a few kitchen utensils. She took no furniture with her, as she would be living with Clara, and anyway she still had her room in the house. She left at dawn for Folkestone, and crossed France, Belgium, the corner of Holland, and was in Germany by mid-afternoon.

She intended to stop at a hotel when she got tired, but still feeling comparatively fresh, decided to drive on through. It took her fourteen hours, but she felt exhilarated as she squeezed into a parking space a few metres from Clara's apartment.

Clara and Mia were listening to an old Dusty Springfield CD when she arrived. She heard the song as she unpacked a suitcase in her room.

*If time were not a moving thing/And I could make it stay/This love we shared /Would always be /There'd be no coming day /No morning light above/To make me realise our love/Is over.*

*And now you walk away from me /And there's no place to put my hand/Except to shade my eyes /Against the sun that comes to warm the land/I watch you walk away somehow; I have to let you go now/It's over.*

*It's too late to tell you how I feel/Our love was real/And yet, there are so many times, that people have to love and then forget/Though there might have been a way, I have to force myself to say/It's over.*

Yes, it well and truly was. Marie and she now lived in different countries. There was irrevocably no way back. She was starting a new life. Marie was too. There was no place in either of their lives for each other.

\*\*\*

On October the first, the entire staff of the Gärtnerplatz theatre assembled in the stalls. The Intendant welcomed everyone back with a pep talk, then took a list from his assistant and began to introduce new members. They were each welcomed with a round of applause.

He began with the dressers and wardrobe staff and continued through the technical departments, the administration, the chorus and the orchestra. Some stood and waved, some barely raised themselves from their seats, cringing as everyone looked at them, and tried to store name and face in their collective memories.

The solo artists came last. There were three new members in the ensemble. They were greeted with cheers and whistles.

"And last but definitely not least, we come to a young woman who made quite a stir at the end of last season when she conducted *Don Pasquale*."

There was a loud wolf whistle from somewhere near the back.

"That is not politically correct, and we are an enlightened theatre here, so please…"

His tone was teasing, and everyone laughed.

"I don't think anyone thought she would be back so soon, but the orchestra, the music director and I were all of one mind. Why wait and allow her to get away, and let another theatre grab her. So please welcome Arabella Cooper, our new conductor."

There was cheering, foot stamping and more whistling. Arabella stood and waved and mouthed her thanks.

\*\*\*

The theatre put on seven new opera or musical productions every season, and two ballets. For the rest of the, on average, five performances a week, revivals of existing productions were pulled out of store and with minimal rehearsal, took their place in the repertory. As the lowest ranking conductor, Arabella would conduct several of these revivals.

She could not expect a new production until the music director and the first conductor had taken their pick. In addition, occasionally a guest specialist would be engaged for a premiere slot, so she knew the pickings were lean. But Arabella had grown up in the system and was frankly delighted just to be conducting a generous number of revivals.

She could still stamp her interpretation on a performance even with the minimum of rehearsal, if she was well prepared. When she saw her list, she panicked and wanted to get on the first plane back to London. She had to learn five operas before January, one of which was the *Barber of Seville,* and she was terrified of Rossini. She rang Sir James.

"What am I going to do," she wailed.

"For starters, you stop yelling and then we can discuss the problems one at a time. Give me the list, in the order of first nights."

"I'm so sorry, Sir James. It's not like me but I'm just overwhelmed."

She gave him the list and they went through it. First off there were two musicals, one of which was a Stephen Sondheim work, then *The Bartered Bride* from Smetana, *Hänsel and Gretel* over Christmas, and the dreaded *Barber of Seville* at the end of January.

"You can manage that, my dear. I'll make out a list of tips and mail them to you."

Which he did, she set to work, and when she wasn't in the theatre, she was at the kitchen table, memorising.

She realised this was an imposition on Clara and Mia, as were her irregular hours, and although Clara pretended not to mind, Arabella knew that it disturbed their ordered existence. She began looking for a small apartment as close to the theatre as possible. It was in an expensive area of Munich, and the rents were horrendous. She had no luck.

James rang one day at the beginning of November. "OK, we have the valuations, and they are really very close to each other, which means they are fair and realistic. If you agree on the price, Ian can get his bank loan and we will buy you out together. It is too much for me alone. What do you think about a hundred thousand pounds."

"James, you have got to be kidding."

"It's great, isn't it. The house is now worth three times what we paid for it. Your share comes out at a hundred grand. And the value will continue to increase as more of the houses in the street get renovated, so Ian won't have a problem getting his loan. Anyway, that apart, how are you?"

"Panicking at the workload, but it's great. It was the right thing to do, although I miss you both a lot."

"We miss you too. Have you seen anything of Marie?"

"No, I told you, it's over. It really is."

"That's tough. But you never know."

"You and Suzanne Weigl are just too optimistic."

"I like being in the company of super stars." They laughed, and he ended the call.

\*\*\*

She was being hit on regularly. Mostly by men, but the odd woman tried her luck as well. A girl in make-up, one of the secretaries, an older mezzo-soprano in the ensemble. The only one who interested Arabella was Claudia, one of the designers.

She was a hot blond, and very attractive. They went out a few times, and did some heavy making out in a bar, but Arabella couldn't let herself take it further. She used as an excuse not wanting to get involved with a work colleague. Claudia didn't see the problem as the design side and the musical side had no direct contact with each other. She was right, but Arabella pulled back anyway.

She also began to get serious fan mail. It was flattering, and ninety per cent was harmless, but sometimes the letters and notes became abusive when she rejected invitations to lunch, dinner, trips to Paris and whatever else they fantasised about. That made her think of Marie, and especially of Suzanne who had had to cope with much worse over many years.

One evening the stage door keeper called the police. It was obvious she was being stalked. She had seen him before, noticed him on the tram, and saw him get off at her stop. The police caught up with him, and the stalking stopped, but she became uneasy about travelling on her own late at night. She redoubled her efforts to find an apartment closer to the theatre. In the few free hours she had, she looked at possibilities, but found nothing she liked. They were mostly too large and too expensive.

She became friendly with Bettina, one of the girls in the company office, and was with her, moaning about the property market in Munich, when a soprano in the chorus came in. She was getting married to a bass in the ensemble.

"Hey, are you are looking for an apartment?"

"Yes, do you know of one?"

"I have a very, very small one bedroom just down the road. But Dirk and I are moving into his house outside the city. If you want mine, I would be grateful for a smooth handover, without having to go to all the bother of painting it up for the landlord. It's a bit old and grungy, but if you are prepared to decorate, and save me the trouble, you could make it nice in no time."

"When can I look at it? Please say now?"

"I must get back to the chorus room, but I'm going home at one o'clock. You could come with me."

They walked across the Gärtnerplatz square, which was more of an oval, and on about fifty metres down the road towards the famous outdoor market, the Viktualienmarkt. They stopped at a high wooden double gate, and she pressed a fob to open it. Inside, a small courtyard had stairs leading up on two sides. They went up two floors on the right side, and she opened the door.

The apartment really was minute. There was a bedroom just big enough for a double bed and a wardrobe, and a living room in which a small sofa faced a wall mounted TV. A bathroom with shower, and a kitchenette in one corner of the living room completed the less than thirty square metres. It was shabby, but Arabella didn't hesitate.

"I want it, I'll take it. If I can afford it, please, please."

They walked back down to the courtyard.

"You even have a very small space down here. Theoretically to park a car, but nothing would fit. But it's fine for a bike or a moped."

On the first Sunday in December, she moved in. With her skills learned on the job in her London house, it only took her two weekends and some late evenings to redecorate, even retiling the bathroom and kitchen. The tiny apartment now looked stunning. And when part of her money arrived from London, she bought herself a second hand Smart. She could just squeeze it into her courtyard space.

\*\*\*

The Christmas show was *Hänsel und Gretel*. Arabella was over the moon to be in charge of this masterpiece, and it was only because it came up every year, and her senior colleagues were sick of it, that she was allowed to conduct it. There was no rehearsal at all. The orchestra could play it in their sleep, and it sometimes sounded as if they were. The audience was mostly comprised of small children with their grandparents, so they didn't notice, and the orchestra knew it.

Arabella was determined they wouldn't get away with sloppy playing this year. As usual she knew the opera perfectly, so she didn't need her score. That way she could keep her eyes on the players and eyeball them when they played badly. She was popular, and they humoured her. The standard improved.

Possibly the worst performance was going to be on New Year's Eve at two o'clock in the afternoon. The orchestra had another performance in the evening, and yet another at eleven on the morning of New Year's Day. This was an important concert, conducted by the music director, and for which they rehearsed all week. Arabella knew they would save their best playing for it. A children's performance in the afternoon would see them sitting back in their chairs.

Arabella entered the pit, determined to get the best out of the performance. And she did, working overtime to motivate them. The applause at the end was typical for a children's performance. They booed the witch and cheered for the Hänsel and Gretel singers.

They usually didn't give the conductor more than cursory applause as they didn't realise who she was. Knowing this, she dressed up, with full make-up, and stiletto heels, and her applause at the end was gratifying, interspersed with some wolf whistles, some of which she thought came from the orchestra.

As her eyes swept over the audience, acknowledging her applause, her heart nearly stopped when she saw Marie sitting at the side of the dress circle. She stared, frozen to the spot, until she realised her applause was dropping, and hurried back through the curtain. When she came out again with the cast, the seat was empty.

She went to her room confused. It could not possibly have been Marie. She was seeing things. Then she remembered Suzanne saying she had performances of *Die Fledermaus* in Munich over the New Year. She checked the State Opera website, and it was true. She had a performance at seven thirty. It was not yet five, so theoretically it could have been Marie, although it was unlikely. She was usually in her dressing room three hours before her performance began. Arabella ran upstairs to the company office.

"Bettina, do you know who had complimentary tickets this afternoon? Did anyone ask?"

Bettina shrugged. "No one asked me."

"Is there a list anywhere?"

"Hold on, I'll look." She rummaged through stacks of paper on the communal desk.

"Just one. Wow, just look at that. Marie Nyman asked to have a seat where she could see into the pit." She looked at Arabella, with slightly raised eyebrows: "Do you know her?"

"I coached her on the Marschallin last year."

"That all?"

"Yes."

"I wonder why she didn't ask you for your tickets."

"She's rather shy."

"Maybe she's waiting at the stage door."

"I doubt it."

There was no one at the stage door. She walked slowly back to her apartment, got into her Smart and drove to Clara's. She was going to see in the New Year with them and stay the night.

The evening went by in a blur. She could see only Marie's face in her imagination. She was as much in love with her as ever.

***

Beth found Arabella a new agent, one of the best in Germany. She began to get offers to conduct concerts, but they were all at least eighteen months down the line. For that she wasn't sorry. She still had her Gärtnerplatz repertoire to learn, most pressingly Rossini's the *Barber of Seville*. She telephoned with Sir James several times.

"Apart from trying to make the music interesting for you and the orchestra, the secret is in maintaining a tight rhythm. Rossini's music can so often fall apart. I presume that is what you have heard in the past, and why you are so scared."

She overcame her fear and after a short week's rehearsal they presented a first night that crackled and fizzed. To everybody's astonishment, not least Arabella's, the leading evening newspaper awarded them the *Cultural Event of the Week* prize. Considering how much the city of Munich had to offer on this front, it was a great honour.

Soon afterwards, she was sitting bored in the company office waiting for Bettina to finish her work so that they could go to a bar together. She sighed for the umpteenth time.

"If you don't stop doing that, I'm going to throw you out. It's so distracting."

"Sorry."

"Here, read this." She handed Arabella the February issue of *Opernwelt*, the leading specialist magazine for Germany, Austria and Switzerland. "There's an interview with your friend Madame Nyman."

Arabella rolled her eyes but picked up the magazine and found the pages in question. The main photo was her usual record company portrait, and there were some additional smaller photos, one of which was of her and Fredrik obviously watching tennis somewhere. With a start she realised that one of the others was a photo from the gala event.

She looked so hot in that leather outfit with the heels, holding the mike suggestively. Arabella sighed again and looked guiltily at Bettina. She was easily recognisable playing the piano.

Bettina leaned over her shoulder and pointed at the photo.

"Not what you would expect from Marie Nyman, is it. I thought they called her the Nordic Ice Queen. Hey, isn't that you at the piano?"

There was no point in denying it. "Yes, it is. She was asked to do a segment of a sponsor's gala. We thought up the act as a team."

"You look fantastic together." Arabella grunted non-committedly.

"Are you sure you were just her coach?"

"Bettina, look at the other photo. At the time she was married to Nicholas Miller. You know him, I'm sure. His new Hollywood action movie is just out. And now she's with her next hunk, look here, Fredrik Rasmusson, ex-tennis champion."

"Scrumptious. She has great taste in men."

"Well, they also have good taste, as you can see." She could barely keep the edge out of her voice.

"Ooh, are we jealous?"

Arabella stuck out her tongue and read the article. It was timed to coincide with the release of a new Mozart Aria CD. She turned to another section to read the review, which was a rave.

"Shall I photocopy the interview? After all there's a picture of you in it."

"Thanks. I can show it to Omi."

The next morning, she walked into the city centre and bought a copy of the CD. That evening she listened to it. The beauty of Marie's voice took her breath away. The aria Per Pietà from *Cosi fan Tutte* was particularly poignant. She seemed almost to be weeping as she sang.

*For pities sake, grant me pardon for the errors of a loving soul...How could this vain, ungrateful heart have broken its promises? My darling, you deserved better for your fidelity!*

\*\*\*

Gradually, the weather turned warmer, and the first spring flowers appeared. The sun was hot for March, an obvious effect of global warming. She remembered as a child playing in deep snow until the end of April, although it probably hadn't been every year.

She cycled regularly to Munich's huge central park, the Englische Garten, and lay sunbathing on the banks of the river Isar. Sometimes Bettina went with her, and two gay friends, one of whom was a tenor in the ensemble and his partner an oboist in the orchestra. They were an attractive quartet, and heads turned when they walked past.

Arabella tanned easily, and her skin was soon a golden colour. Her hairdresser put a few thin golden highlights in her hair, which caught the stage lights. At thirty-one, she was at the height of her beauty.

Sam was guesting at the State Opera, and once his rehearsals were over and his performances began, he was bored. He took to hanging around the Gärtnerplatz canteen, waiting for Arabella. This was allowed. He was a famous international baritone after all.

They were soon aware of the looks and the gossip, but did nothing to discourage it, finding it funny. The situation nearly soured when Matilda arrived for a quick visit over Easter, and she and Sam ate lunch with Arabella between her rehearsals. As she became aware of looks and whispering, she turned to Arabella.

"Do people here always look so oddly at strangers?"

Bettina came to join them.

"Matilda, this is Bettina, who works in the company office. You two do more or less the same job. Bettina, this is Matilda, my best friend, and Sam's wife."

Bettina opened her mouth and did a double take. Then she looked pityingly at Matilda. "Pleased to meet you."

"What have you two been up to?"

Arabella and Sam sat sniggering.

"You can't stop people putting two and two together and coming up with twelve. You know what this business is like."

Matilda didn't look very happy about it, but reassured Bettina. "If it was any woman other than Arabella, the divorce papers would be on his breakfast table next week, but Arabella is head over heels in love with someone quite different."

Arabella kicked her under the table. Sam and Bettina both looked interested.

Arabella looked at Sam and spoke to Matilda. "Well, my soon to be *ex* best friend, I know at least you haven't told Sam, and I'm grateful. And as you well know its tempi passati."

Matilda winked. "It's not what I witnessed recently."

Sam looked curious.

"You were in Munich, doing god knows what with Arabella, while the love of her life…"

"Matilda! Can it."

Matilda grinned. "I'll tell you about it some time. When we're alone."

Neither Sam nor Arabella had a performance on Easter Sunday, and as the weather was still glorious, they all felt like getting some fresh air. Arabella borrowed Clara's car and they drove out to Lake Starnberg. She really loved it there and knew Sam and Matilda would too.

They took a boat trip out on the lake and looked enviously at the houses with gardens running down to the lake. Most had boathouses, and all had private jetties for swimming, fishing or boating.

Sam went to buy beers. Arabella could see the queue was a long one. He would be away for at least ten minutes. She drew breath.

"Stop, I know what you are going to ask. She was with us, singing Agathe in *Der Freischütz*. You knew that I bet?"

"Actually no, I don't follow her schedule."

"She was full on Ice Queen from the first rehearsal. What didn't help was Gemma singing Aenchen."

"Oh hell no. They have almost all their scenes together."

"Exactly. The staff director was Richard, and he came in white faced after the second rehearsal. Apparently, they bitched at each other all day long."

"That's not really like Marie."

"That's what everybody else thought too. But her bad mood went on all week on the rehearsal stage. Then they got onto the main stage and started having trouble with the conductor. No one was surprised. He's awful, but he has a big fat recording contract, and gets good press for whatever reason, and it's hard for a major opera house to ignore someone like that. As you know he's Austrian and has that awful Viennese drawl, and he started picking on Marie. She put up with it for a couple of days. On the third day, she stopped singing and walked down to the front of the stage and in a voice loud and so clear that we all heard it over the relay system said: 'The musical quality of this great house has sunk to low depths since I was here last season.'"

Arabella gasped.

"He just stared at her. To make matters even more embarrassing, some orchestra members were subtly tapping their bows and lightly stamping their feet in agreement. Naturally, Gemma leapt to his defence. After that there was full on war. Sir William had to intervene. Marie offered to withdraw, which Sir William understandably refused to accept. The conductor should have done the decent thing and walked, but of course he didn't. Somehow the ruffled tempers were soothed, and the performances are happening. Oh yes, and Gemma put it about that it was all due to Marie's sexual frustration because Fredrik Rasmusson is away in Australia."

"Maybe it is."

"No way, baby. She asked me to take her up to the press office. On the way, she ever so casually asked me if I still had contact with you. I said yes, and that you were doing incredibly well. She said the music department wasn't the same without you. Later, I asked the press officer what she wanted. She had been looking for photos from the *Rosenkavalier* first night party. She ordered quite a number."

"What does that prove?"

"I asked to see a list. You were on every single one. It wasn't suspicious for anybody who doesn't know. There were loads of Suzanne and Gunter, though none of Gemma." She giggled. "For me, it was clear as day."

Sam returned with the beers, and they relaxed on board, soaking up the sun and enjoying the fresh wind coming down from the Alps. They ate dinner together and Arabella dropped them off at Sam's guest apartment near the State Opera.

She was sleepy when she got home and crawled into bed immediately. She had a lot to think about.

*\*\*\**

At the end of April, she was scheduled to conduct a performance of Stephen Sondheim's *Follies*. It was no hardship. She was a fan, particularly of his lyrics, which were usually translated in German speaking theatres. Luckily it was the Intendant's own production, and he was also a fan of the lyrics, so they were sung in the original English with surtitles.

It would be a noisy performance. The audience was stacked heavily with gay men, and they were usually loud in their appreciation after the numbers.

When in the pit for musicals, the conductor and musicians are not bound by the more formal opera or operetta dress code. Arabella wore skinny leather pants, a full satin shirt tucked into them, and ankle boots. A red leather tie dangled from her open collar. She had been to the make-up girls, and they had fun putting a few burgundy red highlights into her hair and a touch of gel to make it even fuller bodied. The kohl around her eyes was lavish. She looked at herself. More suitable for the *Rocky Horror Show* than *Follies*, but she knew what the audience would be like, and felt like having fun.

She was strangely restless waiting to be sent on. When she turned to face the audience for her applause before beginning, there were a few gasps, and loud applause.

Before the second half, the orchestra manager came by.

"You'll never guess who's in tonight."

"No, I won't unless you tell me."

"One of the greats. Wait and see. Eighth row on the right."

He pushed Arabella gently into the pit, and as she turned to take her bow, she tried to look into the stalls, but the lighting department thought it would be funny to shine a spotlight on her and she was blinded. So much so, that when she turned, she couldn't see her score. It was a good thing she didn't need to read it. She was mildly irritated. They meant well, but it would be a catastrophe for a conductor who was dependent on his music.

At the final curtain, as she waited to be sent on for her solo bow, she asked the stage manager, "Who's the big cheese in tonight then?"

"No idea. Probably some famous drag queen."

She went through the curtain to a roar of applause. She looked down at the eighth row expecting to see an over made up, overdressed transvestite, but instead looked straight into the eyes of a glamorous blonde with her hair in a chignon, wearing a simple elegant black sheathe dress. She was lucky her applause went on and on because she was rooted to the spot.

Marie gestured to her to look right and left and up, and she snapped out of her trance and acknowledged the applause from all over the auditorium.

This time, Marie remained until the end of the applause and stood up clapping with the rest when they gave the cast a standing ovation. The stage manager stopped her.

"Marie Nyman is in tonight. I just heard. Strange choice for her I would have thought."

"Not really. She did sing in a bar when she was younger."

"Is she here for you then?"

Arabella shrugged and went to her room to change. She wondered if this time Marie would come to her dressing room, but she didn't, which was disappointing. She changed quickly into normal skinny jeans, high riding boots, and a sweater.

She couldn't get the gel or the highlights out of her hair, but she did tone down her make-up, leaving just a smudge of kohl, and some lip-gloss.

She could hardly breathe as she walked up the stairs to the stage door, fearing she would again be disappointed. But Marie was there, surrounded by people, and she was signing autographs. When the fans saw Arabella, they began collecting hers as well.

When they were finished, they walked out together. Arabella stopped.

"Why are you here tonight?"

"I have something I want to ask you. Something professional."

"Then contact my agent."

Marie winced and her eyes filled with pain. "Bella, please. Don't let us go on hurting each other like this. It's unbearable."

Arabella looked down. "I'm sorry…What did you want to ask me?"

They stood just outside the door, which constantly swung open. Almost every time it did, someone stopped to say goodbye to Arabella. Some looked curiously at Marie.

"It's not a good idea to stand here. Are you looking for a taxi? We can walk down to the Platz."

"I was hoping we could talk for a few minutes."

Arabella looked at her for long moments. She made a decision.

"Actually, I'm really hungry. There's a small Italian just down the road. Shall we go there?"

Marie looked as if a ton of bricks had fallen from her shoulders.

"Yes, please."

They walked down the road. The pavement was wide, and they kept a metre distance between them. Arabella stopped at a small restaurant and went inside. It was over full, and Marie took a step back, but Arabella continued to walk in.

"Hi, Alfredo."

"Arabella!"

"Table for two?"

"Always. For you." He winked and gestured to the furthest corner of the restaurant where a small table backed up against the wall. It had a reserved card on it.

As they weaved their way between the tables, they were recognised. A lot of the diners had been in the performance. A few clapped.

But when they sat down, they were left undisturbed. Arabella handed Marie the menu.

"I'm not terribly hungry. I…I'm nervous. But let me first tell you how much you have grown as a conductor. It's fascinating to watch."

"How can you tell that with *Follies*?" She laughed.

"I did see *Hänsel und Gretel* as well."

"Yes, I thought I saw you."

"I wasn't sure…about your reaction and I had a performance. And…I was scared."

"The story of your life, Marie."

She winced again.

"I'm sorry."

"It's alright. I deserve it."

Arabella just stopped herself from reaching out to take Marie's hand. "Share a pizza?"

She nodded. Alfredo came to take their orders.

"A pizza to share. *Tonno e cipolle.* With extra black olives and a lot of mozzarella. *Un mezzo litro vino rosso. Acqua minerale con gas.*"

"Si, Signora."

"You remembered."

"What?"

"My taste in pizza. No, please don't say what you're thinking. I don't have any right to say anything about your partners."

"Nor I about yours."

"I don't have one."

Arabella looked at her in surprise, as Alfredo came back with wine and water.

"This house red is a good chianti. I hope you like it." She poured two glasses. Marie sipped at hers.

"Mmmmm. This is good."

"You were saying. About partners. You mean Fredrik Rasmusson is in Australia."

"Probably."

"You don't know."

"No."

"Have you split up with him too?"

"We were never together."

"But all the gossip rags. I even read about it in an inflight magazine."

"Bella... he is as gay as I am. We went to school together. He has helped me through these past months... as a friend."

Arabella choked on her wine and had to take a large gulp of the water, which didn't help much as it was fizzy.

"Did you just say what I thought you said?" Her voice rasped.

"That I'm gay, yes. I'm a lesbian."

The halved pizza arrived.

"This is so good. I'm hungrier than I thought I was. It's a good thing the hotel has a large fitness room."

Arabella chewed on her pizza. She was completely lost for words. She remembered why they were here.

"You wanted to ask me something."

"I showed my record company our gala performance. They are mad keen for me to make a crossover disc. I've told them I want you to conduct it, and I thought we could use the Gärtnerplatz orchestra."

"Marie, that would be sensational."

"I have some ideas for songs, but I want your input. You must decide if you want to do your own arrangements, or if we should get an arranger in."

They finished their pizza and Arabella ordered another half-litre of wine.

"And you?"

"Me, what?"

"Do you have a partner? I can't imagine you don't have. You were beautiful before, but you are now simply breath-taking."

"Even with this hair? It's only for tonight. I'll wash it out later."

"Especially with the hair. You have created a very special image. You are so charismatic. But I always knew you are clever. Is there somebody waiting for you? Am I keeping you?"

"There's nobody."

Marie edged her hand towards Arabella. Their fingers touched on the tablecloth. The jolt was painful. Arabella crossed her legs, as she saw Marie's nipples harden under the sheath fitting tightly across her full breasts.

"But have there been others…after Chloe, the pillow princess?" The grey eyes sparkled with laughter.

"How…oh Suzanne, of course."

"She couldn't not tell me. She thought it was hilarious."

"I wore dresses and skirts for weeks. I'm not a butch. You know that."

"Hmmmm. I saw the boots remember. Do you still have them?"

"At the back of a cupboard somewhere." Marie shifted in her chair. "Did she tell you anything else?"

"She mentioned Dr Jekyll."

"I will never speak to her again."

"She has a guilty conscience about that. She says you would never have gone with her on your own. It was all her doing. And Beth was very much against it."

"I know. It was awful. I take a detour if I have to walk past the Bayerischer Hof. You're not staying there, are you?"

"No. Four Seasons."

"What are you singing here? Sorry, I'm so busy and so in my own little world that I forget to look at the State Opera schedule. Though the last time I looked, I didn't see your name."

"I'm not working at the moment."

"Oh. How long are you here then?"

"A while. I'm not quite sure." Arabella sensed Marie would not say more. They sipped their wine slowly. Although, the restaurant was now nearly empty it was obvious neither was in a hurry to leave.

Marie fiddled with the stem of her glass. Arabella watched the long, elegant fingers and tried not to think about what they were capable of. Her nails were trimmed again.

"Bella, do you know what today is? The date I mean."

"April the twenty seventh. Its nearly the twenty eighth though."

"It's two years since we met in that coaching room. When we had our first little disagreement."

"You know that for certain? I remember it was the end of April."

"I think I…no, you don't want to hear it."

Alfredo came up to them. He looked at Arabella apologetically.

"Yes, sorry, Alfredo. We are keeping you from your bed. I'll settle next week if that's OK."

"Of course."

They went outside. It was raining slightly. Marie shivered. "I'll get a taxi. Look there's one over there." They waved, but it went in the other direction.

"In this weather it will be difficult."

"I know."

"Look, I'll drive you."

"No, please that's too much bother."

"It's not. My car is right here." She pressed the fob on her key ring, and the gates next to the restaurant opened.

"I live here."

"That explains why you have a table and a tab at the restaurant."

Arabella laughed. "That's my car. It could fit onto the back seat of yours. But then again, yours couldn't even get through the gate."

"It's adorable. Like its owner." Marie ran her finger down Arabella's cheek.

"Climb in." She wasn't ready for this. She wasn't going to be hurt again. But her body screamed to touch Marie. She felt the tell-tale wetness in her pants. Better get out of here, quickly, before she dragged her upstairs to the apartment.

She drove the short distance to the hotel. The rain was heavier. She parked just short of the awning. They were in comparative darkness. There was only one porter on duty, and he didn't seem interested in the Smart.

"Are you working on Sunday?"

"No, it's a ballet performance."

"May I collect you? I want to show you something. We could have lunch together and start thinking of songs for the CD."

Her mind said no, but her mouth overrode it. "Yeah, why not."

"I have my car here, so I'll pick you up at your apartment. Is eleven alright? It's number eight, isn't it? I don't have your phone number. Beth said you now have a German one. But mine's the same, for the time being anyway. Text me if something comes up and you can't make it."

Arabella pushed the icon on her mobile and sent her a text.

"Here, just in case you need to contact me. You never know."

Marie took Arabella's hand and rubbed her thumb across the back.

"I'm so glad we could talk this evening." She put Arabella's hand on her own cheek, turned it over and kissed her palm gently. Arabella stopped breathing. Her heart was pounding so loudly she was sure Marie could hear it. Her clit was on fire.

"Good night, my love." She got out of the car and walked towards the hotel entrance. The porter recognised her, gave the Smart a puzzled look and opened the doors. Marie didn't look back.

Arabella groaned and gripped the steering wheel. She drove back to her apartment and sprinted up the stairs. She showered and washed all the gunge out of her hair. Still turned on she got into bed and gave herself the best orgasm she had had for over a year.

\*\*\*

Fortunately, she had no performances to conduct for the rest of the week. She relived the evening continuously. Had Marie said she was gay? After a while she started to doubt it. The conversation blurred in her mind.

She vacillated between wanting to call her and invite her over to the apartment and sending a text saying something had come up and they couldn't meet. She couldn't get into all that again. She couldn't have her heart broken a third fourth and fifth time.

Then she pictured Marie sitting in front of her. The perfect cheekbones, the luminous grey eyes in the candlelight. Her elegant neck, her collarbones screaming to be kissed, the soft skin of her cleavage and the round curve of her gorgeous full breasts.

She was soaking wet. Nobody else had ever, and most likely nobody in the future would ever, have that effect on her body. She thought of Suzanne and Beth and how they knew they were destined for each other. So were she and Marie. But the obstacles remained. Nothing had really changed.

The husband was out of the way, but the parents and her catholic upbringing were still there, and her refusal to come out as well. She was such a private person, and so well known. She wouldn't risk the fall-out.

For the first time Arabella sympathised. She had had no problem being out and proud as a pianist behind the scenes in the opera house, but now she was getting known and gave interviews, she tried to shy away from questions about her love life. It really was nobody's business and had nothing to do with how well or badly she conducted. No, Marie would never want to read salacious gossip about the two of them in the magazines, and she could empathise.

***

She did nothing. It was Marie who texted on Sunday morning. As she heard the ping and her name came up, Arabella felt her disappointment surge. *Here we go again. She's cancelling.* She opened the text: * 'I'm certain I won't be able to park anywhere near you. I will be double-parked outside the gate at eleven. Baci.'

She opened the gate. Marie leant against the bonnet of a huge Audi Q8 blocking the entrance to the courtyard. Her hair was tied back in a high ponytail. She wore skinny jeans and a cashmere pullover. She had designer sneakers on her feet and sunglasses perched on her head.

She looked like a teenager and took Arabella's breath away. Marie pulled her in and brushed her lips with a light kiss.

"Careful, look, there are people about."

"No one's looking at us, and anyway who cares. Are you suddenly shy?"

"I guess everyone will be looking at this vehicle, rather than us. Is it a hire car?"

"No, it's mine. Hybrid. One must move with the times. Get in."

Arabella walked around to the passenger side, and stopped, confused. Marie laughed.

"You want to drive?"

"No, of course not. This is a German car." She hadn't noticed the registration. It had a Munich number plate, she now saw.

"Come on, let's get going."

She walked back and got into the passenger seat. The car, which was a gorgeous pearly ivory colour, had soft dove grey leather upholstery. The cockpit would look at home in a spaceship. Marie reversed, and a three-dimensional coloured image flashed up on the screen.

It didn't take long to get out of the city, and they were soon on the southbound motorway. It had been a cloudy start to the morning, but the sun now shone, and the Alps came into view.

"Where are we going?"

"Surprise."

Arabella shrugged.

The motorway was surprisingly traffic free, and Marie accelerated. Arabella saw the speedometer touch two hundred and thirty kilometres, which was the take-off speed of a jumbo jet. Although the landscape rushed by in a blur, it felt as if they were cruising along. She slowed smoothly and took the exit to Starnberg.

"Great. I love it here."

"I remember."

She parked in the small town. "I'm dying for a coffee. How about you?"

"Mmmm, that would be nice."

They found a café on the waterfront, and sipped on their drinks, content just to be with each other and watch the activity on the lake. It was warm, and Arabella slipped off the light jacket she was wearing over her black t-shirt and black skinny jeans.

Marie looked at her hungrily. "I think you will need to put that on again. Come on, I want to show you something. Then we can look for a restaurant and have lunch. Have you had any thoughts about the songs? You were probably too busy this week."

"No, my week was fine," *except for thinking about you 24/7.* "I have a list in my pocket."

Marie drove them out of the town and onto the road around the lake, although the water was seldom visible. Walls and hedges concealed the luxurious villas with direct access.

She turned into a narrow road with a large private sign, and no entry in large letters. The high hedges concealed everything, except where there was a gap. A row of trees had been ripped out, and a huge crane towered above a massive hole in the ground. Building paraphernalia was spread all over the large piece of real estate.

They passed by and the tall hedge resumed. They stopped at a high gate on the neighbouring property. Marie took a fob off the middle console and pressed. The gate opened. Inside was a tall house dating back to the early years of the last century.

On the left against the hedge to the building site, was a three-door garage. Marie drew the car up to the steps leading to the front door and put the automatic in park. They got out and walked up the four stone steps. She opened the door.

It was cold inside and smelt musty. The large circular hallway led to double doors ahead. On the left were stairs down to the floor below, and up to the first floor where Arabella could see a wide landing with doors leading off. Marie walked towards the double doors and opened them onto a huge, curved room looking out onto the lake.

The entire front was made up of windows, except for two central doors leading out onto a stone balcony. It was empty of furniture, except for an old beer bench placed in front of the doors.

Marie took her hand, and they sat down. Her hand was warm. She rubbed the back of Arabella's with her thumb.

"What do you think?" she said softly. Her voice was uncertain.

"What do you expect me to say? It's perfection." They looked out over the lake. In the distance, the highest peak of the mountain range was probably the Zugspitze.

"I want you to help me decorate it."

Arabella turned to her, and her mouth gaped open.

"It's your house? You own it? But what about Richmond?"

"Up for sale."

"What! Why?"

"There's nothing keeping me in London. Brexit is a real pain. I work more in Europe than I do in England. Why on earth should I stay? I thought about going back to Stockholm, but you had told me about this area, and how beautiful it is. And I hoped…I…I could hardly forget that."

She squeezed Arabella's hand. "Come on, let's look at the rest of the house. I need your fantasy and your decorating flair."

They first went downstairs. Instead of one large room there were two with a lake view, although they were still spacious rooms.

"I thought this one could be the music room, and here next door a guest apartment. This wall can be knocked through for an ensuite bathroom and is convenient for the plumbing because it's next to the utility room."

They crossed the hall to the other side, to a room which had a window onto the side garden. It faced northeast and was naturally cool.

"I don't know about this one."

"Fitness room," said Arabella immediately. "It will always be cool. Perfect for running up a sweat."

"Arabella, that's brilliant. Look, a shower can go in here, in this niche."

They went back up the stairs. On the right was a large kitchen. At least that is what it looked like. The walls were bare, but there were installation points dotted around. It also faced north. Opposite, on the south side, was its twin. It looked out onto the hedge where the crane was visible in the next-door garden.

"That thing won't always be there. I was given the plans. Of course, it will be a modern house, but it will fit in with the rest of the neighbourhood. They are building an indoor pool in the basement."

"Do you know who it belongs to?"

"Juliette something or other. A singer too, but pop I believe. That's the only thing I'm a bit worried about. Parties and drugs and things."

"Not Juliette Simon? She's immensely popular in her field. She sings a sort of folksy pop and appears on those family TV shows a lot. Don't worry. Unless she leads a double life, it shouldn't be a problem. Her image is squeaky clean."

Marie let out a breath. "That's an enormous relief. It had been niggling at me." They turned from the window. "This would make a nice dining room/library. I saw the arrangement somewhere and I loved it so much, that I want one of my own." Arabella smiled and blushed.

"Here behind the stairs is and will be again the guest cloakroom. Now let's go upstairs."

They held hands going up. As the house was almost oval, the top landing was a kind of gallery with doors leading off all around it. Marie opened the central door to the lakeside. She walked to the window, not looking at Arabella.

"The master bedroom of course."

Two doors led off it on the right side, one to a large bathroom, the other to a spacious walk-in closet/dressing room. Both had windows looking on to the side garden and were above the kitchen. The room on the left of the master bedroom was smaller, but also had a lake view, and an ensuite bathroom.

"Another guest room, but only for people I know very well. I…don't want to be eavesdropped on." They looked at each other. Arabella felt her core tighten and heat rose in her stomach. Marie looked away.

She led her around the circular landing to a large room facing away from the lake. It looked over the rear hedge and onto other houses, although they were too far away to be disturbing.

"The least attractive room in the house, but it could be ideal as an office." They walked back downstairs to the living room and stood looking at the lake.

"It's going to cost a lot of money to renovate."

"I'll have a million euros when the Richmond house sale goes through."

"Just for renovation?" Arabella whistled.

"Yes. I think I got a bargain here. People who have this kind of money don't want to do the necessary work, and most definitely don't like the big hole next door. And they probably want something larger. But it's big enough for…come on, let's have a look at the garden."

They let themselves out through the French windows and walked down the dozen steps to the lawn, which sloped quite steeply to the lake.

"You see. The house is half built into the rise here, which is why the lower rooms are level with the garden."

"Yes, it's more or less the same principle as my London house."

"What's happened to that? You are keeping it I presume. For when the Gärtnerplatz engagement ends. If it does, of course. But you will want to go home to London at some point….and to live there again."

Arabella shook her head. "I sold my share to Ian. I still rent the third bedroom. The small one. The men wanted me to stay part of our household."

"Do you miss them? They are so nice. I think of them quite often. You are lucky to have that stability in the background."

"Sometimes, just a little. I've never actually lived on my own you know. I'm incredibly busy, but a bit lonely sometimes."

Marie took her hand again and they wandered down to the lake. There was a small and very wobbly boathouse next to a jetty, which had been renewed at some point. It was stable, and they walked out on to it, and stood close together, leaning on the railing and watching small fish in the clear water.

A pair of swans swam over, bobbing their heads, looking for food. Marie laughed at them.

"Sorry." She turned out her pockets. "Another time. Please come back." They drifted away, barely rippling the water.

"They are monogamous."

"I know. I envy them. Bella..." she sighed, looking down intently into the water, then took a deep breath. "I love you. I've always loved you. From the moment I saw you, I've loved you. From the moment you looked up and you stared at me, and I looked into your blue eyes."

Arabella felt a lump in her throat. She whispered, "I love you too. But..."

"I know. I gave up my right to you when I left for America last year."

"Marie, you broke my heart. I wanted to die. I love you and I desire you so much it makes me want to do crazy things, but I told you back then, I can't be your dirty little secret, even though admittedly it wouldn't be such a hardship here in this house."

They were silent, and both continued to stare into the water.

"Bella, I want to marry you. I want to be Marie Nyman Cooper. I want everyone to know and envy me for having the most beautiful wife on the planet."

Arabella turned to her. "But your parents, and your reputation. You can't."

"My parents know. I couldn't stand the farce anymore."

"What did they say? Do they talk to you?"

"It was hard for my mother. They asked me if I have a new partner. I said no. My father said, *not Arabella? I was hoping it would be.* I told him I had messed up. He told me to go and get you back. And here I am."

Arabella held her face and kissed her gently. Their mouths parted and their tongues explored each other. They both groaned and their hips came together. A boat went past.

There were some whistles and catcalls, but Marie didn't flinch. Time stood still. They gazed at each other.

Arabella sighed. "I'm hungry. Didn't you promise me lunch?"

They locked up the house and drove a little further round the lake until they found a small restaurant with all day service. They weren't in a hurry anymore. Arabella took out her list.

"Shall I just tell you what I have been thinking about?"

"Please do."

"You know I told you my Omi is a Dusty Springfield freak, and I grew up on her music. Well, I think those big ballads she sang in the 1960s are still valid today. Omi told me they are using *You don't have to say you love me* for a new TV series, as background music. And I think there is going to be a biopic at some point. Or perhaps there already is. So, I thought about half the CD could be those, then some modern songs. Gaga and Swift and co., then some original material, which you could commission."

Marie was thoughtful. "It's a great idea. Though I would like to sing *Mockingbird* and *You Don't Own Me*, and a couple of soul numbers as well. And perhaps some big musical songs. The company are quite prepared for a double album, so we could have about two hours of music."

"Wow, sensational. That opens up a lot of possibilities."

It was getting dark, and the sun set over the lake. The snow on the Alps was pink and gold. It was almost too beautiful.

"Nobody would believe you if you painted that."

Marie sighed. "Let's go back. I would very much like to see your apartment." Her eyes went dark. "You drive." She tossed Arabella the keys.

Arabella had never seen a free parking space in the road, but as they arrived, a large combi-van pulled out right in front of Alfredo's restaurant. She slid into the space. They grinned at each other.

"This is meant to be."

"It will never happen again. Don't get used to it. This is a wonderful car, but not suitable for Munich, though it will be great in the winter in Starnberg. But why something so huge?"

"I have developed a bit of a flying phobia over the years. I can't change anything about the intercontinental flights, but at least I can drive myself around Europe. And it will mean I can get home sooner after concerts. I think that is going to be important."

Hand in hand, they climbed the stairs to Arabella's apartment.

"It's tiny I'm afraid."

"But it's totally Arabella. You have great taste…in decorating that is."

"Is that going to be a running gag for the rest of our lives?"

"I hope so, my darling."

They undressed each other unhurriedly, caressing soft skin, renewing acquaintance with favourite parts of each other. They made love. It was hot sex, but it was different. Their bodies clove to each along their lengths. They couldn't bear to be separated.

They rolled over, sometimes Marie was on top, sometimes Arabella. Arabella entered Marie; Marie slipped down to savour Arabella's sex. When each climaxed, it was shattering. They cried out each other's name, and said 'I love you' over again, trying to make up for all the times each had supressed the phrase. They slept, wrapped around each other. The day had been emotionally exhausting.

Arabella woke as the dawn was beginning to lighten the curtains in her bedroom. A hand was fluttering lightly up her inner thigh. Marie was pressed behind her, her breasts against Arabella's back. She felt the hardened nipples sliding gently across her shoulders. She groaned.

"What are you doing to me?" Her hips automatically moved and ground against Marie's sex. The silky hair pressed into her cheeks.

Marie's voice was husky in her ear. "I want you so much." She nibbled on her ear. Then she was flipped over, and Marie lay on top of her. She took a hardening nipple in her mouth and sucked it to a peak.

Her hand was still fluttering lightly against Arabella's inner thigh, tormenting her, when it stopped just short of the part of her needing it most. She reached up and pulled Marie's face to hers and thrust her tongue hungrily into her mouth. Marie ground into her.

"Darling, I need your fingers." She guided Arabella's hand down to her folds at the same moment her other hand entered her, and she began to thrust slowly. Arabella swiped up, then down Marie's wetness, her other arm circling her waist to push their hips even closer together.

"Enter me, sweetheart." Arabella thrust three fingers in deep. Marie groaned. They moved together. Their rhythm was perfect. As it got faster, they both panted and whimpered.

"I can't hold back any longer. Come…come with me, Bella." Marie pressed her thumb against Arabella's clit, and they climaxed together. Both stayed in each other as their walls pulsed in sync.

They lay still, lost in wonder.

"We really are good at this," Arabella whispered.

"Practice makes perfect. I hope you don't have to work today."

Arabella snorted. "Oh, but I do. We begin rehearsals at ten o'clock for *Tosca*. It is my last rehearsed revival this season though. And you are going to have to leave this bed of lust. Your monster can't stay parked where it is without you feeding fistfuls of euros into the meter every twenty minutes. But now, how about coffee and toast?"

"Oh yes, I think I'm hungry. If we do have to interrupt this most pleasurable of occupations for a hopefully short span of time, may I take a shower?"

Arabella took a clean towel out of a drawer and threw it on to the bed.

"Much as I would love to join you, my shower is not built for two. You can only just about turn around in it, but at least the water is hot."

They ate breakfast. Arabella took her shower and dressed. Marie had put on an old t-shirt she stole from a drawer, and was sitting on the bed, showing a great deal of her long legs, when Arabella had to leave. She looked strangely vulnerable and pulled Arabella down to join her.

"What now? When can I see you again? I don't suppose I can come back this evening, can I? I have so much I want to discuss about the house before I go down to Starnberg again. I want to get everything moving. I want to move in at the beginning of September."

"That will be tough to achieve."

"I know. I need to brainstorm with you. But I know you are busy. Can we at least see each other again on Saturday?"

"Marie today is Monday. It's impossible." She got up and moved into the tiny sitting room. When she came back, a tear rolled down Marie's cheek.

"Marie, it's impossible because I can't wait for five days to see you again, knowing you are in Munich. Here are your keys to my apartment. I'm afraid Alfredo is closed tonight, but I can collect some groceries on my way home, and we can cook. I hope very much you will be here when I get back at around five."

Another tear ran down Marie's beautiful face, but she was grinning happily.

"Don't you dare do the shopping. I'll take care of it, and like a good wife, you will find dinner on the table when you come home. Talking of which, can we please get married as soon as possible?"

"Are you serious?"

"Oh, Bella, I've never been more serious in my life."

"Then I have a suggestion. Cooper – Nyman sounds much better than Nyman-Cooper."

\*\*\*

Marie stayed in the tiny apartment all week, only returning to her hotel during the day to change clothes, work out in the fitness room, and on one occasion, driving down to Starnberg to meet a builder who was to oversee the renovation.

Arabella was in the company office, sitting at a table making out a schedule for her rehearsals. Bettina looked at her thoughtfully. For a moment they were alone. Briefly. The office always teemed with people.

"You look different. You radiate something. You also look so exhausted that you don't need your kohl. You have dark rings under your eyes quite naturally."

Arabella grinned and went on with her schedule.

"I heard Marie Nyman was a surprise guest…again…in *Follies* last week. Any connection?"

Arabella looked at her and sighed. "I suppose it won't be a secret for ever. Yes, we are back together."

"Back together? So, I was right. There is something between you. How long has it been going on?"

"Two years. But we've been apart for a year. Please, please keep it to yourself until the dam breaks, which it will soon, if Marie has her way. She wants us to get married."

Bettina squealed and hugged her. "That is so romantic. But I promise. I won't say a word until someone else does, and then I'm going to announce it over the intercom."

"I believe you would too."

\*\*\*

On Friday night, as they lay in each other's arms after hot sex, Arabella cleared her throat.

"About getting married. Are you divorced yet?"

"Yes, that went through very quickly in the States. Nick's starlet girlfriend, now wife, was pregnant."

"You're kidding."

"No, and she had one of those desperately ugly pregnancies. Blew up like a balloon in all directions. It put paid to Nick's interviews and photo opportunities for months." She giggled. "Poor love. They have twins."

"How does she look now?"

"Back to normal, but I doubt she can do her own body shots anymore. All those stretch marks you know."

Arabella doubled up, wheezing. It was several minutes before she could stop laughing.

"You are worse than Suzanne, and that really is saying something. Incidentally, shall we tell them?"

"Yes, and no. I would prefer our wedding to be just us. I don't want to share you with anybody. And then I want to tell everybody and do one big interview in a serious paper together, and then I want a big party in September when we've moved into our house. Or am I being selfish?"

"No, I'm relieved. I can't quite imagine flowers, cakes and wedding dresses and all that stuff. It's not me at all. But I do want a wedding ring."

Marie curled their hands together. "I'm going to get it welded to your finger."

\*\*\*

They spent all the daylight hours that weekend in the Starnberg house, drawing up plans, choosing colours, bathroom fittings, tiles, curtains and everything else which needed to be decided. The builder left a mountain of catalogues and interior decorating magazines, and most considerately, a huge old table and chairs. They spread everything onto it. Marie tended to dither, but Arabella was ruthlessly single minded.

The builder came to the house on Sunday afternoon, and they went through everything until it was too dark to see anymore.

"He's fallen in love with you, Bella."

"Yeah, I noticed. It's going to be useful. For the first time, I think it's possible to finish by the end of August."

"I'm taking no chances on leaving you two alone for a single minute. After I get back from Hamburg at the end of May, we are getting married. I've made all the arrangements. It will take place in the Starnberg registry office. And on the morning after, I have agreed to a major interview in *Die Zeit*. They don't know what it's about yet, but you will be with me of course." She suddenly looked stricken. "I can't organise this over your head though. I know I'm a selfish Ice Queen diva, but just this once are you alright with it?"

Arabella laughed and hugged her tightly. "*Die Zeit*! Then the whole world will know. We'll have to tell family and friends before it's published."

"Yes, I know. That's why I've chosen the week when I know we are both reasonably free."

"You really want to do this? Come out of the closet I mean. You've been locked inside for fifteen years."

"My darling, I can't wait."

\*\*\*

"I think I should meet your grandmother." Arabella stopped chewing on her salad. They were having lunch. Alfredo came over to the table.

"Marie, do you want more water?"

"Si, grazie." She looked at him warmly. He hummed and walked away slowly.

"I don't know what's more useful. Having the builder in love with me, or Alfredo completely besotted with you."

Marie winked and rubbed her stomach. "It's a toss-up."

"I didn't want to bother you with my Omi, but it would be wonderful. I do have a guilty conscience about not telling her."

"Then call her now. Perhaps we can go over this afternoon, but I must change first. We can go to the hotel on the way."

Arabella called Clara. "She'll have coffee on the table at three."

They took the Smart to the hotel. It could be parked in the smallest space, even face on to the pavement.

Arabella sat and watched as Marie changed out of her comfortable jeans into her Ice Queen image. Charcoal pencil skirt suit, stilettos and chignon.

"I haven't seen your uniform for a while. You know what it does to me. I can't wait to get you out of it later. Or at least most of it. You might like to leave on bra, panties and those hold up stockings. And the shoes perhaps."

Marie's tongue slowly licked her top lip. "Oh yeah. Isn't that a little Dr Jekyll? I'll remember this conversation." She slid her hand under Arabella's fitted black V-neck sweatshirt and pinched a nipple hard as she whispered in her ear.

"And while we're on the subject. You remember my birthday and Christmas present? I'd like that as my wedding present too."

"If you don't stop, I will combust here on the spot."

She laughed. "Come on, let's go and meet the family."

Clara let them in. Mia stood a little behind her.

"Omi, this is Marie." Arabella was nervous.

"I know you from somewhere. But I don't think we've ever met. Please come in. Coffee is on the kitchen table. I hope you don't mind, but Mia's and my hearing is not what it used to be, and it's much easier for us if we sit facing you."

Arabella led the way, and they sat around a square table. Small plates and cake forks were laid out, and a plate with a selection of petit fours sat in the middle. Clara poured coffee.

"I've just remembered where I know you from. Arabella brought a flight magazine with her last year. You are Marie Nyman, aren't you? It was an interview about you and your partner, that tennis player. And I think I've seen interviews in other magazines or on the television. But they were with a different man. An actor."

"Omi…I have something to tell you…"

Marie put her hand out and stopped Arabella fiddling with her cup.

"Let me. Clara, may I call you Clara… and Mia." They both nodded.

"Clara, I have been madly in love with your granddaughter for over two years. I would like to ask your permission to marry her."

Arabella stifled a sob. Clara looked straight at Marie. They held each other's gaze.

"If you promise never to hurt her, you have my blessing."

"I promise."

\*\*\*

They stayed with Clara and Mia for a couple of hours. Clara was merciless and wanted an explanation about the men in all the interviews. Finally, she accepted the story and looking at Mia, took her friend's hand.

"I know what it's like to live a fake life. You two are lucky. You have your whole lives ahead of you. We were too bound by convention."

Marie turned to Arabella as they climbed into the Smart. "Let's go back to the apartment quickly. We still have something to do before I drive to Hamburg tomorrow."

They walked to the Marienplatz in the centre of the city. On a corner was an expensive jeweller.

"We are looking for two matching gold bands."

The jeweller didn't miss a beat, though she obviously recognised Marie. They chose a heavy thick ring. They both had beautiful hands with long fingers, and the wide rings looked wonderful. They paid separately with their credit cards. Arabella gulped. She was thankful for the London house money.

They went back to the hotel. Marie had to leave early the next morning for her long drive to Hamburg, so Arabella would stay there for the night. They were walking to the lift, when Marie stopped, took her hand and turned back to reception.

"*Wir sind zur Zweit in mein Zimmer heut' Nacht. Für meine Rechnung.*"
(For my bill. My room is a double tonight.)

Things had certainly changed since their weekend in Vienna.

***

Arabella missed her terribly for the three weeks Marie was in Hamburg. They telephoned and texted multiple times a day. She used the time productively. She had only performances to conduct until the end of the season, so her days were free. Most mornings she studied her scores for the following season.

Some afternoons she went for long cycle rides. When the weather was fine, she spent a couple of hours sunbathing in the Englische Garten. And she prepared for their CD recording. Scheduling was not easy. Marie could not record during the time she was singing opera, as the vocal technique required was so different.

She would be in Salzburg from the middle of June until the middle of August, so they fixed the sessions for the last two weeks of August. The Gärtnerplatz orchestra was officially on holiday at that time, but enough players were happy to earn extra money, and after signing the record company contract, she and the orchestra manager booked them. It also meant that they were given permission to record in the orchestra rehearsal room in the theatre, which was soundproof. The project was prestigious for the theatre.

The record company was delighted with the solution. Suitable venues for recording orchestras were difficult to find. The company put her in touch with Bert Schmidt, who wrote and arranged many of Juliette Simon's songs. He kept putting off appointments, until eventually he asked her to come to his house on the outskirts of Munich. They sat in the small studio in his basement.

"I know I haven't seemed to be very enthusiastic about this meeting. I just can't imagine writing or arranging for an operatic voice, least of all a soprano."

Arabella expected this. She had with her the DVD of the Friends Gala and gave it to him to slot in his machine. It was obvious he couldn't believe what he was seeing. There was a beat before he said anything.

"I'm in, oh yeah, I'm very much in if you still want me. But there isn't much time before the middle of August. How many songs do you want from me? And what about the arrangements?"

"We were thinking five new songs. We can work together on the arrangements. I have the sounds in my head for most of the numbers. The orchestrations for the musical numbers already exist. I want to tweak the Springfield stuff. On her recordings, which she, at least unofficially, produced herself, she pulled the bass and percussion right to the front of the sound. I think we should do this too, but a little more subtly. With our orchestra, we have more instruments available than she had. Do you think you can manage five new songs?"

"I'll play you three which I have already. Two were meant for Juliette, but she doesn't know about them." He winked. "I've got a melody right now in my head which I think would be great for Miss Nyman. Can you write lyrics?"

Arabella gulped. "I can try." They went over to the piano. As Bert played, she thought of her heartbreak when Marie left for the States a year ago. It was uncanny. The words came into her mind, and by the end of the evening, they had a new ballad.

*\*\*\**

Marie sang her last performance in Hamburg. Arabella was expecting her home late the following day, but she was woken at six o'clock by the key turning in the lock.

"Now you know why I have my monster car."

"But its eight hundred kilometres and you had a heavy performance last night. Are you completely crazy?"

"About you, yes I am." She stripped off, went to the bathroom and climbed into bed.

"Now where were we three weeks ago?"

They made love, revelling in each other's bodies and the heat they engendered.

Marie's tiredness overcame her eventually, and she slept deeply until nearly three o'clock. Arabella was loath to disturb her and anyway she loved watching the beautiful woman. She was breathing softly through slightly parted lips, whimpering occasionally as she entered a dream phrase. She dozed too, using the intervening times when she was awake to arrange music in her head.

When Marie woke, stretching and yawning, Arabella had a terrible thought.

"You didn't leave the Audi outside, did you? It will either have been towed away or you will have a horrendous fine."

Marie laughed. "You think I'm a stupid soprano, don't you? No, I left it at the hotel garage and took a taxi. Now…I'm starving."

Arabella made omelettes. "Mmmm, I needed that. This is a fabulous omelette, darling. It's so good to know that I won't have to do all the cooking when we're married, which I must remind you again, is on Friday. You have three days to do a bolt if you're going to."

"I've been thinking."

"Darling, please don't say you've loved your freedom for the last three weeks and you want out." Despite the teasing tone, there was a worried line on Marie's forehead.

Arabella kissed it smooth, taking time to run her tongue over the perfect eyebrows. "No way. I know we want to be alone, but are you sure we don't need witnesses?"

"We don't but I was thinking the same. Let's collect them on Friday morning, show them the house, and have lunch before our appointment at three."

"I love you so, so much."

\*\*\*

They spent the night apart. Marie insisted it was bad luck to flout convention.

They assured one another that they didn't want any wedding trimmings, but when Marie drew up to collect Arabella who was waiting outside her wooden gate, they had to gape at each other.

Arabella wore beautifully tailored cream coloured dress pants and a voluminous dark blue silk shirt tucked into the waistband.

The shirt made her deep blue eyes even more radiant. Marie had on a soft dove grey jersey sheath dress. It moulded to her perfect model figure. Her hair was in its chignon. After feasting on the curve of her breasts revealed by a generous cleavage, Arabella's eyes dropped to the sneakers on her feet.

"My heels are in the car. But we are going to show the house and it's a tip."

Arabella opened the car door and threw in her overnight bag. She would be staying in the comfort of the five-star hotel for their wedding night, and for the planned interview the following morning.

They collected Clara and Mia. The two women looked lovely in lightweight woollen dresses and fought to contain their excitement. Arabella drove down to the Starnberg house. Marie groaned when they picked their way over rubble in the main hall. It didn't faze Arabella. She was used to it from her London days and was not bothered by the destruction all around them at this stage of the renovation.

"It's going well. They seem to be ahead of schedule, which I hadn't expected." Their builder clumped down the stairs, his eyes wide when he looked at Arabella. Marie rolled her own.

"Drink your fill," she muttered. "In three hours from now, she'll be mine, all mine, and I'll put a chastity belt on her if necessary." Arabella sniggered.

Treading carefully, they made a tour of the house. Clara and Mia loved it and were as unbothered by the mess as Arabella.

"Why am I the only one who can't appreciate potential?"

Arabella stood staring at a magnificent fully-grown oak tree on the right side of the garden, about five metres from the hedge, halfway between house and lake.

"I have an idea," but she refused to tell Marie what it was.

They ate a light lunch, although nobody was hungry, and drove to the registry office in the town hall. They located the registrar and waited a few minutes, before he let them into the room. He sat behind a large desk. In front were two old wooden chairs, and behind them seating for a dozen people.

They sat, Clara and Mia directly behind them holding hands. Arabella turned to look at them fondly. *Almost a double wedding.*

It was a decidedly unromantic procedure and consisted almost entirely of them signing documents. They were asked if one of them wanted a change of name and answered that they both wanted to adopt the name Cooper – Nyman. That necessitated additional paperwork. They exchanged rings. The registrar looked at Arabella.

"You may kiss your spouse if you want to." He obviously thought Arabella was the *man* in the relationship.

"That's it?" Marie asked. "We're married?"

"Yes, indeed."

They kissed each other gently on the mouth.

"Would you like a photo?"

Neither had thought of that. Arabella handed him her smart phone. He snapped several of the two of them, and one of all four.

He shook hands all around, and they were shepherded out.

Clara wanted to see the photos, and Arabella mailed her the one of the group. They arrived back at the car.

"Now you must please drive us home immediately. You two should be alone." They didn't deny it.

Arabella parked the Audi in the hotel garage, and they took the lift to the top floor. Hand in hand they approached the last door on the corridor. Marie opened it with her key card.

"The bridal suite. I'm sorry I can't carry you across the threshold."

Arabella threw her bag into the room, and putting her arms under Marie's hips, she lifted her from the ground. Marie let out a small shriek, then gripped firmly on Arabella's bulging biceps. She was carried through the open door of the bedroom and put down gently on the huge bed.

There was a champagne bottle in a bucket of ice, and a covered plate of fresh canapés standing on a table across from the bed. On the floor was a large vase full of at least three dozen white long-stemmed roses.

"No, you're not romantic, are you? No wedding trimmings you said. Marie, it's lovely, and so thoughtful, and I must admit I'm now rather hungry and thirsty. I was too nervous at lunchtime."

"So am I," Marie's voice was husky, "but first let's drink some champagne and eat a few of those canapés before they go stale. We have the rest of the night ahead of us."

"Much longer than that, my darling wife."

They drank half of the champagne, and on empty stomachs, both felt a slight buzz. Arabella unpacked her outfit for the interview and hung it next to Marie's clothes. She put her bag next to the bed and reached over to Marie. Slowly she undressed her.

It took time because their mouths could hardly bear to be apart. Finally, she lay naked in the middle of the bed, and watching Arabella, parted her legs slightly. She glistened, and Arabella gushed even more in response. She undressed herself and reached into her bag for the strap-on and the lube.

Marie leaned over to help her with the buckles. She shook her head at the lube.

"No need." Her pupils were enlarged. Arabella started to slip down between her legs, but she was stopped and flipped onto her back. Marie straddled her hips and placed herself directly above the dildo, so that it was touching her entrance. She lowered herself, pushing down the full extent so that the base knocked against Arabella's clit, causing her to gasp.

She ground herself into her hips. Arabella reached up and cupped the heavy breasts, massaging them and flicking her hard nipples.

"Bella, this is not going to take long. I'm dying here." She started to push herself up and down, each time connecting with Arabella's clit. Then she whimpered and held her breath, as her leg muscles went tight, and she climaxed.

"I'm sorry, darling."

"More, Marie, I'm very close." Marie continued pumping, twitching slightly as her after waves hit. Arabella's hips arched to meet hers, and to get the maximum benefit as the base banged into her clit. It was a delicious agony.

She groaned as her orgasm surged. Marie kissed her neck, then her lips and pushed her hands through her hair. Their breathing slowed.

"I'm not finished. Fuck me, my love… please."

She rolled onto her back and opened her legs wide. Arabella knelt between her thighs. Marie watched her. With one arm supporting her weight, she put her fingers deeply into her folds and gathered her own juices. She rubbed them along the shaft and pushed gently into Marie, who rose to meet her.

Their rhythm was slow at first. Marie's breath hitched with every thrust.

"Faster, darling." This time they came together, and Arabella thought for a second she might black out. Her spasms were never ending. Judging by Marie's shudders, it was no different for her. Arabella began to cry softly, and Marie held her tightly. A tear ran down her own cheek. They couldn't speak.

Then Marie whispered. "I am enormously privileged to have experienced that with you. I will never ever forget it."

She pulled the cover over them both, and they fell asleep. They woke very much later and finished the champagne. They didn't talk much. The sex had been close to a religious experience, and both wanted to hold on to the miracle for as long as possible.

\*\*\*

They woke the next morning and stared at each other.

"Am I dreaming, or are we actually married?"

"You're not dreaming, we are, breakfast will be here in ten minutes, and the journalist arrives in an hour and a half."

"Help, I'm first in the shower."

Marie waited in a hotel robe to let the breakfast trolley be wheeled in. She had ordered enough for six, and the waitress could hardly disguise her curiosity. She tried to peer into the bedroom when she saw Arabella's shadow flit past, but Marie blocked her view. "Now, now, it's only my wife, and she's probably naked."

The girl blushed scarlet, stammering her thanks for Marie's generous tip.

"Marie, was that a good idea? She might sell her story to a gossip rag."

"In this hotel, she would be sacked on the spot, and anyway, on Wednesday evening it will be on all the news-stands."

The journalist called from the lobby and was sent up. She led the cultural section of the paper and was herself lesbian. Marie had insisted she would only give the interview to her personally. A photographer accompanied her. Fortunately, the suite did not have *honeymoon* written all over it. The white roses on their own were not incriminating. The bedroom door was firmly shut.

"Thank you for coming here to do this interview, and on a Saturday morning as well. There is a reason for the timing."

They had talked about what they would wear, knowing they would be photographed. Marie chose a deep burgundy pencil skirt suit. She had only just put her hair up in time, but no one would have known. She was steely calm and immaculately turned out.

Arabella had on a short pale grey denim button down skirt and jacket and wore her cream cavalry boots. This last article of clothing had contributed to Marie almost being late.

"I happened to be in Munich this weekend, and it is my pleasure. It is also my pleasure to meet Arabella Cooper, who I have no doubt will herself soon be the subject of a portrait interview."

She unashamedly raked her eyes up Arabella's body, ending by focusing on her lips. The vein in Marie's neck stood out.

"I read that you have worked together, and of course you now live in Munich. How nice to see you here." She managed to snap her attention back to Marie. "I would like to concentrate on the new production in Salzburg. I think we will hold the interview back until July. It's good publicity for you, and the festival."

"We can of course talk about Salzburg, but that is not the reason I wanted to give this interview, and why I hope you will reconsider the timing, and include it in next week's edition."

"Oh no, I can't do that. The timing is too tight. I need at least a week to write it up. Unless, of course, there is a very pressing reason."

"I think there is." She fixed the journalist with a steady look. "You see, I got married again yesterday."

"Congratulations." The photographer nodded in agreement. He was busy getting his camera ready.

"Arabella is now my wife."

To her credit, the journalist became totally professional, and they discussed how they would present the interview. The paper was much too serious for the article to be salacious, so they talked about coming out, and how it affected a woman professionally at this moment in time, and about Marie's catholic upbringing, which contrasted strongly with Arabella's more liberal childhood. Future plans for both of them were noted and they mentioned the crossover CD. The photographer snapped away more or less discreetly.

"Thank you for this. Thank you for giving it exclusively to my paper."

"Do you think you can get it into next week's edition."

"Oh definitely. I'll be writing this all day and night if necessary."

"I would like to read it and see the photos before they go to print."

"I don't usually agree to it, but in this case I understand. If you give me your private email address, I'll send it as soon as it's finished."

She turned to Arabella. "Shall I send it to you as well?"

Marie's eyes turned cold. "One copy will be enough thanks."

The journalist laughed. "My reaction wouldn't be any different, I assure you."

They left. Marie collapsed onto the sofa.

"Is it going to be like this with you for the rest of my life? I could have hit her when she stood there drooling over you."

"Marie, my darling, my wife, my everything that is precious. You have just outed yourself to the entire world, and all you are worried about is a dyke looking me over?"

"I have my priorities."

\*\*\*

On Wednesday afternoon, they hit the phones. They made a list. Arabella would begin with her parents, James and Ian, Matilda, Bettina and some other close friends.

Marie headed her list with her parents, Fredrik and Nick.

But first they called Suzanne and Beth together. They had recently returned from Australia and New Zealand and didn't know about the reunion. Marie used her phone. Suzanne answered sounding sleepy.

"You are not both in bed I hope, at three o'clock in the afternoon."

"Hello, stranger. Yes, we are, but it's not what you think. Jet lag after three months spent in the Antipodes is absolutely crippling. But how are you? Your usual morose self… or even more depressed?"

"Better thanks. I got married again on Friday."

There was dead silence in Berlin. Then a sigh.

"Marie, I'm happy for you, but I wish you could face facts and do the right thing with your life. Fredrik, I presume?"

"Suzanne, my new spouse wants to have a word with you."

"I've only ever met him once for five minutes, but alright. I suppose we will have to get to know each other better. Put him on."

"Hi Suzanne. How's Beth?"

"She's fine thanks…Arabella, what are you doing on the line. Not a ménage à trois surely? Not with uptight Marie."

Marie took the phone back. "Arabella is now my wife, and I'm the happiest soprano ever, and we can't wait to see you and tell you everything, but right now we have a thousand people to call before they read about it over their breakfast cereal tomorrow. In *Die Zeit*, if you want to buy a copy."

There was no point in continuing with the conversation because Suzanne was lost for words, and Beth was yelling at her in the background.

"We love you both," they chorused, and cut the connection.

The call to Cardiff did not go as expected.

"Hello, Mama, I've something to tell you. Is Father there?"

"Yes, he is. Darling, we know."

"How, what? Oh of course, Clara. She promised not to tell anybody."

"I know she did, but she couldn't resist sending me the photo of the four of you."

"You haven't told anyone, have you? It's not public until tomorrow morning."

"I might have mentioned at the gardening club my daughter getting married to a famous opera singer."

"Mama!"

"But I didn't say who."

"And Father? Is he OK?"

"We are both thrilled about having the most beautiful daughter-in-law anyone could wish for. Clara is completely crazy about her. And we can't wait to meet her."

"She's in Salzburg in the summer, but I will come over to you for a week. And we both want you to come and stay in September when we move into our new house."

"We'll be there."

\*\*\*

The news was the anticipated sensation, but they stayed true to their pact with *Die Zeit* and gave no other interviews. There were a handful of abusive letters and mails, far outweighed by the hundreds they received supporting them and admiring their courage. Marie left the hotel, and they holed up in Arabella's apartment, cooking, making love, and working on the CD project.

Occasionally, they slipped down to the restaurant and ate in their discreet corner. It was a wonderful honeymoon. For an international singer like Marie, luxury was staying put, not getting in a plane to stay in yet another hotel.

In the middle of June, she left for Salzburg where, together with Suzanne, she would star in a new production of *Cosi fan Tutte*. Arabella drove the hour and a half trip with her to help her settle into her rented apartment next door to Suzanne's. They had a hot date with her and Beth who naturally wanted to know everything about the reunion.

Arabella was nervous for Marie being on her own. She feared the paparazzi, who swarmed around Salzburg during the festival. She was more than glad that for as long as the first act was being rehearsed Suzanne would always be with her. Beth promised to be around as well. There was no doubt Marie would be harried by journalists and reporters, at least until a new scandal took over the headlines.

They had been having an argument for weeks. Marie was determined to change her professional name to Cooper – Nyman. Arabella was not happy, and Marie's agent was completely against it, which only made Marie more stubborn. Beth's quiet good sense finally persuaded her to drop the idea, but only if the title of the CD could be *COOPER – NYMAN ROCK*. It was agreed, and Arabella took the morning train back to Munich.

\*\*\*

The Gärtnerplatz season ran until the middle of July. Arabella conducted her performances, began rehearsals for the new season's operas, and worked with Bert Schmidt on arrangements. Her new agent kept coming up with future offers, mostly concerts, but there was also one for a new opera production in Hannover. She went first to Bettina, who looked at the scheduling and more often than not had to shake her head.

If there was any chance of her getting time off, she went to the Intendant. He was not always happy. Sometimes he agreed, sometimes he didn't. They were both aware, although no one confronted the elephant in the room, that she would not be able to continue as a permanent member of the ensemble after the coming season. She was missing too many career opportunities. It made her sad, because she knew how much she owed the Gärtnerplatz theatre. Her agent was clear though. It couldn't go on like this.

Once a week, she drove her Smart down to Starnberg to meet the builder. He sighed like a lovesick puppy but had finally understood the situation. It didn't stop him giving their project his priority and Arabella was grateful. The renovation was progressing well. She discussed her tree idea with him, and he agreed to do the work.

She flew back to Cardiff immediately after the season ended. She enjoyed the few days with her parents. They were happy for her, although she knew her mother would love a grandchild. Marie never mentioned children.

Arabella banished the thought. She flew back after five days in Wales, having again deepened her tan lying next to the pool.

Marie drove back every Saturday afternoon and stayed until Sunday night. Arabella stocked the fridge with food. They left their bed only to eat. They were blissfully happy.

The premiere in Salzburg was on the last Saturday in July. Arabella spent the final rehearsal week with Marie, and attended most sessions, trying not to be an interfering partner, but giving her advice if asked. The first night was a huge success for the singers, if not for the production.

There were five performances scheduled with days off in between. Marie checked out of her apartment, and they returned to Munich. Arabella drove her there and back for the performances. It wasn't officially allowed, but they didn't advertise the fact, and nobody queried it. They went down to Starnberg twice a week, and otherwise worked on the recording programme.

The performances were a triumph for Marie. She was showered with roses from adoring fans. It was noticeable that the proportion of gay boys and girls had swollen her fan base. And when Arabella collected her after the performance, and they left the artists entrance, they were mobbed. On the last night, the theatre sent security personnel to protect them.

***

Marie had three days to ease her voice gently into the right place technically. They agreed on only two two-hour sessions a day, so as not to take a risk with her vocal cords, but in the event, as the recording progressed, she could manage five hours without feeling any strain.

Arabella conducted from the piano, and Bert was always present, fixing notes, checking balance and even conducting, if a song was too complicated for Arabella to do both. Marie loved Bert instantly, and the feeling was mutual. It was a happy and fulfilling ten days, after which the material had only to be edited. Together with the producer and engineer, Bert oversaw this phase.

Arabella and Marie would hear the first cut, which allowed them a level of objectivity the others had to struggle for, after having spent many hours weighing up various versions. It was an effective system.

The record company was pushing for a cover photo session. They decided to recreate the *Friends* gala situation, wearing the same clothes.

The photographer was delighted with the session. After looking at the shots, Arabella went into the changing room and got back into her jeans and sleeveless black t-shirt. Marie was still talking to the photographer when she came back out. She picked up the bag containing her clothes and made for the door.

"Aren't you going to change?"

"No. We have the car. No one will see me."

Arabella drove the Smart into its tiny parking space.

"Is there something wrong? You've hardly said anything. As far as I could tell, there are some good photos."

"I'm sure there are."

Marie walked up the stairs ahead of her, her butt stretching the tight leather of her skirt.

Despite being worried, Arabella watched hungrily until she reached the top step.

"Get your ass up here, as of immediately."

She swallowed hard and followed meekly.

Marie kicked the door shut behind her and pushed Arabella hard against it. She crashed their mouths together and pushed her tongue in roughly. Then she pulled back, her eyes angry.

"Have you been unfaithful to me?"

"No…what are you talking about?"

"I saw you ogling the photographer's assistant as she stood there holding up the light."

"Marie, have you gone crazy? I never even noticed her."

"Get into the bedroom."

She did as she was told, conscious that the colour had drained from her face. She saw a flash of doubt in Marie's eyes, then she was pushed roughly, and fell back onto the bed.

"I didn't say you could lie down. Stand up and strip."

Trembling slightly, Arabella did as she was told until she stood, covered in goose bumps in front of a fully clothed Marie. She could feel her sex, the arousal coating the apex of her thighs. Her nipples hardened until they were painful. She put her arms up to cover them, but Marie growled, so she dropped them.

"Now you can lie on the bed."

Marie rummaged through a drawer and drew out one of Arabella's leather ties. She gently pulled her arms above her head and tied her wrists together. She stood looking at her, and the tip of her tongue slid over her top lip. Arabella squirmed.

"You like that, do you?" Arabella nodded. "Then beg. What do you want me to do to you?"

Arabella couldn't speak. She opened her legs wide, offering herself. She was going to climax without even being touched.

Marie topped her but was now gentle. She kissed down her neck and sucked gently on her nipples. The leather skirt and bustier rubbed against her body and she arched her back to feel more. Marie slid down and breathed on her folds but didn't touch her sex.

She pulled Arabella up by her waist so that she was on her elbows and knees. Marie was kneeling behind her and ground into her butt. The leather was so tight that Arabella could feel her mound straining against it. Marie slapped her, but the touch was feather light.

Then she put her hand between Arabella's legs and stroked her folds, before entering with three fingers. She began thrusting and Arabella pushed back against her hand for maximum penetration. Marie's fingers curled inside her, and she exploded.

Marie whispered in her ear. "My darling, I love you so much. I'm sorry if I scared you. I was so mad with desire in that studio, I couldn't resist. Please forgive me."

She rolled her over onto her back and gently loosened the tie. Arabella could only look at her in wonder. She pulled Marie towards her, quite roughly pushing the tight leather skirt up so that her legs could straddle her. The tops of Marie's stockings were now visible, and she let out a groan.

She pulled her down to her lips. Marie wore a thong. Arabella growled and used both hands to rip it apart. She swiped up her folds, tasting the copious arousal. She pushed into her and thrust hard. Marie rode her hand, supporting herself on her arms either side of Arabella's head.

She pulled her hips down again and sucked on Marie's clit, which was red and swollen. It sent her over the edge and her contractions pulsed against

Arabella's hand. Eventually she slid down Arabella's body and they lay panting. When their breathing evened out, Arabella gently undressed her.

They lay under the covers at peace. Arabella cleared the rasp in her voice.

"That was wild, and exciting and hot as hell, but I don't really think it's either of us. Do you?"

Marie giggled. "I think we should probably put Dr Jekyll to rest. I love you in leather sometimes, but the sado-masochistic thing is for others. I had intended to slap you around, but I couldn't. I can't hurt you. I love you too much."

***

The last few days of August and the first few of September went by in a mad rush. The house was finished. Some of Marie's furniture arrived from London, though she sold most of it with the house. She hadn't liked a lot of it. But bed linen, and kitchen utensils, and a few good pieces of antique furniture were unloaded and brought into the new house. Naturally the contents of her music room, including the grand piano, were in the moving truck.

They still had to buy a great deal, and they were sometimes too tired for sex at the end of the long days.

They weren't entirely alone with the work. The builder gave Arabella the best birthday present she could wish for, when he brought along a housekeeper from the nearby village. In this wealthy area, they were almost impossible to find.

Arabella interviewed her. She was nervous about her reaction to their relationship. This was a strongly catholic region. She decided to be honest.

"I don't care about your sleeping arrangements," Wiebke told her. "I don't like cleaning up after men. The bathrooms..." she shuddered.

Wiebke would clean three times a week and was available if they needed her for extra duties. She had two teenage children. A boy and a girl. They were old enough not to need babysitting.

At last, they were all three more or less satisfied with the state of the house, and Marie and Arabella could move themselves in. They locked the front door and went to lie in the living room, cuddling on the huge comfortable sofa facing the lake.

It was hot. Arabella wore only a sleeveless top and shorts, Marie a linen dress. They watched the sun set over the water.

"I'm not moving house ever again. I'll be buried here in the garden." She stroked her fingers lightly over Arabella's biceps, whimpering softly.

"You do realise we have a party to give in just nine days' time?"

"I know, we were mad to suggest it, but so many people were disappointed about our secret wedding. I think I would have lost half my friends, including Suzanne."

"Can we please have the day off tomorrow and stay in bed. I want to give you at least a dozen orgasms."

"Then we'll have to take the following day off as well. To recover. I'm getting old you know."

"You're only thirty-eight!"

"And that's another thing. Your birthday went under completely in July because we were so busy. I'm going to do something about that right now." She yawned. Arabella laughed.

"I think that had better wait for tomorrow too. Come on, sleepy head. Let's see how comfortable our huge new bed is."

"You've waited so long; I don't suppose another few hours will make any difference." She yawned again. "But tomorrow morning…" She growled like the MGM lion.

The bed was very comfortable. They slept holding each other tightly.

\*\*\*

The garden party was planned for Saturday afternoon and evening with brunch on Sunday for whoever was still there. Arabella's tree construction was ready just in time. It was a large wooden deck surrounding the oak tree trunk.

On the side nearest the house, it was level with the lawn, but because of the slope down to the lake, it was held up by stilts which increased in length the nearer it got to the water. There were two long tables either side of the tree, and it was possible to sit forty people. The leaf canopy gave natural shade during the summer months.

Marie's parents arrived on Friday evening, as did Suzanne and Beth. The Nymans would sleep in the downstairs apartment, Beth and Suzanne in the guest room next to the master bedroom.

"There is no way I'm letting my parents sleep next to us. They might hear something. I don't mind Suzanne. I wonder if we will hear them. It might be a turn on."

Arabella thought back to her stay in Berlin. "It is."

Arabella's parents were staying with Clara and Mia, and they would all drive down on Saturday. Ian, James and his soon to be wife Samantha flew over, as did Nick and Tasmin, thankfully without their twins. They had a live-in nanny in Los Angeles. Nick was starting a film in London, or else they probably wouldn't be there.

Fredrik, Bettina, Matilda and Sam, Bert Schmidt, and twenty other close friends and colleagues were also expected. The food was catered, with Wiebke in her element bossing the kitchen staff about. Marie and Arabella would make the Sunday brunch themselves.

They were lucky with the weather. Late summer on the lake was glorious. As expected, it was stressful for them both, having so many people, many with diva egos, to cope with, but there were no mishaps. At first, the new in-laws were wary of each other, but by the end of the evening they were on first name terms, and there was talk of a visit to Stockholm.

Marie's mother had still to relent with Arabella, but Anders hugged her tightly when they arrived. They said the last goodbyes at midnight and fell into bed. They did hear Beth and Suzanne and it was a turn on, but they managed to keep their own noise level down just in case the sounds penetrated to the guest room downstairs.

Brunch was a much quieter occasion. Apart from the in-house guests, the Coopers came back from Munich, and Fredrik and his young tennis professional were there too. They were obviously much more than coach and pupil. Marie was glad for her old friend.

Everybody lazed about in the garden and in the small rowing boat Arabella bought from her friend the builder. It was getting too cold to swim, but Fredrik and Mats braved it.

They all left during the afternoon, except for the Nymans who would stay another week. Arabella was glad she had to work for at least three days of that.

It was Marie's last week before she left for Chicago for two months. They closed the doors and windows every night for fear of being heard. Ulrike Nyman said nothing and gradually stopped looking quite so disapproving.

The last Saturday of September was a beautiful day. There was a very slight autumnal chill in the air, but it was still possible for Arabella to wear shorts and a t-shirt. Anders bought two fishing rods, and he and Arabella sat on the jetty, rods extended, watching the fish in the calm water. Marie and her mother lay on loungers on the wooden deck, speaking Swedish in low voices. Arabella intended to secretly start taking lessons while Marie was away.

The oak tree rustled in the gentle breeze. The leaves were beginning to turn brown and get brittle.

Arabella looked up. Marie was watching her. Blue eyes met grey ones. There was a spark, and this time Arabella knew for certain she hadn't imagined it.

\*\*\*

# Epilogue

*Six months later*

The lawn was a mass of colourful wildflowers. Marie and Arabella were working in the music room, simultaneously enjoying the view and preparing for Marie's first Wagner role, which would be Eva in *Die Meistersinger,* scheduled for June and July. Although whether it would happen then, neither of them knew for certain.

Marie returned from Chicago, and sat Arabella down, which was fortunate, or she would have fallen. She had consulted doctors. She wanted a child before she reached the age of forty.

It was a bombshell for Arabella. When they made love with the strap-on, Marie often mentioned her regrets that Arabella could not impregnate her, but otherwise it wasn't a topic of conversation they shared. But now Marie had concrete plans. She wanted Arabella to be donor impregnated, using a blonde Scandinavian.

When Arabella became pregnant, the egg was to be transplanted into her own womb. She would bear the child. It was the nearest they could get to being natural parents. Arabella was sceptical that such a complicated process could work, but they were starting all the necessary tests the following week.

They told nobody except their parents. Both mothers were delighted, and they eagerly committed themselves to taking turns staying in Starnberg to help if and when the time came.

Arabella came to a compromise with the Gärtnerplatz theatre. She would leave the fixed ensemble but have a guaranteed new production and two revivals to conduct every season. The rest of the year she would freelance.

There was already a tentative offer from the Munich Chamber Orchestra. She would most likely be invited to take over the music directorship in eighteen months' time. It was a dream come true to have her own band, and that it was in Munich was icing on the cake.

Marie had work in her calendar for the next six years, but it would all be dependent on baby plans. In any case, she was trying to cut back on her intercontinental work, maintaining enough to cement her standing as an international star, but subtly increasing her work in mainland Europe. The State Opera in Munich was prepared to offer her whatever role she wanted to sing, so she would be doing at least one new production at home every season.

They kept the little apartment near the Gärtnerplatz, buying it outright when the elderly landlord offered to sell. It was useful to be able to rest there between sessions or to stay overnight during the strenuous last two weeks of a rehearsal period.

*COOPER – NYMAN ROCK* was a huge success and even made the charts in Europe. They had occasionally been on a TV show to promote the disc, performing a couple of numbers, but Marie could seldom take time out from her schedule to make the necessary vocal changes. A tour was out of the question, despite the offers, which poured in. They agreed to make a follow up disc in the summer.

They were just about to take a break and go out into the garden for some fresh spring air, when the doorbell rang. Wiebke had finished her work for the day and gone home. Arabella got up from the piano bench and made for the door.

"I'll go darling. And get rid of them. Whoever they are. I'm better at it than you are."

Standing on the top step was Juliette Simon, holding a bottle of wine. They were aware she had moved in over the last two weeks. The finished house was large but attractive, the garden had been landscaped, and the hedge replanted. No loud parties had yet disturbed the peace.

On a step below her stood a muscular man with magazine good looks. *A Marie type.* Arabella recovered from her shock at seeing the face which weekly adorned many magazine and television publications. She wore only light make-up and was as beautiful in the flesh as in print.

"We've just come to say hello. We are your new neighbours. I'm Juliette, this is my husband Thorsten. I want to apologise for all the noise you have been subjected to for so many months."

She had a slight accent. Arabella remembered reading Juliette Simon was Italian. Her German was perfect. She handed over the bottle.

"That is so sweet. Come in. We were just about to take a break. I'm Arabella by the way. Please come downstairs."

She led the way into the music room. Juliette's gaze went immediately to the platinum disc hanging on the wall.

"This is Marie, my wife." Juliette looked startled. She obviously hadn't known. Thorsten said nothing when he was introduced but shook Marie's hand.

"I had heard we are sort of in the same business, but of course you are high art, and I'm just a kind of folk singer."

Considering she was a highly paid one judging by the size of the house next door, Arabella thought that a bit coy. But the penetrating, intelligent eyes suggested she was not a simpering bimbo.

Marie cleared her throat. "I'm sure our respective schedules are packed for months, but when the opportunity arises, Arabella and I would like to invite you both over for dinner."

"We would love that. Let's keep in touch. We don't want to disturb you when you are obviously busy," They turned to leave, and Arabella decided not to offer them a drink. Juliette had already reached the top of the stairs and stood by the door.

When she came back, Marie was in the garden sitting on a chair outside the music room. Arabella joined her, taking her hand.

"Bella." There was a warning note in Marie's voice. "Not again, please, or I will cancel all my engagements forever, lock and bolt the doors and throw away the key."

"What are you talking about?"

"Don't be dim, darling. She couldn't keep her eyes off you."

"You're imagining it. What about the hunk? Isn't he something for you?"

Marie rolled her eyes. "I wonder if he can read and write."

Arabella pulled Marie onto her lap, so that she straddled her hips. "It could be interesting having them as neighbours, but right now, I think we should go upstairs for a nap. Good idea?"

Marie's voice was husky.

"That is a very good idea."

## THE END

Ingram Content Group UK Ltd.
Milton Keynes UK
UKHW021827260423
420831UK00003B/23